"This has been a great year for reading for me. One of the highlights was discovering author Keith Dixon's Sam Dyke Private Investigator series. I've read several of these now and they just keep getting better. I've now found my favourite: 'The Secret Sharers'. Brilliant!" – Reviewer Enrico Graffiti on the last Sam Dyke Investigation.

Sam Dyke has been described as 'Crewe's answer to Philip Marlowe' by industry magazine *The Bookseller*. *The Innocent Dead* is the latest instalment in this series.

Also by Keith Dixon

The Sam Dyke Series

Altered Life
The Private Lie
The Hard Swim
The Bleak
The Strange Girl
The Secret Sharers
The Innocent Dead
The Lonely Grave
The Second Guess (short story)

The Paul Storey Thriller Series

Storey
One Punch
The Song of Geneva Chance

Standalone Novels

A French Darcy – a Romance
Actress – a Contemporary novel

Essays on Writing

The Idle Writer
Crime Writing Confidential

Blog

www.cwconfidential.blogspot.com

Webpage

http://www.keithdixonnovels.com

THE INNOCENT DEAD

KEITH DIXON

A Sam Dyke Investigation

Semiologic Ltd

The Innocent Dead
A Sam Dyke Investigation

For Claude

THE INNOCENT DEAD

PROLOGUE

WHEN THE CAR stopped suddenly he looked up from his iPad and glanced through the front windscreen.

He knew they were close to home because he recognised the hedges and the twist of the road ahead. But the car didn't usually stop here. There was never any traffic to obstruct them. And it was the wrong time of day for cows to be herded along the road from one field to the next, the red-faced farmer twitching a long cane against their waggling backsides. That didn't take place till an hour later.

There were no cows but there was a black car angled across the narrow lane. He saw that its doors were open as though the driver had just stepped out to go somewhere and would be back in a moment.

He switched off his iPad and folded down its cover.

Harris, the chauffeur, pressed a button and there was a heavy clunk as all the doors in the vehicle locked.

Their eyes met in the rear-view mirror and then Harris' eyes flicked past him to look through the rear window. He said, 'Shit.'

Now he noticed a man had appeared at his door. He couldn't see much of him but he saw the man was wearing black gloves. Another man was standing in front of the car. He wore something over his face, a woollen mask. The man at the front was pointing a gun at Harris, through the windscreen. Then he lowered it and shot one of the front tyres. The car sagged.

The man raised the gun again and waved it twice, sideways.

The doors unlocked and Harris got out. He walked towards the man with the gun.

Then suddenly his own door was yanked open and a hand fell on his shoulder, pulling him from the back seat.

This man smelled like a dirty clothes basket and was tall.

But then everyone was tall to him.

He was ten years old.

CHAPTER ONE

A FULL FIVE minutes after passing through the entrance gates, the house came into view.

Although to call it a house was like calling Buckingham Palace a beach-hut. The driveway I was travelling along curved in a great arc between wide, scissor-cut lawns, leading towards a circular, gravel-encrusted courtyard. The obligatory stone fountain—two cupids entwined—sat in the middle of the circle, as dead as Ancient Greece. The mansion itself was faux-Victorian, but a very high-class faux. A phalanx of windows on three stories reflected the sky and its scudding clouds while to one side a large orangery, its roof white and domed, seemed to be clinging on to the main building by means of an intricate network of Virginia creeper and ivy. The place was well-tended but didn't look particularly well-loved.

As I drove closer I began to see more of the near side of the house, angling towards the rear aspect in another series of square regimented windows, some of them open to combat the effects of the stifling heat. In others I could see reflected the tops of working buildings clustered around the rear of the house—perhaps accommodation for staff, or garages, or stables or, for all I knew, camps of itinerant labourers milling about aimlessly, waiting to be let loose to tend the gardens or perform other mundane tasks.

I'd seen the estate from above, from Google Earth, and the mansion showed up as a massive brick of a place surrounded by open lawns to the front and rambling forest to the rear. I'd also found it listed in a local estate agent, where the asking price was £5.5 million. Even for Prestbury, apple of the North West's eye, that was steep. I wondered why the owner, Mark Ware, was selling. Had the cash run out? Or was he bored with all the greenery? It was a question I might not ask him — it didn't pay to be rude to clients.

I stopped my car and climbed out, then stood for a moment, stretching, turning to look over the roof of the vehicle beyond a low wall, letting my gaze fall away over the half-mile of flower beds and lawn towards the distant road. There was no traffic out here: less than two miles from Prestbury, it was isolated, cut off, a planet to itself. I rather liked the idea of being separated from people. Lately I'd been getting too close to them. It hadn't been good for me.

I crossed the gravel to the massive front door and after two minutes' searching found a cord that when pulled seemed to ring a bell somewhere deep inside. The sun beat down on the back of my neck and I felt myself heating up like a lobster in boiling water: nowhere to go but still hoping for the best.

The door was opened silently by an Asian woman in a smart pale blue jacket and skirt, her hair tied in a bun on the top of her head. She looked to be about forty though I'm notoriously bad at guessing women's ages. I think her lips were pulled in a tight scowl before she even opened the door, and my actual appearance did nothing to soften her assessment.

She lifted her chin once. 'Yes?'

'I'm Sam Dyke. Here to see Mark Ware.'

'You have appointment?'

'It's a long way to come up that drive without one.'

The scowl was unremitting. 'You wait here.'

The door closed and I continued to boil. I had little time for rich people with staff, though naturally that wasn't the staff's fault. Sometimes, however, the staff seemed to think bad manners were necessary to maintain the rich person's high opinion of themselves.

The door opened again and the woman stepped back.

'You come in, please.'

I did so and after a couple of paces came to a dead halt. My mouth had probably opened when confronted with the sheer size and scale of the hallway in front of me. Black-and-white check tiles stretched away towards a panelled wall in which there were four doors, two of them closed. A massive oak cupboard with half a dozen doors and what seemed like a couple of hundred shelves stood to my right. To my left an elaborate curved staircase ascended first to a mezzanine or balcony—I don't know the technical term—before taking a break and carrying on upwards to another floor hidden from view above. Several large oil paintings hung on the walls of the mezzanine. These weren't depictions of faded ancestors but appeared to be modern landscapes full of swirl and dash. There were more rooms up there and I could see high ceilings and large glass chandeliers.

The Asian woman had been watching me, seeing my response, perhaps basking a little in the reflected glory.

She said, 'Follow, please,' and headed towards the staircase. Our footsteps rang crisply on the tiles until we reached the carpeted stairs, where they were muffled by the warp and weft of deep Axminster. At the top of the first flight of stairs she led me past the manic landscapes and along the mezzanine, turning left to push open a panelled door nearly twice her height.

We entered a large room painted mostly in white and furnished with expensive cream leather chairs and sofas. A grand piano stood in the far corner, its lid open and with the traditional set of photographs arranged on its shiny top, and there was a fifty inch television set hanging on the wall. From where I stood it looked as big as a stamp.

More pictures were grouped on the wall between two open french doors that gave on to a wide balcony — but these were enlarged photographs, the kind you pay a specialist studio to take of you and your children against a white background, playful, fun, capturing a moment in your lives you'll perhaps never know again.

I didn't have any of those photographs. When I was growing up that kind of ostentatious 'fun' was considered indulgent and middle-class. Looking at the photos of the young couple — the man handsome but already grey at the temples, the woman a blonde beauty with large blue eyes, the child, seven or eight years old, staring frankly at the camera — I felt a surge of envy together with a growing kernel of dislike that was perfectly unfair. These were my clients, and that was their son. I had no need for any feelings whatsoever towards them.

I should have kept telling myself that.

CHAPTER TWO

THE ASIAN WOMAN was still with me. She took a step forward and made a 'please sit' gesture with her hand. She waited until I was reclining like a pasha on one of the white sofas before she turned and floated out of the room, closing the door behind her.

I was there because of a curt phone call the previous evening, just as I was leaving my office. The man on the phone introduced himself as Mark Ware and then asked whether I knew who he was. Afterwards, I had the feeling he only agreed to meet me because I didn't know the answer to that question.

Surrounded, now, by this extravagant display of wealth, I told myself I should indeed have known him—local hot-shot businessman, CEO of Denning Electronics, suppliers of complex countermeasure systems to the Ministry of Defence and parallel agencies worldwide. In his early forties, he'd been made head of the company a couple of years ago, having risen quickly through the ranks in a small but dynamic pharmaceutical company based in London. He'd been given a Golden Hello—which probably paid for this pad—and a salary that would have kept a small African nation afloat for several years.

To say I was surprised by his phone call would be an understatement: I thought he would have had People to do that for him. Even his People would have had their own Sub-People to talk to menials such as myself.

So when he found out I didn't recognise his name he invited me out to talk to him. He wouldn't say why but said it was urgent. I can resist anything but urgency in a rich client.

Though now I was confronted by the spoils of his job, I was getting a little acid reflux in my stomach. When I worked in Customs & Excise, as it was then known, I'd broken down my fair share of drug-dealers' doors. I wouldn't say they had as much money as Ware, but whatever they had, they splashed it around. Exhibitionism seems to be a drug more addictive than heroin when the money gets into your system. It didn't sit well with me then and it still didn't.

I was roused from this philosophical crisis when the door opened again and I stood up in an automatic response.

The man in the happy family photographs came in. He was older, greyer and seemed altogether not happy. He lifted a grim smile to his lips and stuck out a hand, which I shook.

He said, 'Mark Ware. Sorry to keep you waiting.'

'Sam Dyke. No problem.'

His build was trim and athletic and he had the good looks of a minor television actor, someone who'd started out merely pretty but had weathered and acquired character over time. He was wearing jeans with an arrow-like crease and a pullover by Dolce & Gabbana. Whatever was bothering him wasn't going to interfere with his dress-sense.

'Mr Dyke, thanks for coming, please, sit.'

We sat at opposite ends of the cream sofa, turned awkwardly towards each other. The air of control transmitted by his body-language was almost palpable. I felt like the gardener summoned to be grilled on how the roses were doing.

He said, 'If you didn't know who I was last night, I daresay you've done your research now. Am I right?'

'Google is the detective's best friend.'

'So you'll know my position and what I do. Not that it should make any difference to this conversation, I realise that.'

'What is this conversation about, Mr Ware?'

'I just wanted to be clear. No misunderstandings. My strength as a leader has always been clarity, at least that's what people have said. Though of course they could just have been licking my arse.'

'It's a popular occupation in large companies.'

'Of course, you'd know that, having worked for the Excise.' He caught the flicker of acknowledgement that crossed my face, and explained parenthetically: 'I can use Google too. Most of the time I'm surrounded by people who'll do what I want without asking questions. That's all well and good but at this moment it's irrelevant. I need someone competent … and discreet.'

'I'm as competent as I'm allowed to be and as discreet as the next person. Mr Ware, would you like to drop a hint as to what this is all about?'

'It's just …'

'What?'

'I don't know you. I find it hard to talk about this.'

I stood up. 'Let me know when you find the guts to do it.'

'No, please …' He looked up at me, his face now agonised. 'I'll tell you, of course I'll tell you. Please, sit down.'

I hadn't intended to leave but sometimes you have to force their hand. Clients are often embarrassed or guilty or find it difficult to open up to a stranger. Sometimes you have to prove to them that your time is valuable.

I sat down again and there was a pause I didn't interrupt. Eventually he turned away from me and stared through one of the open french windows. The day beyond was filled with warm air and blue skies but I could tell it meant nothing to him. His massive gardens and over-substantial house could have been fabricated out of matches for all the strength they were able to provide.

'I have a son, Mr Dyke. Lucas. Ten years old. Little blond terror. Do you have kids?'

'A son.'

He nodded, then took a piece of paper from his pocket.

'I should probably have kept this somewhere safe, but I can't seem to let go of it. As though it'll read differently next time I look.'

He handed it across. It was a sheet of graph paper torn from a standard exercise book, used by children everywhere. There was writing on one side:

> *We'll be in touch. No police if you want him back. Go*
> *to work. Say nothing.*

Ware watched me finish reading the note and turn it over. There was nothing on the reverse.

He said, 'Two days ago Lucas was coming home from school. Our driver had picked him up and they were half a mile from here when they came to a car parked across the lane. Harris, the driver, stopped and another car came up behind him. Seemed to be one man in each car. One of them shot the front tyre and got Harris out. The other one took Lucas from the back seat. They gave Harris this note and made him walk back.'

'And you haven't told anyone?'

He snorted and gestured towards the note. 'Would you? If it was your son?'

'Could Harris give any descriptions of any kind? Anything unusual about the car, the men?'

'Harris is good, ex-cop, worked in the Met. But there was nothing. License plates were covered up. Men were average height and build, wore masks and gloves and dark glasses, said nothing, did it all through gestures.'

'What time was this? Where were you?'

'I told you, it was after the end of the school day. I got the call from Harris at about four-fifteen and came straight home. My wife was on the way already.'

'You have a driver but he was driving neither you nor your wife? Does he take Lucas to school and back and that's it?'

He grew exasperated and some colour came into his face.

'I was in a meeting in Manchester that was due to finish after six o'clock. My wife was at the hairdresser. She would normally have picked Lucas up but she didn't want to lose her appointment, and Harris was free because he was hanging around waiting till it was time to fetch me. He would have brought Lucas home then driven into Manchester later on.'

'And he would have left Lucas with the woman who let me in.'

'Mrs Chau, yes. Lucas doesn't need much looking after as long as he's got his iPad and the TV.'

I leaned back on the sofa and glanced at the family photographs on the wall facing me. They were like a mocking commentary on the situation in which the Wares now found themselves.

I said, 'So what do you want me to do? You know what my advice is going to be.'

He lowered his eyes. 'Go to the police. Tell them everything.'

'Any reason not to?'

'How about the fact we're scared shitless something's going to happen to Lucas? Will that do?'

'It may have already happened. If it hasn't, the police are still your best option. Resources, manpower, contacts. I'm outgunned.'

'My research says you've dealt with some high-profile cases in the last few months.'

'I'm flattered. PR doesn't come cheap. The note says no police—that might include me, if you push the definition.'

'My wife wants to do something, anything. It's been two days of hell for her—for me as well, of course. We haven't slept, barely eaten. We're just waiting.'

I sighed. 'What will they want?'

'Who?'

'The kidnappers. Will it be money? You're not short of it.'

'What else would it be?'

'Influence. A decision made on someone's behalf. In someone's favour.'

He glanced up, searching my face. When he spoke he sounded dubious, as though the idea had never occurred to him. 'Is that likely?'

'They're making you sweat so they're not after money in a hurry. Perhaps there's something else on their wish-list. Any big decisions coming up for you? From what I read, your company supplies equipment to most Western defence agencies. Do you sub-contract work out, new contracts to be drawn up, work offered to the smaller fish to fight over … stuff like that?'

He shook his head confidently, ruling out the possibility. 'Nothing. The pipe-line for the next eighteen months is all in place. There's nothing on the table for at least another six.'

I stood up and went to look through one of the open french windows. As I expected, the view was startling—the garden fell away in little swoops and hollows of colour, the shape defined by artfully-placed trees or bowers or low rough-brick walls; but beyond, across the road where Lucas had been kidnapped, the Cheshire countryside continued in its stately progression, green and profuse and untroubled, an occasional knot of cows punctuating the greenery like brown paint spatter.

But it was a world of nature and although well-concealed, an incorruptible violence lurked just below the surface. Evidently Mark Ware and his wife hadn't expected it to come marching through the front door and seize their child with its rough and uncaring hands.

As I was thinking this, the door behind me opened again and I turned to find the most beautiful woman I'd ever seen walking towards me.

CHAPTER THREE

THE PHOTOS ON the wall didn't do her justice. They'd caught the angled planes of her face and the deep colour of her eyes, blue as a Greek sea, but the camera lens couldn't capture the elegance with which all the sundry parts had been put together—the ligatures, the smooth joints, the precision with which the neck connected collar-bone to jaw-line, the tension of the skin as it moved across the brow and down the cheek towards the delicate chin.

She was a marvel of genetic engineering.

Today her blonde hair was piled roughly on top of her head and she wore just a trace of pink lipstick. No ear-rings, just a wedding-ring on her finger. A simple white blouse and pale cream slacks. No ostentation. She didn't need anything to draw attention to her physical presence—you couldn't help but look.

And this was on a bad day.

I shook the pale hand she held towards me.

She said, 'Mr Dyke, Roberta Ware. Everyone calls me Bobbie. So, can you help us?'

Mark Ware had stood up. He seemed diminished by her presence, as though his own life-force recognised a stronger being.

He said, 'Mr Dyke thinks it would be best to tell the police.'

She looked me up and down. 'That's impossible. You read the note.'

'But you still called me.'

'I'm going out of my mind. I had to do something. If calling the police is all you can think of you're no use to us. I'm sorry you came all this way.'

'I said the police were the best solution to the problem. I didn't say they were the only solution.'

She studied me again. 'Has anyone offered you anything to drink?'

'Coffee would be good. White, no sugar.'

Behind her, Mark Ware moved to a telephone next to the door. I heard him murmur into it.

Bobbie Ware reached out a hand and drew me back towards one of the sofas, then sat on it next to me. Unlike her husband she had no difficulty looking me straight in the eye. I had no problems with it either.

She said, 'You've got to help us, Mr Dyke. I'm going mad worrying what they're doing to Lucas. It's money, isn't it? They'll want money. We'll pay anything … poor little mite …'

Now she looked down and I saw in the tremor of her hands the fragility in her no-nonsense pose. She was holding herself together with sheer will-power.

I said, 'If it's money they're after they'll be in touch soon. They'll look after him because he's the meal-ticket. They know you'll want proof he's still alive. They hid their faces with masks and dark glasses so neither he nor Harris could identify them, which means they've planned thoroughly and intend to get away with it. If they … do anything to Lucas, it's worse for them if they're caught.'

She nodded, as though she'd already thought of all this but was grateful for the reassurance.

'It's this house. We're bloody miles from anywhere. As soon as we got here I didn't like it. Now we can't get rid of it.'

'They'd have got to you wherever you were. It's a pro job — or at least someone with brains has thought it through.'

'We have to drive miles to get anywhere, Lucas can't just go next door to a friend's house, he has to be chaperoned, chauffeured … we should have moved back into town.'

Mark Ware said, 'Bobbie … let's not go over that again.'

She turned on him. 'Why the fuck not? The poor kid's got no friends except a tablet and a TV. And a Vietnamese woman whose English isn't even her second language …'

'It's not helping. We've got to think sensibly.'

She stared at him for a moment longer, then seemed to shudder and drew a long breath. Finally she turned back to me.

'Mr Dyke, what can you do for us? Obviously money's no object but you can't talk to the police about this. To be honest, part of me doesn't want you to do anything, in case, you know … but I can't just sit around waiting. It's killing me.'

'My best advice is still to tell the police. They're experienced in this kind of thing, keeping out of the way, persuading the kidnappers nothing has changed. Who knows, there may be CCTV footage from Prestbury they can use.'

'Please, don't make that suggestion again.'

'I'm putting all the cards on the table.'

In response she stood and went to the grand piano, plucking a framed photograph from its shiny black surface. She sat down again and handed it to me. It was a 10x 8 school photograph of a young boy with straight blond hair and a crooked grin. He wore a grey pullover and a red tie was pushed up against his thin neck.

Lucas Ware.

Bobbie Ware said, 'What would you do if it was your child?'

I had no reply. I understood completely. I hadn't known Dan when he was growing up, but now he was a young adult I knew I'd do anything to keep him from harm. I handed the photograph back and she placed it carefully on a small table at the end of the sofa.

She seemed to become conscious that her back was towards her husband. She left the sofa she and I were sitting on and went to take her place next to him, giving him a small, forgive-me smile as she did so. Their hands found each other and they sat waiting for me to unfurl my expertise like a magic carpet.

I said, 'Okay. I'll do what I can.'

As best they could, they both smiled. Bobbie Ware said, 'Thank you.'

'But we need to discuss what exactly you want me to do. There isn't much to go on.'

'We're in your hands. How do we start?'

I began by telling them my rates and by adding that I might use a colleague, Belinda McFee, for some leg work, and gave them her rates too. The talk of money seemed to irritate them—they both frowned as though it were inconsequential.

I said, 'Let's go over the story again. Lucas was taken when you were both away from the house.'

They nodded.

'Who would know that?'

They glanced at each other. Mark Ware said, 'Harris, of course, and Mrs Chau.'

Bobbie Ware added, 'And Debra.'

I raised my eyebrows.

'My assistant. She wasn't here at the time but she knew I was having my hair done and we were meeting later to discuss one of my projects. I'd told her Mark was going to be out till seven-ish so we'd have time before dinner.'

'Anyone else?'

They looked at each other again. Mark Ware said, 'Not that we can think of. And believe me, we've been thinking about it.'

'And you can trust all of these people?'

'Implicitly. Harris has been with us for nearly five years, from when we were still in London. Mrs Chau started when we moved to Manchester a couple of years ago. And Bobbie was at school with Debra.'

I'd taken out a small notebook and had written down the names. Before I could ask the next question there was a small knock on the door and the housekeeper, Mrs Chau, entered with a tray containing a single cup of coffee. She set it on the glass table in front of me and then retreated, nodding once. I took a sip while she left the room.

I said, 'So what's the house routine? How do you organise yourselves in this Disneyland?'

Between them they began to describe their family life — Mark was driven in to Manchester most days, where his company offices were based, and then Harris would come back to the house and help out with driving duties where he could. His duties seemed to include more than sitting in the driving seat waiting for instructions. He kept track of who was where and organised the transport timetable, keeping both Mark and Bobbie aware of what he could or couldn't do for either of them. As he was paid out of Mark's salary, he had first call on his time. But there were long stretches of the day when he could ferry Bobbie around to her various project meetings, which were often in Manchester anyway. She didn't like driving in the city unless she absolutely had to.

'What are these "projects"?'

She shrugged. 'Mostly charity work. This is Cheshire. Lots of bored women—farmers' wives, businessmen's wives, footballers' wives … they have time on their hands and brains, so they want to get involved in something. Mark has a big profile and I'm not unknown around here, so I help out where I can.'

Mark was away a lot on business, home and abroad, so Bobbie stayed at home to look after Lucas and keep the house running. She usually took Lucas in to school and picked him up at the end of the day, driving her own car. When she couldn't manage they organised themselves so that Harris did it. And if that didn't work, there was a floating parents' car pool they could call on as a last resort.

'Is there a cook, a housekeeper?'

'I like to do my own cooking but Mrs Chau looks after the rest. Cleaning, washing, keeping the place looking nice. I offered to get in a maid service but she said she can manage. Out of all the rooms in this place we only use half a dozen on a daily basis and she can look after those.'

'Does she live in?'

'Not now. She used to but about a year ago she told us she'd bought a house in Liverpool with her savings and wanted to spend more time there.'

'That's a long commute.'

'She only does half days. She can get everything done in the time she's here and the rest of the day's her own.'

'What about Harris?'

'He has his own accommodation at the back of this building. I don't mean a flat, it's a separate house, a barn conversion done by the previous owners.'

'No Mrs Harris?'

'Not these days. He'd just divorced when we took him on. He left her in London. No kids. He was glad to get away, go somewhere new. I don't know what his domestic arrangements are now and I don't care. He can do what he likes in his house.'

'Those are extensive gardens out there … does Mrs Chau look after them as well?'

'We contracted a father and son company in Prestbury. The previous owners used them and recommended them and we've had no reason to change. They never step inside the house. We barely even see them. They bring their own tools except for the ride-on mower, which is kept in a hut around the back. I seriously doubt they'd have anything to do with this.'

'Why? If you don't know them well, how could you judge their character or motivations?'

'They're gardeners, for Christ's sake. Settled in the village for years, decades. Why would they muck that up?'

'The thought of money can really confuse some people.'

'You can talk to them if you want. Pearson. Harry Pearson and son.'

Bobbi added, 'John.'

I said, 'It sounds like your routine would be easy to work out. On days you, Mark, are not abroad you're in Manchester, being the leader of men. Mrs Ware—'

'Bobbie.'

'—you're likely to be here or if not, then in Manchester.'

'Someone would still need to know the exact details of where we were going to be, and when.'

'Why? All they'd really need was the time Lucas was going to be picked up from school. Whether Mrs Ware was driving or Harris, it wouldn't make any difference. In fact it might have been safer if the lady of the house was behind the wheel rather than an ex-copper. Makes you think, doesn't it?'

'What, Harris? Don't be stupid.'

'Can I talk to him?'

'Of course. When do you want to start?'

'Now.'

CHAPTER FOUR

MARK WARE SAID he'd take me through the house to see Harris. He called first, using his mobile, then led the way out of the lounge, down the stairs, through one of the hallway doors that had been closed when I entered the house, and along a corridor that was tiled and smelled of disinfectant. At the end of the corridor we opened out into a kitchen of almost industrial size, then passed through into a mud-room with green wellington boots lined against one wall and overcoats hanging on hooks ranged on another. Like everywhere else, it was spotless. Mrs Chau earned her money.

A final door led out back to a gravelled yard. To the left was an open barn, inside of which I could see the ride-on mower Bobbie Ware had mentioned. The barn also contained two huge piles of firewood laid out in neat ranks. Somewhere in the house was a wood-burning stove and maybe an Aga so Bobbie Ware could cook in the accepted style. Straight ahead was another building that to judge from its construction had also been a barn once but had been re-purposed into a solid-looking house with a fresh paint-job and double-glazed windows.

Mark Ware knocked on the door and it was opened immediately. A man in his late fifties appeared in the doorway. He had short grey hair thinning at the front and drooping bags beneath his eyes. He ignored Ware and looked at me with frank displeasure.

Here we go again, I thought, with the suspicious cop routine. As soon as they knew what I did, their eyebrows closed together and their lips pursed as though unwilling to let any potentially treacherous words out.

Ware said, 'George, I've brought Mr Dyke to have a conversation. About ... you know. Tell him what you told us. Don't hold anything back.'

He made a move as if to step forward into the house but I put out a hand.

'That's okay, I can take it from here.'

He looked startled and then relieved, as though he couldn't bear to hear the story all over again.

'Right, fine. I'll be in the house when you've finished.'

He backed away as though waiting for a farewell, but neither of us said anything. Harris remained in the doorway, obdurate and solid. He was shorter than me but the barn conversion had a raised front step so he looked me directly in the eye. He was wearing formal black trousers—perhaps part of a uniform—but with a tee-shirt covering his sagging chest.

He said, 'Got special powers, have you?'

'None that I know of.'

'Able to sniff the air and tell which direction they went in? Read tea-leaves? Do a bit of dowsing with a compass over a map?'

'Can I come in, or do you want to continue the job interview here?'

He snorted. 'You can come in but you haven't got the job.'

He turned and went inside. The space opened up into a single large room with an area sectioned off for the kitchen, and a sofa facing a TV console of the kind you don't see much any more, the wooden sort with spaces beneath for a VHS player and a few tapes. Rows of DVDs were lined up on shelves either side of the television and more of them were ranged in Ikea bookcases behind the set. Not much of a reader, then, but a hell of a couch-potato.

He said, 'I'd offer you tea but I've just run out. And coffee. Shame, that.'

'Milk?'

'It's gone off. All lumpy.'

'Can I sit down?'

'Free country.'

There was an armchair next to the sofa and I sat in it and made myself comfortable. He remained standing just inside the door, still not giving an inch.

I said, 'So when you let these two men take your boss's ten-year-old child, what were you thinking? What passed through your head?'

His face darkened and he took a step forward before catching himself. His face and the half-moon of flesh above his tee-shirt went red.

'I don't have to answer to you.'

'The Wares think otherwise. Like me, they're wondering if there's anything else you could have done. Like me, they're wondering whether you put yourself before the boy. Let him take his chances rather than you get a bullet in your leg.'

'You bastard.'

'Come on, then. Tell me otherwise. Describe what happened. Tell me what choices you had.'

'I worked fifteen years in the Met. I saw what bullets did to bodies.'

'Looks worse in ten-year-old bodies.'

He moved further into the room, his actions sluggish and leaden. I wondered whether he'd been drinking—then realised he was probably devastated by shame.

That wasn't my problem. I looked around the room. On the walls of the kitchen section there was a calendar showing a week per page rather than a month. Scribbled handwriting filled the mornings and afternoons—this was the agenda Harris kept to tell him where he was supposed to be at any given time. The next couple of days were filled sketchily. Ware had been told to carry on going to work but he wasn't about to do any more than absolutely necessary.

Harris said, 'Two black nondescript saloons, perhaps Passats. I'm not a car person but they weren't fancy like Mercedes or Audis. One was across the road in front of me, door open. First thought: an accident, driver's wandered off. I stop, get ready to open the door when the first man appears out of the hedge, big gun held straight ahead of him, police or armed forces pose. Couldn't ID the gun.'

'Let me guess, you're not a gun person.'

'I look behind—second car's pulled up to the bumper, no room to manoeuvre.'

'And no one's said anything.'

'I lock the doors, start to get my phone out. First man kills the front offside tyre. Waves his gun at me. What am I going to do?'

'The car's not armoured?'

'Get real. Standard issue Bentley. Nice to drive but built for the roads in Cheshire, not Syria.'

'Even with Ware's job? Arms manufacturing?'

'Desk job. Pen pusher. Lots of big decisions but never picks up a rifle. It's all "counter-measures"—computers, in other words.'

'What were they wearing?'

'Black jeans, black pullover, wool masks. Dark glasses, wraparound. Like being held up by Bono.'

'So you get out of the car.'

'Man keeps his gun on me, reaches in a pocket, hands me the note. I hear the rear door of the Bentley opening and see the kid being yanked out by the other guy. Same clothing, maybe a fraction taller. He takes him back to his own car, the one behind mine, shoves him in the back seat.'

I sat up. 'So he puts him in the back then gets in the front to drive?'

'Yes.' The same thought occurred to him as to me. 'So there's someone in the back to watch him …'

'You didn't see anyone?'

'No, my man taps me on the chest with his gun, gets my attention, points me down the road. Still saying nothing. I hear the other car reversing—there's an opening in the field twenty yards back so he probably reversed into it and went out through Prestbury.'

'And you walk back here.'

'I'd gone a hundred yards when I hear the other car leave.'

'Didn't it have to squeeze past the Bentley?'

'No, there's another junction on the road, takes you out between the fields to the farms then out the other side. They'd looked at their maps.'

'What then?'

'I run back to the Bentley but he's taken the keys and anyway, the front wheel's a mess. It's a ten minute walk here. I phone Ware at his office, he tells me not to phone the missus but she's en route anyway, left the hairdresser. Arrives five minutes after me. Asks all sorts of awkward questions, like "Where's my child?" Ware turns up an hour later by taxi and all hell breaks loose. I'd had to tell her and show her the note because I'd turned up without the kid, hadn't I? But he wasn't happy. And she wasn't happy. Pardon my understatement.'

I closed my notebook.

'Going back to when they left you on the road … You ran back to the Bentley but didn't use your mobile?'

'Guy took it with the keys. I'd left it on the dash. Probably thought it would give him another ten minutes.'

He'd sat down on his sofa and relaxed. Perhaps he liked telling his side of the story. He would have had a rough ride from the Wares when he turned up without Lucas and with a story about armed men.

I said, 'Any theories? You being an ex-copper and all.'

'Don't put too much weight on that. Last five years I was behind a desk too.'

'You must have had some thoughts.'

'Money, first. Look around. They wouldn't miss the odd million.'

'But you don't think it's that.'

He shrugged. 'I'll wait and see. Put it this way, I'd be very surprised if it wasn't money.'

'But.'

'You get a nose for these things, don't you? Look, it was two days ago and still no follow-up? No phone-call or message in a bottle? They're waiting to see what happens before they take the next step. If it were a couple of rough diamonds on a caper they'd have called by now, got the ball rolling.'

'Do you think the Wares should bring the police in? Given your experience?'

'Yes, if you want size ten boots all over it and a dead kid in a field. On the other hand …'

'What?'

'The Wares took their bloody time pulling your chain, didn't they? What was that about?'

'You can't blame them. They're worried I might be taken for police.'

'Not by anyone with two working brain cells.'

CHAPTER FIVE

I COULDN'T BE certain, but I didn't think Harris was involved in the kidnapping. He had a cushy number and he knew enough about police operations to know kidnappers were usually caught. You could argue his inside knowledge meant he'd be smart enough to get away with it, but he had the demeanour of someone who couldn't be bothered. He had his DVDs and a nice house and probably a nice pension on top. He'd retire in a couple of years and buy somewhere in Spain, start looking for a companion amongst the widowed expats with dangerous tans and thinning hair.

As I crossed the yard from Harris' house back to the main building I saw a movement behind the kitchen window. I pretended I'd seen nothing, but when I opened the door into the mud-room I moved swiftly into the kitchen.

Empty.

It was more like a canteen than a domestic kitchen, with a free-standing Aga and a separate double-oven, a huge breakfast bar with a shiny granite top in the centre, and two large Belfast sinks side-by-side overlooking the yard, each with their own double-drainer. The house must have been used for entertaining large numbers of people from time to time, Ware's clients or defence ministry muckamucks.

Turning, I saw there was another doorway into the kitchen apart from the one I'd used. I went through it and was suddenly lost in a warren of small rooms and narrow corridors, all interconnected—probably part of the original farmhouse before the bigger mansion was built on top.

I kept moving until I found another corridor. I guessed I was heading west, towards the orangery, and just as I had that thought I came out into a small round foyer with the ironwork structure of the orangery visible on its far side, through a high opening. Trying to look casual, I strolled across and passed through the doorway into a glass-sided octagon with yet more views over the garden. Although at one time it might have nurtured fruit trees the space had now been tricked out as a fairly standard conservatory, complete with bamboo furniture and a glass-topped table. A musty smell of earth hung in the air and I saw there were two wooden raised beds in use housing small shoots that were being nursed to full growth. There were two large greenhouses in the gardens outside so this small nursery must have been an area for the Wares' private use.

Mrs Chau was sitting on a padded bench that ran inside the curve of the windows. She had turned so she could look out through the glass, into the garden. She gave no sign she'd seen me come in.

From this angle I could tell she'd probably been attractive when younger. Although she'd thickened around the middle she still had the long, straight back and slim legs of a woman in her twenties.

She spoke without turning towards me.

'It's a beautiful house, isn't it?'

Her accent had vanished. She spoke with a cultivated English voice that could have belonged to the original owner of the mansion.

I said, 'I've never seen a private house with such large rooms.'

She glanced at me, her eyes cool. 'You don't like it.'

'Too extravagant for my taste.'

'So you're a socialist. My former employers used to laugh at people like you. They used to say you were just envious of what other people had. As soon as you had any power, they said, you would be as obnoxious as any right-wing government.'

'Your former employers sound a little prejudiced towards the common man.'

Now she turned on the seat and looked up at me, her hands clasped together in her lap, her lips thin. A little more intelligence had come into her eyes than I'd seen when she let me into the house.

'My former employers were the British Ambassador to Hanoi and his wife. Of course they were prejudiced.'

I felt my eyebrows rise before I could stop them. She saw the movement.

'Yes, I haven't always been a housekeeper. I was responsible for the running of the embassy's civilian staff. They placed great trust in me.'

'How did you end up here, cleaning bathrooms?'

She shrugged. 'Things change. A man made a promise to me that he didn't keep. I landed in this country with a small child and an address. As you see, I've managed to make my way.'

'Where is your child?'

Her eyes hardened. 'Our early times here were difficult. The strain was too much for him.'

'I'm sorry.'

'Don't be. His suffering was great and when he died it gave me more freedom to travel and find work.'

I fetched a bamboo chair and sat facing her.

'Will you answer some questions for me?'

'I have nothing to tell you.'

'You were here when Harris arrived back, after the kidnapping.'

'I don't want to talk about this. It's not my affair.'

I stared at her, returning her own coolness in my eyes.

'We're discussing the life of a child. Doesn't that matter to you?'

'You say that to me, who lost a boy at six years of age? How dare you.'

'Then imagine how the Wares must feel.'

'I know how the Wares feel. But I have nothing to tell you.'

She turned back to the view and stared at the gardens but I saw her eyes were unfocused. I wondered what she might be thinking about, living in an English house far from the heat and press of Hanoi. And then I knew.

I said, 'I understand you have your own place now, that you don't live here any more.'

She nodded.

'Why was that? I'm sure they gave you a very nice room, the run of the house. No commuting home every night.'

'It's more convenient for me.'

'I find that hard to believe.'

'It's true. When I lived in it was easier for them to call on me even outside my official work hours. And I have friends elsewhere, you know.'

'I'm sure. And of course if you go home at night you don't have to be around Lucas. Who is … what, ten?'

'That's correct.'

'And if your boy had lived, how old would he have been now?'

The question hit her like a slap; she cringed away from me but said nothing.

I said, 'I understand what it must be like for you, in someone else's house, a wonderful house, with an active ten-year-old running around everywhere. It must have been hard to take.'

She maintained her silence for a minute and I didn't interrupt. Then she said, 'They're unlike each other and yet so alike. They play computer games and don't play sport. They listen to the same music, wear similar clothes, though of course Lucas' clothes are much more expensive.'

She said this last phrase with barely a hint of bitterness.

'But you don't want Lucas to come to harm, do you?'

'What does it matter to me? I've lost one child. I can't afford to have feelings for another.'

'And yet you do.'

She lowered her head and when she finally spoke her voice was barely audible.

'I will talk to you but you can't treat me like a person who doesn't care. It's not right and it's not true.'

'I'm sorry, I didn't intend to do that.'

She nodded. 'What do you want to know?'

I felt bad, like a bully who's got his own way because he's bigger and stronger. I cleared my throat.

'When Harris arrived back the afternoon of the kidnapping ...'

'Yes.'

'How was he?'

'What do you mean?'

'Was he calm, angry, flustered?'

'Yes.'

'Which?'

'All of them.' She raised her head to look at me and her voice gained some strength. 'When he arrived he was angry. I suppose he felt his professionalism had been challenged.

Then, while we waited for Mrs Ware to arrive, he calmed himself so he could talk without alarming her. Later, when Mr Ware arrived, he became flustered under their questions.'

'You were there?'

'I brought tea. I heard a good deal of what was said.'

'They blamed him?'

'Not really. He kept saying they had guns and he didn't want anyone shot.' She added acerbically, 'Least of all himself.'

So her view of Harris agreed with mine.

'And what's happened since that day?'

'Mr Ware has gone into work for the last two days. He arrived home earlier today to speak to you. Mrs Ware has stayed home, in case … in case there's a call, or he comes back. Harris stays in his house. Mr Ware drives himself to work. I don't think he can bear to be in the same vehicle as Harris.'

'They had the Bentley fixed already?'

'No, Harris arranged for that to be towed to a garage the same night. Mr Ware uses his private car. I don't know the make. I think it's German.'

'Is there anything you can tell me about their conversations, anything that strikes you as odd?'

She gave a bitter laugh.

'At the moment everything is odd. What is not odd when your child has been kidnapped and you can tell no one about it?'

'But how are they dealing with it?'

She sighed. 'To be honest I haven't seen them much since that night. But that afternoon …'

'What?'

'From what I heard, Mrs Ware wanted to call the police anyway, despite what it said on the note.'

'And Mr Ware?'

'I think he just wanted to follow orders.'

CHAPTER SIX

I LEFT MRS Chau and her bitterness in the orangery and headed back in the general direction of the lounge where I'd first met Mark and Bobbie Ware.

I'd just entered the hall when Bobbie called my name from the other side, beyond the sweeping staircase. She came into view trailed by another young woman, who was dark-haired and slim and attractive enough so long as she didn't stand next to Bobbie Ware.

Bobbie strode forward and the young woman followed, almost sheepishly, I thought, as if she didn't want to be introduced. Obviously my cachet as a private detective was wearing thin.

'This is Debra, my assistant. She's here on another matter but I thought you ought to speak to her as you're speaking to everyone else. Did you find Mrs Chau? I asked her to intercept you on the way back from Harris.'

'We've spoken. Interesting woman.'

'Is she? I really wouldn't know.'

I wondered which version of herself Mrs Chau projected when dealing with the Wares—the uncivil servant or the haughty, slightly elitist administrator with better things to do than wash clothes.

Bobbie had turned to Debra.

'You can use my office. Tell Mr Dyke whatever he wants to know, and I'll see you later. Come and find me in the pool when you're done.'

She strode away and I watched her go, wondering whether I could get an invite to see her in the pool, too.

Debra stuck out a hand, which I shook. 'Pleased to meet you. Shall we go to the office?'

She turned away before I could answer and led me through yet another door at the back of the hall and then along a short corridor to a flight of stairs. I was beginning to get the impression that all the important happenings in this household took place upstairs. Downstairs it was kitchen, pool … what else? Garage? Dungeon?

At the top of the stairs we entered a part of the building that was decorated in a more workaday style than the expansive lounge—grey carpet, plain walls, a sense of businesslike activity rather than domestic leisure.

Debra guessed what I was thinking. She spoke over her shoulder.

'Bobbie and Mark have their offices on this side. They try to keep this part of their lives separate from, you know, family stuff.'

'You were at school with Bobbie?'

'I was.'

She opened a door and led us into a medium-sized room—for this place—that contained a wide desk, an expensive leather office chair and a two-seater sofa with a low table in front of it. The view from the window overlooked the rear courtyard, with Harris' converted barn dead ahead. You could see straight down into his living room-cum-kitchen.

Debra sat on the office chair and twirled it so that it faced the sofa.

'Please, take the sofa, it's more comfy. I really don't know what I can tell you. By the time I arrived that night they'd all calmed down.'

I realised that although she'd been straightforward and businesslike, she was actually very tense. Her hands were knotted together in her lap and her eyes were rimmed with red, as though she hadn't slept.

I took out my notebook, trying to look professional and unthreatening. I said, 'I understand. I'm just gathering information. Why don't you tell me how it works here. How come you've ended up working for Bobbie in the first place?'

She hesitated and looked down, as though fascinated by her hands. 'Can I just say, I'm not comfortable about any of this?'

'Why?'

'I don't understand why they haven't contacted the police. But please don't tell her that!'

'I suppose you've seen the note. Can you blame them?'

'I know, I know … but we're just hanging around, waiting to hear something. It's not right.'

'They hired me.'

'Well, without meaning to be rude, who are you? What can you do that the police couldn't?'

'I agree. I told them that myself.'

Her eyes widened. 'Did you? What did they say?'

'Bobbie wanted to do something, even if it's on the quiet.'

'And do you think you can do anything?'

'I don't know yet. Probably not, especially if I'm supposed to be operating in the dark.'

'It's all so … terrible. I was scared to come in today. What if something happens to one of us? What if they kidnap someone else to make a point?'

'That's not likely, is it? If the kidnappers want money then Lucas is the one who can get it for them.'

She drew a big sigh and seemed to gather her courage.

'Well I think this is a waste of time but if you want to ask me questions I'll do my best.'

'We're all very grateful.'

She looked at me sharply, hearing the reproach. I held her gaze until she looked away, embarrassed.

I said, 'Back to the question: how did you wind up working for Bobbie?'

'Is that relevant?'

'It helps me get a picture of the set-up here.'

She shrugged. 'Well, look at her. It was always obvious she was going to be someone, or do something. She's not just beautiful, she's bright. I hate her.' She uttered a little laugh. 'Kidding. She's actually a very nice person, too. We were in the same year at school but I didn't know her that well. She went down to London to Uni, I stayed up here. Next thing I knew she was married and popping up in the papers and the fancy magazines, Tatler, that kind of thing. She studied languages but it's not the easiest degree to get a job with, unless you go to Europe, Brussels. So she was married almost straight out of university. She and Mark were quite the couple. He became one of the youngest ever CEOs of a pharmaceutical company, she was the glamorous wife, then mother.'

'What were you doing at that time?'

'I had a good job, working in a small PR company in Manchester. It was okay but limited. As you can imagine, most of the big work gets sucked into the London firms. I bumped into Bobbie at a party somewhere just after they'd come north and the next day she rang and asked whether I'd consider working for her.'

'When was that?'

'A couple of years ago.'

'So what's it like, working for someone you were at school with? Must be strange …'

She hesitated and her hands twisted in her lap. She was probably considering how loyal she should be. 'Yes and no. We laugh a lot. If you saw her in different circumstances you'd see she's a lot of fun. Of course all this has devastated her. Lucas is a nice boy, as ten-year-olds go.'

'Do you have kids?'

'Not yet. I'm getting married next month and that's on the agenda, as they say. Tick-tock.'

'You're still young.'

'I'm the same age as Bobbie and she's got a ten-year-old.'

This was a subject where she seemed definitive, so I moved on and asked her about her work routine.

'There's no routine. It can be quite chaotic. Bobbie's involved in lots of different charities—she and Mark visited the Far East on holiday some years ago and I think it woke something in her, a sense of responsibility.'

'Where did they go?'

'I'm not sure … Cambodia, I think, Vietnam, Bali, places like that.'

'Mrs Chau?'

'Yes, she's Vietnamese. But I think that's a coincidence. They got her through an agency in Manchester then kept her on privately. I dunno, maybe the fact that they'd been to Vietnam made Bobbie more disposed towards taking her on.'

I wrote this down for something to do, though in fact I rarely referred to my notes. 'So back to you—you don't have regular hours?'

'I do a lot of work from home—telephoning, email, writing invitation letters. We often meet in the evenings, between four and six, after she's fetched Lucas from school. He gets playtime to himself and we have a couple of hours before Mark gets home. Sometimes I come by in the morning but not often—she usually goes out after she's dropped Lucas at school: shopping, meeting friends, coffee.'

I asked a few more questions about how it worked between her and Bobbie, then said, 'So tell me about that evening, the day Lucas was taken.'

She shifted her position in the chair as though trying to compose herself. 'As I said, it all happened before I got here. We were due to have one of these evening meetings, planning a charity dinner somewhere. She hadn't phoned to tell me not to come—probably forgot, given the circumstances. Anyway, when I come to work I drive around to the yard and come in the back door so I don't have to bother Mrs Chau with answering the front. Also, it's quicker to get here, to this office, up the back stairs. So I came into the house and of course Bobbie's not here in the office so I went through to the main living areas and looked in rooms until I found them in the big lounge.'

'The one with the happy family photos.'

'Yes. You'd think they'd want to take them down. They're like a slap in the face, aren't they?'

'Who was there in the room?'

'Just Bobbie and Mark. They'd spoken to Harris but there was nothing more they could do if they weren't going to phone the police. So more conversation with him was pointless. From what I gathered he kept telling them they should phone someone, he knew some names, ex-copper and all that … blah blah blah. So rather than argue with him they just sent him away. They probably couldn't bear the sight of his stubbly chin.'

'I'm not sure they blame him.'

'Really? They're more generous than I am, then.'

'How were they when you arrived?'

'Shell-shocked. They kept staring at each other, Bobbie would burst into tears and he'd try and put an arm around her and she'd shake him off. It was pretty horrible.'

'And you didn't know what had happened at first.'

'Of course not. I hadn't seen anybody since I came in.'

'So who told you?'

'She did. As soon as I walked in the room. It was as if she had to tell someone, let someone else into the secret. Then they made me promise I wouldn't tell anyone else. Which I completely get. I stayed a couple of hours, just offering comfort … stupid, really. They were beyond comfort.'

'And have you?'

'What?'

'Told anyone else.'

'No, of course not. Not with Lucas' life presumably at stake. Poor kid.'

As she told me this she blushed slowly from her neck upwards. I made some more notes to give her time to stew in her lie. I wondered who she'd told.

I said, 'So you're getting married?'

The change of direction startled her.

'Yes. Charlie.'

'What's he do for a living?'

'What's he got to do with anything?'

'Nothing, just curious.' I smiled cosily. 'One of the qualifications for being an expensive private detective.'

'He's a retired footballer.'

I nodded. 'Some money in the bank, then.'

'He didn't play in the Premiership. But still, yeah. Not bad. We're going down to London. Where his family are.'

'What will you do down there?'

'He's starting a sports agency with a couple of friends. He's asked me to help him set it up, you know, like office manager. I'm looking forward to it.'

Her face was very bright and intense now, thinking about this new phase in her life.

And yet …

There was a brittleness in there, too, as though the overpowering optimism was masking something else.

I said casually, 'Sports agents are big business these days. Presumably he's got lots of contacts. And offices in London—not cheap.'

'He can afford it. Besides, he's got someone who's going to back him.'

'Oh, who? Some famous sportsman?'

Her face clouded briefly. 'The little devil won't tell me. Says it's going to be a surprise. He's like that, keeps stuff to himself.'

'It's a man thing.'

She smiled warily. 'That might be true, but I can't say I like it much.'

'And you haven't told him about what's happened here?'

She glanced away too quickly and the blush reappeared.

'Of course not. I promised.'

'I know, but sometimes things are too juicy not to share, aren't they?'

She held my eyes nervously but said nothing. Perhaps she was worried she'd give herself away.

I put my notebook in my pocket and she breathed out as though she'd been holding it in for the duration of the interview.

I said, 'So, Debra, any ideas about who might have kidnapped Lucas? Have you given it any thought?'

She did a double-take, recoiling from the suggestion.

'Why would I have any idea? Of course I've thought about it—we all have. But honestly, are any of the people we actually know likely to be involved in something like this? Isn't it more likely to be some gang looking for easy money from a rich person?'

I stood up. 'Someone knew the routine, knew that Bobbie and Mark were out of the house.'

'Did that matter? They'd still have Harris to deal with.'

'I suspect he was less likely to throw himself in front of Lucas than Bobbie was. Don't you?'

'So you think one of us—I mean, those of us who work here—has set it up in some way? That's not many suspects, is it? Three of us, if you count Mrs Chau.'

'I'm not saying that. But information has a way of leaking out of any closed group of people. Someone might have said something unknowingly to someone else.'

'Goodness' sake, that means anyone we've talked to in the last six months might have said something to someone. That's likely to be a lot of people.'

'And it's my job to narrow them down.'

CHAPTER SEVEN

TOWARDS THE END of our conversation Debra and I heard footsteps in the corridor and a door open and close nearby.

She said, 'That'll be Mark. Distracting himself with work. Don't tell him I said that!'

So when we'd finished I asked her to point out his office to me and after she'd gone to find Bobbie in the pool, I knocked on his door and heard him tell me to come in.

Unlike Bobbie's this room had no view. The walls were furnished entirely with bookcases, though not all of them were full of books. Looking at the vases, sculptures, pictures and other tasteful knick-knacks that crammed the shelves, I had the sense of a mind that moved swiftly from one enthusiasm to the next. The books scattered between the objects ranged from histories of Chinese art through memoirs of the Second World War to outsize books depicting Victorian architecture—with a special focus on canals—and a small section of contemporary fiction. I could see nothing on modern warfare or military hardware.

He sat behind a desk that was a twin of Bobbie's but where hers was tidy and well-organized, his was scattered with pieces of paper, half a dozen pens, a Lenovo laptop pushed to one side and a half-eaten sandwich on a plate. He was on the phone, turned sideways to me, and when he saw who it was he raised a single finger but carried on talking.

I sat in the chair the other side of his desk—which was about fifty upgrades from the one in my own office—and tried not to listen to his end of the conversation. Which turned out to be impossible.

It seemed to be about the finalisation of a contract to supply something extremely expensive to the defence department of an allied European country. A port in South America was mentioned. The discussion was about delivery dates and completion stages and sign-offs. The fact he was comfortable to talk about it while I was in his office suggested either there were no secrets being revealed, or he was careless. Given his role, and despite the state of his desk, I thought it probably wasn't the latter.

But the conversation wore on.

I glanced at my watch both to check the time and to give him a hint.

He held up his single finger again and I tried to relax.

We'd now gone into the realm of the Power Play. Ware was demonstrating to me, unsubtly, that I was a hired hand and his work was more important than mine. Given the situation in relation to Lucas, I thought that was odd.

After another few minutes I stood up.

At which point Ware told his colleague to hang on, then said he'd phone back, pressed a button on his phone, and turned to face me.

'Sorry about that. Different time zones. I have to make calls at all sorts of odd hours. This job isn't all free meals and roses.'

'How important is it to you that I find Lucas?'

He frowned one of those frowns people who are high-up in organizations affect to show that what you've said is so far beyond their comprehension as to be almost unintelligible—perhaps even rude …

'Don't you think that's impertinent?'

'It might be if you were my boss. But you're not.'

He stared at me, his darkly handsome features trying to compose themselves. Then he laid both his palms on the table, as though putting down the weapons.

'Please, sit down. You're right. I'm so used to people being nice to me I sometimes forget my own manners.'

I lowered myself into the seat again, thinking we'd reached an accommodation. But evidently not, because he leaned towards me and said, 'On the other hand, please don't forget I have a business to run. A very big business. Earning millions of pounds per annum and employing many thousands of people around the world. I can't just stop functioning, much as I might like to.'

'Does Mrs Ware understand your priorities?'

'She knows what I do for a living and that it provides the lifestyle she's now enjoying. I'm not going to apologise for that. I work damn hard and have done for almost twenty years to get here.' He paused and I noticed how sallow and blotchy his skin had become in the two hours I'd been there. He added, 'I'm taking you on trust, which I almost never do. I can't afford to. You'd be surprised how much of my life is run by statistics and probabilities and straightforward research. I have teams of people using science and mathematics to produce software that we sell. Yes we're an arms manufacturer, but it's defence work in the true sense. We don't sell bombs and rockets and bullets. We sell the ability to detect those things so that other weapons systems can do something about it. Do you understand what I'm saying?'

'Not really.'

'This is a step in the dark for me. This uncertainty. Not knowing you or what in fact you can do for me. All the research I've done on you means nothing when it comes to you and I sitting across a desk discussing the life of my son.'

'I've made no promises.'

'I know. You haven't even offered a contract.'

'In this case, perhaps it's better we don't have one. I'm guessing you know where I live by now. And I certainly know where you are.'

'That sounds like a threat.'

'It wasn't intended as one. More like mutually assured security.'

We looked at each other across the desk.

Then he said, as though the matter—whatever it was— had been concluded, 'So what's the next step? You've talked to everyone? Do you have any thoughts, anything we should be doing? Anything we *can* do. Except for contacting the police, of course.'

'I have plenty of thoughts. They haven't yet been worked up into ideas or concepts and I'm a long way from a project plan with milestones.'

'You don't have to use sarcasm, Mr Dyke. Bear in mind I don't know how your business works, what your process is. I've got no criteria by which to evaluate your success or failure. Other than asking lots of questions, what is it you do?'

This was said so aggressively I was taken aback. The shift in his attitude from when I arrived to now was marked and bizarre.

I said, 'I'll go and have a look at the place in the road where the kidnapping took place. I'll follow up on one or two things I've heard this afternoon. I'd rather not talk about them if that's okay with you. Or even if it's not.'

'Do you want to be paid in cash, cheque or bank transfer?'

I knew this was his way of trying to reassert our roles.

I said, 'I'll invoice you afterwards. You can choose how to pay.'

He laughed grimly. 'So it'll be a brown paper bag of unmarked notes under a bridge in Westminster. That's what our critics think, so why not?'

'An arms manufacturer has critics? I find that hard to believe.'

'Are we done for the time being? I should get back to my call and I don't want to delay your investigation.'

I stood up again. He didn't offer to shake my hand and I didn't extend my own. I turned and left the office, hearing the tones of his handset as he redialled.

I stood in the corridor, getting my bearings and thinking hard.

If I didn't know better, I'd have said Mark Ware didn't want me to find his son.

CHAPTER EIGHT

I'D PHONED AHEAD but Dan's Renault Clio wasn't in the drive when I arrived in front of his house. He'd owned it a couple of weeks and I knew he sometimes went out for a spin just because he could.

However, when he turned up five minutes after seven o'clock that night he was carrying a gym bag and looking sweaty.

I met him on his drive as he was reaching for his key.

'What is it—weights? Circuits? Heavy bout of chess?'

He glanced at me. 'Tae-Kwon-Do. They've just started a new class.'

I nodded approvingly. I knew he'd been pretty good as a teenager but recently a computer keyboard was more likely to catch his attention than a Tae-Kwon-Do Front Snap Kick. It was good he was taking time from a screen to look after his body.

He said, 'I'm too heavy. Too much sitting around.' The door opened and we went in. He said, 'I've got to shower.'

He left me in his sitting room and went upstairs and I heard the bathroom door close.

I wondered why he hadn't looked me in the eye yet.

I didn't have much time to think about it because the doorbell rang. I opened it and Belinda McFee stood on the doorstep. As it was evening she'd let her hair down and I saw it was getting longer. She usually kept it just long enough to tie in a ponytail but now it was starting to lengthen down her back. She wore a tight leather jacket, unbuttoned, over a white tee-shirt and black jeans. She looked like an Extra from Rebel Without a Cause.

She said, 'Oh, hi,' as though she hadn't expected to find me there, despite the fact I was the one who'd invited her down for a strategy discussion. I felt a pang of guilt for asking her to drive forty minutes just for a conversation. I'd thought she liked these discussions between the three of us, but looking at her face now I wasn't sure.

She walked past me into the kitchen and poured herself a glass of water.

'Where's Dan?'

'Shower. He won't be a moment.'

'Okay.'

She went back into the sitting room and I followed her like a tame poodle. All the dynamics were wrong. Something was going on.

I said, 'Everything okay?'

She sipped from her drink.

'Well, since you asked …'

'What?'

She sighed. 'Don't take this the wrong way, but I've got clients, Sam. My own clients. I've come down as a courtesy but you can't keep relying on me to drop everything and come a-running.'

This was a new wrinkle. So far in our relationship I'd been a mentor and she'd been an apprentice, though a highly competent one. I hadn't intended for the association to develop in that way, it just happened because of our relative years of experience.

At that moment Dan appeared in the kitchen, dressed but rubbing his hair on a towel.

He looked from one of us to the other, taking it in. He said, 'Is this it? The Discussion?'

'What discussion?'

'Belinda and I had a talk the other day. We decided you needed sorting out. Since that thing in London you've been inside your own head.'

The 'thing' in London had been a job where I'd nearly — and stupidly — fallen in love with a client. Unfortunately for me it had all been a set-up. She'd been stringing me along to help her father do a number on a security firm — another defence contractor, of a kind. I'd rumbled it just in time but it left a sour taste in my mouth and screwed me up for a few weeks. I knew I hadn't been functioning at the top of my game since then. I thought I'd got past it, but from what Dan and Belinda were implying I might have been over-estimating the speed of my recovery.

I said, 'So what's this — an intervention? You haven't got a priest outside waiting to talk to me about the twelve steps, have you?'

Belinda turned to Dan. 'I told you he wouldn't listen.'

'I'm listening but I don't know what I'm hearing. You've sprung this on me when I wasn't prepared.'

Dan wrapped the towel around his neck. 'Dad, we can't be doing with all this moodiness.'

'Me?'

'You don't talk to us for days and then when you do it's all an emergency and you want us to do something for you yesterday. We're not your staff, you know.'

'Don't I pay you for your time?'

'That's not the point!'

'Then what is? I thought you wanted to be part of the firm, the Dyke Dynasty, Private Investigators to the stars.' I turned to Belinda. 'And I thought you were learning the ropes from an old hand.'

'Who's about eighteen months ahead of me in the detecting game.'

'I can't help that. I never promised anything.'

I seemed to be saying that a lot lately.

Dan said, 'Of course we'll carry on working with you. But you could treat us with a bit more respect. Stop expecting us to drop everything else we're doing just because you need a fact checking or a house watching.'

This stung because it was true and I knew it. I had a habit of taking their willingness to help me for granted.

I said, 'Look, I'm sorry. You're right. I get over-committed to what I'm doing. I shouldn't just expect you to be there for me when I need you.'

Dan said, 'Dead right,' then turned and went back upstairs to the bathroom. Belinda and I went through to the living room and she sat down and smiled up at me the way you smile at a naughty child you can't help liking.

'There, was that so painful?'

'Oh, drop it, Belinda. I've said I'm sorry.'

'I'm beginning to think you didn't mean it.'

'I don't like being managed.'

'Sam, you've been awful these last few weeks. No one could talk to you. You snapped our heads off.'

'That's not true.'

She made a disbelieving sound with her lips. 'You have no idea.'

'No one said anything.'

'We just did. You don't know how tough that little scene was for Dan.'

'He's a grown-up. He can take it.'

'Doesn't mean he has to like it. He looks up to you. He doesn't like to see you in a bad state.'

I didn't have a snappy answer to that so I turned away. I could hear Dan's footsteps upstairs.

Belinda said, 'Was London bad? The end?'

She'd worked with me on the case but hadn't witnessed the ending, when I'd confronted Emily and her father. He'd held a gun on me while his daughter left for the airport, destination unknown.

I said, 'It could have been. I fell a long way in a short time, probably because I was ready for something after Laura. Lucky for me I was still paddling in the shallows when I found out Emily wasn't who I thought she was. Another couple of days, though …'

'Are you still getting postcards? Last I heard it was Italy.'

'Not for a few weeks.'

She nodded and said nothing else because Dan had come back in. Perhaps she didn't want to embarrass him by talking about his Dad's love life.

I said, 'Okay, you two, point taken. I'll try to be a bit more gracious about how we work as a team in future.'

Belinda put two fingers down her throat and Dan laughed. It broke the ice and I then told them about the kidnapping of Lucas Ware and the strange little community that lived in the big mansion just outside Prestbury. I didn't tell them my suspicions about Mark Ware because I didn't quite believe them myself.

But, true to form, I did ask each of them to do a couple of things for me.

CHAPTER NINE

AT LUNCHTIME THE following day I followed a taxi weaving its way through Manchester streets until it pulled up outside a bar that was trying hard to be cool and fashionable. The bar had gone the understated route, with minimal signage, pale colours from Farrow and Ball, and inside doubtless some quiet abstract art on the walls, above the neatly organized banks of leather sofas and chairs. From the street it looked as though it was trying to hide itself, to be discreet and not worthy of anyone's attention.

I pulled up twenty yards behind the taxi and told myself I was growing cynical as I got older and further removed from the target market of faddish behaviour.

Despite my response to Dan and Belinda's comments the previous night, I was disturbed. In general I tried to demonstrate that I didn't need other people, but I knew myself well enough to recognise it wasn't true. I couldn't bear my own company for too long and found ways to distract myself from listening to the voices inside my head. If those two had found my behaviour selfish and isolating then I must have been acting very strangely, because I was certain it wasn't the real me.

A tall slim man in his early thirties climbed out of the taxi and threw a fistful of notes through the window. Now that was nice behaviour. Perhaps they'd argued in the cab, or the driver had offered some critique of the man's skill on the pitch.

Charlie, Debra's fiancé, crossed the wide pavement and went into the bar and I drove around until I found an empty parking meter in a parallel street. After Dan had found Charlie's address the previous night I'd got up early and parked outside the house he shared with Debra in south Manchester. She'd driven off mid-morning and half an hour later he'd stepped outside the front door and waited a couple of minutes until the taxi had arrived. Twenty minutes later, here we were.

The streets were busy with lunchtime shoppers but that was good because some of them would have gone into the bar for a drink and maybe a bite to eat. The more people around, the better chance I'd be able to have a civilised conversation with him. I set my shoulders to casual and pushed open the front swing door, adjusting my eyes to the darkness within.

Inside, despite the dim lighting, he was easy to see. He was standing at the bar with two or three men and just taking delivery of a pint of beer.

His arm was around a woman in her early twenties who wore a tight dress and whose hair was a cloud of blonde. Interesting.

I found an empty table and pretended to be looking at the glossy menu. Charlie was the centre of attention. He might only have been a second division player, but he seemed to have plenty of reflected glory. The men around him were older, perhaps in their mid- to late-thirties, and had spent a good part of their lives enjoying a drink, to judge by their midriffs. Charlie had been a defender, so was over six feet tall and had the slimness that all professional athletes have, even though he'd been let out of his contract several months ago. Debra had been a little free with the truth when she said he'd retired — in fact, a little research on the sports pages told me his disruptive behaviour at a string of clubs had meant he had gone from top flight to middling clubs in about three years, finally terminating with his latest team buying him out of his contract and waving goodbye. I hoped Debra knew what she was getting into.

But perhaps that was part of his charm.

The woman on his arm certainly seemed to think so. She knocked back a series of short drinks while bantering with the men and getting comfortable with Charlie, leaning into his side and at one point taking his wallet from his inside pocket to pay for another round.

After twenty minutes Charlie broke away and headed for the rear of the room, where a door led through to the toilets.

I rose swiftly and followed him.

The toilets smelled of summer and were decorated with pale blue tiles, four urinals placed against one wall and three stalls facing them. Charlie was unzipping as I entered and I went and stood next to him, though I didn't unzip.

I said, 'You're Charlie Welsh.'

He glanced at me but said nothing while he commenced his release. After a while he finished off, zipped up and went to one of the two sinks and ran water.

'I don't do autographs.' His voice was light and London-inflected.

'Not asking. Just interested, wondering what you're up to these days.'

'None of your business, mate. See you around.'

He was drying his hands on thick paper towels. He turned and found me directly in front of him. He was tall enough to look me in the eye but was probably twenty pounds lighter. He frowned.

'What do you want? Get out of the fuckin way.'

'I understand you're going down to London, is that right? Start up a sports agency.'

The frown deepened. 'Where'd you hear that? Not common knowledge yet.'

'Is it true?'

'None of your fuckin business, mate. Now piss off before I stick one on you.'

Something in his attitude needled me, despite the fact I'd been the aggressor.

I said, 'Please don't try that. That blonde you're with won't want to see you in a heap on the floor.'

He looked surprised. 'What are you talking about?'

'And I'm sure Debra doesn't want to read about you in the evening papers, found in a bar with an unknown blonde.'

'You're off your fuckin rocker, mate.'

He pushed himself off the edge of the sink and raised his hands to push me away. I knocked them down, twisted, kicked his legs from under him and levered him swiftly to the ground. He fell hard on his right shoulder, unable to roll with the fall.

'Ow, shit! I'm going to have you for that.'

'Stay down.'

He looked up. There was something in my voice he'd responded to.

He said, 'Who the fuck are you? What do you want?'

Staring at him, I realised I didn't know. Part of me sensed he had nothing to do with the kidnapping of the Wares' child—he was a bit stupid and probably full of vainglory, and I couldn't see him being caught up in a serious criminal act.

I stepped back. I said, 'Watch yourself.'

I turned and was walking away when I heard him scrabbling to his feet.

From behind my back he said, 'And that blonde is my sister, you fuckin wanker.'

I closed the door behind me and walked straight out of the bar and into the street, which seemed suddenly noisy and full of people I didn't want to see.

I CLIMBED BACK into my car and sat without starting the engine. My hands were trembling and I'd broken out in a slight sweat. What had that been about? I'd handled trickier situations without losing my temper. Was he really so obnoxious that I'd had to take him down a peg? Or was he just a normal guy fed up of people talking to him in places where he was just living his life?

I closed my eyes and ran through the scene again. Had he been so unreasonable? Had I really been provoked?

Probably not.

I thought again about what Belinda and Dan had said to me the night before, about my biting their heads off at a moment's notice. And my second meeting with Mark Ware, when I'd demonstrated the kind of impatience with him that a child of eight might have shown.

Perhaps I was closer to the edge than I thought. Perhaps what Emily had done to me in London had twisted some inner mechanism out of true, so I'd lost my balance in some way.

It wasn't other people, it was me.

I put my hands on the steering wheel and lay my head there for a couple of minutes, trying to calm down.

Then I realised that the vague buzzing I could hear wasn't taking place in my head but was coming from my pocket, where I'd placed my phone when I entered the bar.

I took the phone from the pocket and saw it was a call from Belinda. She was on observation duty elsewhere.

She said, 'You should get here, Sam. Something interesting's going on.'

I said, 'Okay,' hearing my own voice like a distant whisper.

I put the car in gear and drove away, relieved to be on the move, going somewhere. Anywhere.

CHAPTER TEN

THE SEFTON PARK area of Liverpool was packed with houses built in the early part of the twentieth century, bland semi-detached family homes that had been knocked about to accommodate larger gardens or extensions or granny flats tacked on to the rear.

The road in which Mrs Chau lived was five minutes from the Park itself, where ranks of Victorian town houses marched along cheek-by-jowl like rows of elderly governesses dressed in faded finery.

As far as I knew she owned her own house, so maybe property prices here had collapsed to such an extent that even someone of limited means could buy a lot of square footage.

Belinda's pink Volvo stood out in the street like a rock and roll singer in a church choir. A couple of the houses were being upgraded and two skips full of broken brick and window frames squeezed the available free space. I parked as close as I could then joined her, levering my legs into her passenger seat.

She was halfway through a ham sandwich and nodded at me over it.

I said, 'Got a spare one of those?'

She shook her head. After a moment she finished chewing and pointed down the road.

'That one with the green windows. That's her.'

'Okay.'

She folded together the packaging of her sandwich and pushed it into a plastic bag which she deposited on the tiny back seat. Then she dusted her hands together to get rid of crumbs.

I said, 'You sounded urgent on the phone.'

'I know. Before I show you something, I just want to ask you a question.'

My heart sank. I'd had enough introspection for one day. On the forty minute drive from Manchester I'd had time to re-order my thinking and regain my focus. I didn't want to visit everything all over again.

She must have seen my expression but she carried on.

'Just tell me why we're not letting the cops know about this. We could get in real shit for hiding this kind of thing.'

'Listen, Belinda, do you want the work or not?'

She swayed back, not expecting my aggression. Calculations whirred behind her eyes.

'It's not that simple, is it? I can want the work while feeling uncomfortable about it.'

'Then why did you agree to help out last night? You were quite clear you had your own clients. You could have said no.'

'There's a ten-year-old boy involved.'

'Exactly. The Wares think that if the kidnappers get a sniff the police are involved, well, it wouldn't be good for Lucas.'

'We're no better.'

'We're further under the radar. What if the kidnappers have someone working undercover in the cops? Or ways of getting info from them? I'm pretty confident than neither you nor Dan is going to blab in the nearest cop-shop.'

'But if our involvement comes out in the end we could be charged with all sorts of stuff.'

'It won't come to that.'

'Says you.'

'Look, Roberta Ware asked me what I'd do if it were Dan who'd been kidnapped. Would I tell the police? Probably not. But would I move heaven and earth in other ways to help him? Probably. That's where we're at right now.'

She'd been watching me while I spoke but now she looked away and I could tell she had no answer to that.

I was disappointed that she seemed, bit by bit, to be losing confidence in me.

I wasn't just disappointed. I was hurt.

EVENTUALLY SHE SAID, 'Let's take a walk,' and climbed out of the car. I followed and joined her on the pavement. Mrs Chau's house was thirty yards down the road, but she turned and walked in the opposite direction, towards the centre of town.

She ambled along, talking to me as she went. 'We're going to stop outside a house that's for sale, so look interested. Pretend we're a young married couple. Well, not so young in your case. Actually we're looking at the one the far side of it.'

'What should I say?'

'Doesn't really matter, does it? Just let's not argue. We don't want to draw attention to ourselves.'

'You drive a pink Volvo with leopard-skin seats.'

'I'm full of contradictions, me. Now just stop here and pretend to look at the house.'

I did as I was told and saw a typical three-storey, red-brick Victorian town house, though it had lost some of its original lustre. It had a cracked window pane and one of the stained-glass windows in the door had been replaced by a square of hardboard. Spindly weeds grew nearly a metre high in the small front garden and the cream paint was chipping away from the concrete bow windows. Even the hardboard For Sale sign was cracked with age and coming away from its post. Two purple and two blue wheelie-bins stood outside, adding a splash of colour where none belonged.

I said, 'Why are we looking at this?'

'We're not looking at this. We're pretending to look at this because your Mrs Chau walked out of her front door at ten o'clock this morning, went to the house next to the one we're currently looking at and let herself in with a key. She was carrying two shopping bags. An hour later she came out without the shopping bags but carrying a black rubbish sack, which she took back to her own house and stuffed into the wheelie-bin in her own front yard. I'd call that suspicious behaviour.'

'Did you see anyone else when she went in?'

'Nope. She just turned the key and entered. And nobody was visible when she came out.'

I walked sideways a couple of steps, still ostensibly looking at the For Sale house, but with my eyes sliding away to inspect the one next door. It was in slightly better condition than its neighbour, with no broken glass, though the front yard was equally weed-ridden. There were thick curtains on all of the windows but no lights showing. A telephone line went into the house from the nearest post and there was a satellite dish nestled beneath the eaves, sucking entertainment from the skies.

As I turned my attention away, a flicker of shadow crossed the downstairs front window.

I said casually, eyes straight ahead, 'See that?'

'What?'

'I thought I saw movement inside.'

'Imagination, Sam. Seeing what you want to see. But let's play the game, just in case.'

She pushed open the gate of the sale house and walked up the path. I followed her and we spent a minute or two peering through the downstairs windows as though working out how to lay oak flooring or re-plaster the walls.

Eventually she said, 'That's enough, I'm bored now,' and we walked back to her car.

Once inside I said, 'So at ten o'clock she takes two bags of shopping to the house, stays an hour, then comes out with a sack of rubbish.'

'You're quick. You can recite back to me exactly what I say.'

'So what are the options? It's an elderly neighbour who can't look after herself. Mrs Chau is being a Good Samaritan, fetching her shopping, cleaning the house, taking out the trash.'

'Or, there's a houseful of her family smuggled in from Vietnam. They're waiting for papers or something before they can be let out.'

'Or, she's hiding a criminal so no one knows where he is.'

'Or, it's a battered wife hiding from her husband and Mrs Chau is running a hostel in her spare time.'

We paused. She said, 'Or, we could just knock on the door and find out.'

Thinking about what had happened in Manchester an hour before, I felt I should be more cautious.

'Too much at risk. We can't go blundering in. What if Lucas is in there with a knife to his throat, or wearing an explosive vest? We've got to find out more.'

She shrugged. 'You've changed. Six months ago you'd have battered down the door and knocked a few heads together.'

'You're exaggerating.'

'Not by much. I quite liked that Sam Dyke. You got things done.'

'At a cost. Besides, perhaps there's more at stake now.'

'I know. I'm teasing. Mostly.'

I told her to keep watch for the rest of the day in case she saw anything else. Then I went back to my own car and sat for a while, thinking. I wondered whether she was right and I was being more cautious than normal. But why wouldn't I be? We knew nothing about the house or what Mrs Chau might be doing. It was probably something entirely innocent, maybe even good-hearted. The last thing I needed was to go barging in again, as I had with Charlie that morning, making unfounded allegations. Belinda said she was unhappy with my caution because we should strike while the iron was at least tepid, if not hot. I told her I wasn't certain about any of the assumptions we were making.

What was certain was that I needed to find out more about the house, its owner and its occupant. I phoned Dan and hoped he wouldn't give me another earful.

CHAPTER ELEVEN

I WAS BACK in my office by the middle of the afternoon, catching up on the post and email and telephone messages. There was no post and no one had thought to leave a telephone message, but I had some interesting emails from universities in America telling me my grant was waiting for me to pick up and there were some nice ladies on Facebook who wanted to be my friend. I deleted them, attractive though the offers were.

I thought about Mrs Chau and her morning activities, and I thought about Charlie Welsh. Was the woman in the bar really his sister? She was awful cuddly with him, but I supposed if she was a younger sister she might have a different kind of relationship with an older brother … perhaps he'd always looked after her and been the father figure. Also, I'd seen her reach into his jacket pocket and take out his wallet to pay for drinks; so he was either very comfortable with a female friend handling his money or she really was his sister and she was used to having access to his things.

As for Mrs Chau, I had no idea. My favourite theory was she was kind-heartedly caring for a neighbour who couldn't look after her- or himself. I thought I'd seen a fast-moving shadow behind the window, so if there was someone there he or she wasn't immobile, but there could be a number of reasons why the person wouldn't leave the house to do their own shopping: agoraphobia, a disfiguring injury, lack of transport.

Whatever it was, did Mrs Chau's behaviour have any relation to the kidnapping of her employers' child? Or did this shopping arrangement exist before?

I knew I had to go back to the Wares' place that evening, for two reasons. First, to talk to Mrs Chau again to see whether I could find out what she'd been up to that morning; and secondly, to check out Mark Ware's thinking. The more time that passed since our conversation the previous evening, the more I was sure he'd been acting oddly. He'd begun by being concerned but eager to help. By the time we said goodbye it was almost as though he'd forgotten who I was, as if I were a plumber performing a minor repair whose name he didn't need to remember.

Rather than call to make an appointment I drove out to Prestbury as the commuter traffic into and out of Crewe thickened, and with hold-ups through Congleton and Macclesfield it took me the best part of an hour to turn through the wide gates of the Ware's magisterial estate. The sun had started its descent but the front of the house was still bathed in gold like a Pharaoh's palace.

A ring of the bell brought Mrs Chau's unforgiving face to the door.

'Do you have an appointment, Mr Dyke?' She didn't bother with the cod-Vietnamese accent.

'Not this time. You'll be seeing a lot more of me, Mrs Chau.'

She nodded and stepped back, then turned and led me towards the same lounge as the day before. I followed her slender figure upstairs.

She saw me seated, then as she turned to summon one of the Wares to deal with me, I said, 'Have you remembered anything more?'

She looked at me, her eyes grave. 'I told you everything yesterday. Why do you think I would remember anything else?'

'Often the first questions merely start the process of remembering. When the person you're talking to has had more time to think about the facts, more memories float up.'

'That isn't so in this case.'

'So you're sure there's nothing else you have to tell me? Some changes to the house routine? Some odd visitors, perhaps someone who came once to fix a light or mend a tile? Someone who claimed to be lost and asking for directions? And your own routine, any changes there? Anything you think we should know about?'

She bore all this without a change in her expression.

'I told you everything yesterday. I have nothing more to add. I'll fetch Mrs Ware. Perhaps she'll be able to answer your questions with more certainty than I can.'

She was good. No change in breathing, no flush of the neck, no glancing away. Just a steady, slightly condescending gaze, as though my efforts at ferreting more information from her were like the attempts of a child to snaffle one more sweet before going to bed.

I thought about challenging her, asking what she was doing delivering groceries to another house in her street … but it struck me that a cunning silence might be more effective, at least until I had more information. I let her go.

Five minutes later Bobbie Ware fizzed into the room, looking slim and tall in pale blue pants and a fitted blue blouse with short sleeves and with its top two buttons undone.

She said, 'I wasn't expecting a daily report. Don't think you have to check in every day if it's better for you to be out and about.'

I shook hands with her. Her fingers were slender and she withdrew them quickly, as though anxious to get on with the conversation.

I said, 'I'm sorry about dropping in like this. Has there been any contact from the people who've taken Lucas?'

I was careful not to use the word 'kidnappers': it seemed so definitive.

She sat in the sofa opposite and leaned forward, giving me a view of the top of her breasts. For some reason I didn't think it was accidental.

She said, 'Nothing. It's been three days now — what are they playing at?'

'Turning the screw. Getting you worried. And perhaps checking whether there's any police activity in the area.'

'Then perhaps you shouldn't come. What if they trace your car and find out you're a private investigator?'

'Unlikely. It's not easy to get into the DVLA database.' I didn't tell her my son did it for me occasionally. One of his more impressive skills. 'They'll probably think I'm a work colleague or a family friend. If they're even watching.'

She said, 'Have you checked out the Pearsons, the gardeners?'

'Not yet. Listen, I wanted to ask you something.'

'What?'

Again I chose my words carefully.

'I know this is a really difficult time for you both … but how are you coping? Are you holding it together?'

She frowned. 'Of course not. That's a strange question to ask.'

'I want to be certain we all know what we're doing. I'm sure it's stressful for you and it's easy to make bad decisions in these circumstances.'

'I don't know what you expect me to say. Neither of us is sleeping well. Mark is distracted, which isn't helped by having to go into work every day when he doesn't want to. He's only doing it because the kidnappers' note said he must. Christ, he often worked from home anyway, but he daredn't do that now in case they're watching and think it's suspicious.' She paused. 'Plus, he's angry and seems moody. He's not talking to me much.'

Her eyes had flicked away while she said this, as though she were actually telling herself, revealing his behaviour in the act of describing it.

I said, 'How does he feel about my involvement?'

'Let's just say I had to twist his arm. I'm the one who researched you so like a typical man he resisted doing anything because it wasn't his own idea.'

She smiled sadly at me, as though I too would recognise this masculine foible. To punctuate this disclosure she sat back on the sofa and tucked her legs under her behind. It threw her body into a curved shape that I couldn't help notice. She wore her sexuality like an expensive dress that clung to her in all the right places.

I wondered why she was allowing herself to behave like this. Perhaps she was practising on me because she could. I was no threat to her so she could be free with a display of who she was. Or perhaps being married to a captain of industry wore thin when she didn't see much of him. Or maybe she just wanted to check everything was still in working order.

It certainly was but I didn't want her to know that. So to distract myself I stood up and went to look at the various photos on the grand piano. The photo of Lucas was still there alongside other family shots—a white beach, with Bobbie bent down and hugging Lucas from behind; the three of them on a small sailing boat, wearing orange life-jackets, a choppy sea in the background; Mark and Bobbie in formal dress holding hands in front of a coastline at night that looked like Amalfi, taken from a higher slope.

She had to turn awkwardly to see what I was doing. I'd disturbed her pose and when she spoke her voice was cool and matter-of-fact.

'Is that it? Is that the only reason you came all this way? Checking our psychological health?'

'What do you know about Harris, his career before you hired him?'

She waved a hand as though brushing off details. 'Mark does all that stuff, hiring and firing.'

'Can I talk to him?'

'Not today. He won't be back till nine: transatlantic conference. Real work for once.'

'How can he concentrate with this going on?'

She shrugged. 'He has to. He can't tell anyone in the office what's going on and the place won't run itself. He's always been good at compartmentalising. And to be honest, although he doesn't want to be there, the work's probably keeping him sane.'

I thought again what a cool reaction this family was demonstrating. Their insides must have been twisted in knots. They must have spent every waking minute worrying about the trauma their son was suffering. And yet ... they carried on their lives because a hand-written note told them to. They didn't call in the experts. They didn't collapse in a heap on the ground. Admittedly they'd called in some professional help—me—but I was beginning to think I might have walked into an episode of the Addams Family. I couldn't imagine how they functioned from moment to moment while they waited for news of their son, who was probably being kept in a dark room somewhere and fed fast food on paper plates.

If he was still alive.

I said, 'We got distracted. I asked about Harris.'

She sighed, 'All I know is he worked for the Met for years. You can tell by looking at him he's a cynical old boot. Usually reliable, though. I feel sorry for him right now because he must be feeling terrible. It's hard to blame him.'

'You don't think he could have done more?'

'And got himself and Lucas shot? How would that have helped? I don't think he could have done much different. Do you?'

I shrugged. 'You can't tell what the options are unless you're there. Does he drink?'

'Not that I know of. He stays on campus most of the time. Watches his videos. Doesn't have visitors. If he's involved in this I don't see when he would have organised it, quite frankly.'

I moved closer to her and to the questions I really wanted to ask. 'What about Mrs Chau? How did you come across her?'

Bobbie shifted her position again and looked up at me from her large blue eyes. I noticed how subtle mascara enlarged them. Even at home she maintained the image. With great effort I stopped myself looking down the front of her blouse.

'When we moved to Manchester we had a big house in Wilmslow and needed someone to look after Lucas, do some housework, that kind of thing. Like an au pair. But I didn't want to entrust him to a twenty-year-old from Oslo, so we found an agency that hired out mature women who were multi-skilled, so to speak. Housework, children, cooking if necessary. We had Mrs Chau on trial for three months and she was excellent. After the trial we made her an offer higher than the agency rate she was getting and she came to live with us. A year ago she said she had a place in Liverpool and wanted to change the arrangements. So she doesn't work full-time now, but that's okay because Lucas doesn't need the same level of looking-after he did when he was younger. He's more self-sufficient, like his dad.'

'Do you know anything about her past?'

'Mrs Chau? Only that she had very good representations from the Embassy in Hanoi.'

'Why did she come to the UK?'

'I have no idea. Doesn't everyone want to come here?'

I ignored the question and sat facing her again. 'I've been wondering how she could afford to buy a house in Liverpool. The area she's in isn't cheap. Did you lend her money?'

'What's this about? Do you think she's involved? She seems loyal and she'd be stupid to jeopardise what she's got here …'

'I have to ask these questions, don't I? That's why you're paying me. I have to do the kind of thinking you and Mark can't do—or won't do.'

She took this as an insult. Like her husband she seemed to have a low threshold when it came to being affronted.

Unlike him, however, she had better control of her emotions. She took a moment and composed herself.

'No, we didn't lend her money. We didn't think it was any of our business, quite frankly. We had no idea what cash she might have brought over from Vietnam, or anything she might have received from the father of her child.'

'You knew about that?'

'It came out in the interview. I wasn't there but Mark told me about it afterwards. He thought maybe it gave her some understanding of what it was like to have a young boy, how to deal with him and so forth. Not that being a nanny was her main job. But it helped if she had experience with children.'

'No idea who the father was?'

'None, and I don't care. I expect it was someone in the Embassy, don't you? A quickie in one of the guest rooms.'

'Have you been to her place?'

'No, why should I?'

Before I could answer the question the door to the lounge was pushed in and Bobbie's assistant, Debra, walked through and headed straight towards me as though guided by laser technology.

CHAPTER TWELVE

DEBRA LOOKED UP at me with focused intensity and came to a dead stop. Her breathing suggested she'd run up the staircase. She said, 'Where do you think you get off talking to Charlie like that?'

'Debra—'

'Why were you even talking to him at all? I told you all that stuff in confidence and you go and throw it straight back in his face. Now he doesn't trust me.'

'I'm sorry, I have to look at everyone's connections.'

'Just because he's a footballer you think he's got no brains and knows lots of shady people.'

Bobbie said, 'Debra—'

But Debra was barely conscious Bobbie was there. She jabbed a small finger into my chest.

'I don't know what you're playing at but keep away from him.' Now she turned to Bobbie and explained. 'He saw Charlie this morning and beat him up in the toilet of a bar. Can you believe it?'

Bobbie's eyes flicked towards me and I couldn't read what I saw there—surprise? Concern? Interest?

I said, 'It wasn't like that.'

'So what was it like, Mr Tough Guy Detective?'

I debated how much I should tell her and concluded I didn't owe Charlie Welsh anything. 'He was in a bar in Manchester with some friends. I wanted to talk to him but I waited until he went to the toilet so his friends wouldn't hear what I said. He got angry and tried to push me away, so I just … restrained him. He wasn't hurt.'

'You should see the state of his suit. Ruined.'

Bobbie said, 'We'll replace it, Debra. Call it expenses.'

'Don't bother, I quit. I was going anyway, I'll just bring it forward a couple of weeks. The atmosphere in this place is horrible right now. No disrespect, Bobbie, this must be hard on you. I can't imagine.' She took a big breath, calmer now, and looked back at me. 'I know he's got a temper but he's not the sort to go looking for a punch-up. He said you had a weird expression on your face. He was scared of you. What do you expect, confronted by a stranger in a toilet? He wasn't pushing you to start a fight. He wanted to get away.'

She turned and walked towards the door, then stopped and turned around again. 'I'm sorry, Bobbie. I'll finish that newsletter and the round-robin and send them. Then that's it.'

'Are you sure that's what you want to do? We should talk about it.'

'That's okay. My head's in London most of the time anyhow. This way it'll be easier.'

She walked out of the room. Bobbie stood up and made a face at me, an 'oh-dear-what-have-you-done?' grimace.

'I'd better go after her. Don't leave.'

She walked quickly across the carpet and I heard her calling Debra's name as she followed her down the staircase.

I let myself fall into a chair and stared at the ceiling for a minute, then gazed around the room. There were more landscapes on the wall facing the french doors and a glass cabinet holding various pieces of china statuary. I wondered who was the collector and decided it would be Bobbie—I suspected Mark didn't tend much towards aesthetic appreciation.

After a while Bobbie came back in and I stood up. I sensed I might be wearing out my welcome.

She said, 'I calmed her down. She's mild as a mouse normally. You must have really upset her man for her to get that angry.'

'Have you met Charlie?'

'Once. Let's just say I entirely understand your position.' She gave a rueful smile. 'In a way I'm glad she's going now. She knows she's been distracted by the move to London. This job's become more of an irritant to her than anything else. And the atmosphere around here must have been awful the last few days.'

'I'd better go.'

'Have you got what you came for?'

'I'm not sure.'

'Why's that?'

'It's the kind of thing you only know after the event. You keep asking questions and talking to people and see what pops out of the woodwork.'

'Like Charlie?'

'Like Charlie. Only I'm pretty sure he's not involved in this.'

'Glad to hear it. Why?'

'He's not a master criminal. He couldn't even stay upright in the toilet.'

I said it with a smile and she smiled back.

'I'll see you out.'

We walked down the staircase side by side and she opened the front door for me. The sun was in our faces and still carried some heat. She touched my arm.

'I'm not sure we've said thank you for what you're doing.'

'I haven't done anything yet except irritate a few people.'

'Something tells me you're used to that.'

'Not only used to it, I'm a world-class expert.'

We said our goodbyes and I climbed into my car. I drove away feeling uneasy, as though some mechanism I didn't understand was working inside me and throwing me off-kilter each time it revolved. I thought about Bobbie Ware and the shape of her body and the curve of her neck and the dazzling clarity of her eyes, and why she was so keen I should see and appreciate all these characteristics. Was it entirely unconscious, the reflexive behaviour of a woman who all her life had been praised and appreciated for her beauty? Or was it a deliberate choice, an attempt to draw me into her orbit should an interest need to be declared in the near future?

I hadn't driven as far as Prestbury when Dan called. I pulled over to the side of the road and took his call. He'd found the name and address of the owner of the house Mrs Chau had visited. It had been an easy enough search for someone of Dan's talents.

Where he'd surpassed himself was in trawling his various databases to discover that the house owner, a man called Ted Mason, was an ex-convict.

At last I was beginning to accumulate information I could do something with.

CHAPTER THIRTEEN

AT THREE O'CLOCK in the morning the street had a spectral, unworldly air, like a film set waiting to be populated by actors who would give it life. The streetlights fizzed and one flickered intermittently. Earlier a dog had howled in the distance but it had been quiet now for half an hour.

Belinda and I sat in my car until we were certain every neighbour was asleep, then we slipped out, closing the doors quietly and crossing the road and heading towards the house. Despite the heat of the day the evenings were still cold and I zipped up my jacket. Belinda had already done up hers.

We stood by the gate and looked at each other. She'd tried to convince me that the 'shadow' I'd seen in the window must have been the reflection of a shifting cloud pattern. She'd spent all day in the car and seen no signs of life or movement at all.

But I still wasn't persuaded. Otherwise, why was Mrs Chau taking loaded bags inside?

I nodded and we went up the path to the door. She stood guard while I broke out my lock-picks and had the Yale open in less than a minute. I pushed and the door swung slowly in.

Immediately I was struck by the smell of the place—musty and sweet at the same time. It was reminiscent of something but I couldn't remember what. Belinda turned on the torch app of her phone and shone it on to the worn tiles of the hallway, moving it slowly upwards to show the doors into the downstairs rooms. A substantial flight of stairs rose up on our left but there was no hint of movement or noise from the upper floors.

I stepped inside slowly and walked to the first door, pushing it gently open. Belinda came to my shoulder and her torchlight revealed a standard layout—TV, armchairs, a sofa, pictures on the wall. The TV was an old-style cathode ray tube edition, not a modern flat screen. The whole atmosphere was reminiscent of my parents' front room when I was growing up, though it wasn't perhaps as grand as this.

The room behind was the dining room—a bare table and a sideboard and half a dozen chairs. I was beginning to get the sense that the house hadn't been redecorated for forty years or so. Had we been able to see them clearly, I suspected the carpets in the rooms would have been patterned and threadbare along the most-used paths.

I whispered, 'Looks as if no one's been here for years.'

She pointed down the corridor and whispered back. 'Kitchen.'

We tip-toed along the tiles and went into the kitchen that sat at the rear of the house. I closed the door behind us, found the light switch and turned it on. A fluorescent bar hummed into life above us, revealing in a sudden glare an unexpectedly modern kitchen. A large fridge-freezer stood in one corner and there was a microwave, a kettle and a toaster sitting on a long counter-top, none of them looking particularly old.

Belinda said quietly, 'Anybody home?'

I opened the door of the fridge and saw most of the goods I supposed Mrs Chau would have brought—fresh milk, butter, a pack of yoghurts. I opened the freezer and pulled out a drawer: it was stacked with microwaveable ready-meals. Then I looked in the salad drawer at the bottom of the fridge: one lettuce, still in its plasticated wrapping. I pointed towards the sink where a single dirty plate lay in a bowl ready to be washed.

I said, 'We should go. Someone's here.'

'We still haven't learned anything.'

'We'll find another way. I don't like this.'

'It was your idea. I said we should knock on the door.'

'My ideas aren't always the best.'

Before she could open her mouth to argue, the kitchen door slammed open.

I took a step back towards the rear of the kitchen while Belinda was forced into the counter.

A boy of about sixteen had appeared in the doorway. He had black hair that was spiked up from sleep and wore a tee-shirt and thin track-suit pants, but no shoes—evidently he'd got out of bed and come straight downstairs. He'd taken an aggressive stance and he glanced feverishly from one of us to the other as though he might attack at any second.

We could have handled an attack from a sixteen-year-old boy, despite the fact he was carrying a curved knife almost twelve-inches in length.

But Belinda and I paused a moment because of another aspect of the boy's behaviour. First, he had the high-cheekbones and oval eyes of someone from the far East.

And also he was shouting at us in a language which I guessed was probably Vietnamese.

CHAPTER FOURTEEN

I THINK THE boy was confused to find two of us there. His eyes moved uncertainly from one of us to the other while he kept up his stream of invective.

I glanced quickly at Belinda and she nodded. Then she said, 'Hey!' loudly and the boy turned to her. That was my opportunity to step forward quickly, grab the boy's wrist and turn it back so he had to bend and then release the knife, which he did with a grunt. I took it, stepped back and laid it on the kitchen counter out of his reach. The boy fell silent and raised his arms defensively. Belinda closed the door behind him and he jumped.

He was now trapped, barefoot and only half-dressed. He didn't know what to do. I showed my palms placatingly and stepped back, making sure I kept myself between him and the knife.

He looked nervously at us. I spoke to him quietly in English, even though I thought it was a futile gesture.

'Don't be afraid, we're not here to hurt you.'

No flicker of comprehension passed across his face. Now he wasn't shouting he looked even younger and more skittish.

Belinda said, 'Now what?'

'Mrs Chau's got some questions to answer, for one thing.'

'Do you think he's alone?'

I turned to the boy. 'Are there more upstairs, or are you alone?'

Again, no recognition that I was speaking a language he might understand.

I said, 'I'll go upstairs and check it out. Will you be okay here?'

She pulled a face at me, then moved to the kettle and filled it with water. She raised it to the boy with a question on her face, then replaced it on the counter and switched it on.

She said to me, 'We'll talk politics while you investigate. I think he was all mouth and no trousers.'

'Watch him with that knife.'

She nodded, then started looking for cups while I opened the kitchen door and went upstairs.

As I went up the first flight of stairs the smell that I noticed when we entered grew stronger. It was an odour I wasn't likely to forget. At the first floor I opened a couple of doors and found what I might have expected—a teenager's untidy bedroom, a bathroom that smelled as though it had been recently cleaned—Mrs Chau—and a further bedroom being used as a TV and games room: a large flat-screen television attached to a PS4, a laptop on a desk, an iPhone and various sets of portable bluetooth speakers.

A third bedroom was empty except for a suitcase. I opened it but there was nothing inside. I'd wondered briefly whether I'd find Lucas in the house but my instinct told me that wasn't likely.

I stood on the landing and looked around. I knew from seeing the house from outside there was another floor, probably a converted attic, but instead of a second flight of stairs all I could see above me was a drop-down door like those used to access lofts. If there'd been stairs leading upwards they'd been taken out in favour of the more difficult option. Convinced now that there was no one else in the house, I switched on the landing light and, against one wall, saw a pole with a hook on the end. I used it to pull down the trap-door, which also lowered a staircase mechanism.

With the door open I could see the loft was already brightly lit. I went slowly up the metal steps and peered over the threshold and into the roof space. It was as I'd thought. The floor had been strengthened with thick boards of MDF and a network of lamps hung from the beams overhead. The windows to the front had been carefully boarded up. The inside of the walls and the roof itself had been layered with reflective silver insulation, both to keep the heat in and to stop light escaping at night, when the lamps remained on. Before me row upon row of green plants were laid out neatly, all about four feet tall, in full leaf and flourishing in oblong plastic tubs. There were probably a couple of hundred plants ready to go.

I went downstairs, turning off the lights as I went. In the kitchen both Belinda and the boy had cups of tea in front of them though the boy hadn't touched his. She'd even found a biscuit but it lay forlornly next to his cup on the counter.

She said to me, 'So what gives? A youth hostel?'

'Nope, a cannabis farm.'

'You're kidding.'

'In full leaf. Won't be long before it gets cut and sold on.' I turned to the boy and said, 'Cannabis. Do you know that word?'

He looked confusedly at me and then at Belinda. He was small but wiry and I felt he might make a dash for it any moment. I saw Belinda had cagily hidden the knife.

I said, 'The question is, who owns it? Is it the guy who bought the house?'

'Mason?'

'Yes. Or is someone else using the property without his knowledge? If he's an ex-con he might have the contacts, but I might just be jumping to conclusions.'

'This changes things, doesn't it?'

'The cops are fighting a losing battle against these farms. I read somewhere they closed down four hundred of them last year in Merseyside, but they keep springing up. Funnily enough, it's Vietnamese gangs who are in charge of most of them.'

'We have living proof. So young chappie here is head gardener?'

'They find someone young and without anywhere to go — usually an illegal immigrant they've brought in themselves. They make all sorts of threats about their families back home to keep them on track. Besides, the youngsters don't speak English, they have no money, they don't know anything about the UK except what they've seen on Downton Abbey …'

'So what do we do about him? We can't leave him here. As soon as Mrs Chau comes he'll spill the beans and she'll vanish and this poor kid will probably be knocked off by the gang.'

'Whereas if we take him they'll just assume he's run away and they'll draft in someone else to take his place.'

'We should tell the cops. Let them sort it out. If the farmers have got Lucas, this would be a way of grabbing them.'

'I don't want to bring the police in if we can possibly manage without.'

This exasperated her. 'Why? We can't look after this kid and we can't hide this operation without getting in real shit ourselves. You keep wanting to do this to me, Sam. It's not my favourite part of your personality.'

'If we bring in the cops and they come mob-handed it'll tell the people who've got Lucas we're on to them. Then who knows what will happen?'

'If the cops find out afterwards that we knew about this and didn't tell them, they'll have our heads.'

'Let me worry about that.'

'You can worry about your head, but I've got one of my own to worry about.'

'I'll deal with it.'

'How do you intend to do that?'

'With charm and grace, as always.'

She blew air out of her cheeks and looked away.

'It still doesn't help us with Gunga-Din here. What do we do with him?'

'You're right, we can't leave him. But I can't take him.'

'And you think I can?'

'I didn't say that.'

'You're making this really difficult.'

'Just stating the obvious.'

We avoided each other's eyes for a minute. Then she said, 'I might know someone who'd look after him. Get him into the system.'

'Without reporting him?'

'At least at the beginning. But she couldn't keep it quiet for ever. She's got her own job to think about.'

'Who is it?'

'I'd rather you didn't know. But she's legitimate, part of the system. Our backsides would at least be partially covered and not flapping in the wind.'

'I've always loved your turn of phrase.'

She scowled. 'Never mind that. How are we going to do this—your car or mine?'

We decided it was safer to take both cars in the end. We didn't want either of them in the area if Mrs Chau or the people she worked for came around. We would strap the boy's hands together and put him in my passenger seat.

I said, 'When can you call your friend?'

She glanced at her watch. 'Certainly not at a quarter to four in the morning.'

I gestured to the young boy. 'Well perhaps he'll learn English while we wait.'

Sometimes I surprise even myself.

CHAPTER FIFTEEN

FORTY MINUTES LATER we were in Knutsford Services, the only place we could think of that was open at that time in the morning. Luckily, Belinda and I were both starving. She ordered a burger and we bought another for the youngster. I chose chicken nuggets.

Despite the early hour there were still travellers so we found a table remote from everyone and talked quietly. I'd taken the youth back upstairs before we left so he could get dressed and pick up anything personal he wanted, though I confiscated his iPhone. When I looked at it there were no numbers in the contact list but lots of music and games in its memory. He hadn't objected when we'd used his own belt to strap his hands together in the passenger seat of my car. It was as though he knew it was the price to pay for threatening us.

We'd turned off all the lights in the house and left quietly. The next time Mrs Chau turned up she was in for a surprise—part of me hoped it wouldn't land her in trouble with her bosses. Despite myself, I liked her.

I inspected the youth sitting opposite me. He'd dressed himself in torn blue jeans and a white tee-shirt under a denim jacket. His hair was combed flat and his untied hands lay in his lap. He was pretty unremarkable. His face was long and his eyes were flat, uninterested. He had some adolescent spots on his cheeks that his diet of microwave meals had probably exacerbated. Once we'd reached the Services I'd untied him and he'd been docile enough and had waited quietly while we ordered. In the dim light he seemed underfed and pale, his fingers and arms as thin as a young girl's, but he looked at his burger with distrust and picked desultorily at his fries. He didn't touch the Coke we'd placed in front of him.

Belinda said, 'Reckon he's homesick?'

'For which home?'

'True. We don't know how long he was stuck in that house or even whether he could get out.'

'I expect he thought Mrs Chau was watching him so he'd better not try anything.'

Belinda nodded. 'So next question: who's paying her? Or do you think it's her operation?'

'Hardly likely. She's tough but not that tough. Besides, how would she sell the product?'

'So she's been run by someone else. One of these Vietnamese gangs you mentioned.'

I thought back to the conversations I'd had with Mrs Chau. There'd been nothing in what she'd said that suggested she was in debt to anyone, which was the usual way immigrants found themselves performing illegal—or cheap—jobs for villains. But having said that, she was cagey and smart and probably worked on the basis that I'd underestimate her in one way or another.

I also wondered whether the story she'd told me about her dead son was true. Could it be this youngster sitting next to us? I couldn't believe she'd have enrolled her own blood into working in the cannabis farm—for one thing he seemed older than the ten years she'd suggested for her son—but I was beginning to see there were multiple strands attached to the threads Belinda and I were pulling on.

I noticed the boy was sneaking glances at my chicken nuggets. I picked up the cardboard container in one hand, then leaned over and lifted his untouched burger. I held them both before him, asking him to choose.

Immediately he pointed to my nuggets and I handed them over. He started to devour them, adding fries into the mix as he went.

I looked at Belinda and raised my eyebrows.

The boy stopped eating for a second, looked at me, and said, 'These are good. Can I get a Sprite, too?'

Perhaps we'd caught a break.

UNFORTUNATELY, THAT WAS all we got from him. I asked a series of questions but to each one he shrugged and went back to focusing on his nuggets.

My impatience amused Belinda.

'Face it, Sam, he outsmarted us. He heard everything we said and didn't even have to bribe us with fast-food.'

She was right but that didn't placate me. I gestured to her and we moved away a couple of yards, keeping him in view.

I said, 'Can you take him? If we wrap his hands together again so he can't grab anything?'

'Where am I going?'

'You said you had a friend.'

'It's barely six o'clock in the morning, Sam.'

'Do you know where she lives?'

'You're joking, aren't you? I can't turn up outside her house with a stray youth in the back of my car like an escaped prisoner.'

'So what's your better idea?'

She stared at me. 'All right, I haven't got one.'

'We'll take his belt off and wrap his hands to one of his legs so he can't move.'

'You'll cut off his circulation and I'll have a dead Vietnamese prisoner in the back of my car.'

'I didn't know you were so squeamish.'

'And what are you going to do?'

'I might just go home and sleep, like a sensible person.'

She glanced at the boy. 'While I baby-sit.'

'I know it's unfair but I've got something to do later and I can't spend all day dealing with juvenile delinquents.'

She paused for a second, looking at me with something like disappointment in her face. 'You do realise this is exactly what Dan and I spoke to you about? Expecting us to jump because you need us?'

'If I could think of another way around it, I would.'

She said bluntly, 'I'm not sure that's true,' then turned and sat next to the boy again.

Twenty minutes later I strapped him into her passenger seat, his hands tied with a length of rope from the boot of my car, the rope then looped around the seat's safety-belt. As I leaned over him to test the knots I felt him looking at the side of my face.

I felt sorry for what we were doing to him, treating him no better than the people who'd placed him in charge of growing cannabis in an attic. I hoped Belinda's friend would be able to help him.

When I'd finished and closed the car door Belinda drove off without saying anything. I watched them head south — she would have to drive to the next motorway junction before being able to turn and come back north again — and I hoped she'd be okay. I knew I'd annoyed her and was giving her a lot of responsibility she could do without … but I had to sleep before taking my next step.

I would need all my available wits, however meagre they seemed at that moment.

CHAPTER SIXTEEN

TED MASON LIVED in the West Derby area of Liverpool, a region that ranged from working-class red-brick terraces through to high-toned mansions owned by people who, when their pensions finally accrued, would probably make the journey down to Berkshire and Kent, where their spiritual homes lay.

Mason's house belonged to neither extreme of wealth and was just comfortable, with a short pebble drive leading to a double garage and a well-tended rose-garden out front. There was a wooden fence, with gate, to the side of the house and I had the sense a sizable garden lay behind.

For an ex-convict he'd done well for himself.

Before I pressed the bell I rotated my neck and stretched my arms above my head, getting the fatigue out of my bones. I'd slept until two o'clock, then woke to find two messages on my mobile. The first was from Dan—he'd checked the Wares' gardeners, the Pearson father and son, and found nothing to suggest they might be involved in this kind of villainy; they'd operated out of Prestbury for years and were well-regarded in the area. The second message was from Belinda to say that her contact in the Liverpool Careline service had thrown a fit but taken the young Vietnamese boy with her and promised to go slow on the process of entering him into the system.

So I said a mute thanks to Belinda, crossed the Pearsons off my list and drove north yet again, tracking down the address Dan had found for the owner of the cannabis farm.

The bell was answered by a well-tended woman in her fifties. She had hair that was too blonde for her skin tone and wore a necklace of square gold pieces. Her expression was aggressive.

'What do you want?'

'Is Ted in?'

'Who wants him?'

'Can I speak to him?'

I thought we were going to continue this question-tennis indefinitely but she suddenly turned her head and screeched her husband's name over her shoulder. There was a rumble from further in the house and then he appeared in the hallway. She backed away but stayed behind him so she could hear what I said.

Mason was a bit shorter than me and had gone shapeless in the chest and upper arms. He wore a short-sleeved Lacoste shirt and peered at me through squinting eyes. I didn't know whether it was because he needed glasses or because I was silhouetted against the sky. His voice was a low, heavily-accented Liverpool drone.

'What can I do for you on me day off?'

'Do you own a house near Sefton Park?'

'Which house?'

I recited the address. His expression didn't change.

'What of it?'

'I should come inside.'

'What for? Who the fuck are you? Are you with the bizzies?'

I took a step forward and Mason and his wife both stepped backwards. We were in a hallway that was carpeted and neat. An open door to the left led into the lounge. I could hear the television playing.

I said, 'Let's go in there,' and walked in to the room.

'Hey! What the fuck are you doing? This is my 'ouse, you can't just walk in.'

'Turn the television off and I'll tell you what's what.'

Mrs Mason found the remote and turned down the sound. It was probably the best I could expect.

I said, 'That house. Who lives there?'

'None of your fucking business. Joan, call the police …'

'Did you know someone's growing cannabis in the attic?'

'How do you know?'

'I just do. So, is it your business or is someone else taking advantage of your kindly nature?'

His wife said, 'Ted, what's he on about?'

'Never mind. I'll deal with it.'

I glanced around the room. I didn't know why Mason had gone to prison but I guessed it might be for crimes against interior decor. There was a profusion of floral printwork on the sofa, the chairs, the cushions and even the wallpaper. Mrs Mason—I hoped it was her—had a collection of small furry animals that occupied the mantel over the gas fire, and on a table in front of the window stood several foot-high pottery statues of Regency women in demure poses. A small bookcase contained romance books by Georgette Heyer and tales of SAS derring-do by Andy McNab. This was an interesting relationship.

Mason had been sizing me up. He said, 'So what if I own the house. I don't live there.'

'You rent it out?'

'None of your business.'

'The police will really like your attitude when they knock on the door.'

At this he licked his lips and glanced at Joan.

'Look, I'm clean now for two years. I don't need this kind of bother.'

'So who's it rented to—just give me a name and I'll get out of your hair.'

'I can't do that. Privacy laws, ain't it? Besides, I don't know who actually lives there.'

'But you know who rents it.'

He said nothing, but that was a reply in itself.

Then, almost half-heartedly, as though he had to offer a show of strength, he raised his arms to push me away. I caught both arms, spun him and pushed him with more vigour towards the sofa. His feet caught on the carpet and he fell to his knees with an 'Oof' sound.

I said, 'Don't be so daft, Ted. Just give me the name.'

Joan had stood and watched and I realised that she'd lit a cigarette, as if better to enjoy the show. She made no attempt to go to her husband's aid.

Mason turned himself and stayed on the floor with his back to the sofa. He said, 'You didn't hear it from me.'

'Wild horses, etc.'

'What?'

I sighed. 'Wild horses wouldn't drag it out of me.'

Joan said to her husband, 'Haven't you heard that? I've read it.'

'Shut up, Joan. Fetch me a cup of tea.'

'Yes, Massah.'

But she turned and took the cigarette and its noxious smoke out of the room.

Mason said, 'Wynter. With a Y. Came recommended.'

'Where am I likely to find him?'

'How the fuck do I know?'

'Where would you go if he didn't pay his rent? How would you find him?'

'I'd look on the fucking contract, which unfortunately I haven't got at my fingertips right now. I'll get my secretary on it straightaway.' He got wearily to his feet. 'Not that he'd ever run out: he's paid two years in advance.'

I put my hands in my pockets now we were having a cosy chat. He collapsed backwards into the sofa and rubbed the back of his head as though it were bruised.

I said, 'That must have seemed odd. How much was it?'

'Six hundred a month. You do the sums.'

I did. It was over fourteen thousand pounds.

'So he paid all that money and doesn't even live there. Didn't that make you wonder?'

'I was too busy counting money to speculate, wasn't I? Just the windfall I needed.'

Joan came back in with a cup of tea. Mason took it without a word of thanks and sipped. Joan lit another cigarette.

Mason said, 'Are we done here? Visiting hours are over. Now fuck off and don't let me see you again.'

When I left the room Joan followed me out and held the door. Her face had softened a little, despite the fact I'd manhandled her husband.

'In case you're wondering, this house is mine. First husband. Ted lost everything when he went down. Accounting error, that was what it was. Inland Revenue didn't like it, though, so he did a few months. He's not been the same since.'

I paused and didn't know what to say. I suddenly felt bad that I'd bullied him. This was the second time in a couple of days I'd been physical with someone—it was as though something was taunting me, some atavistic mechanism that forced me to strike out at the slightest threat.

I said, 'Tell him to get his affairs in order. And for god's sake stop smoking that vile stuff, it'll only make him worse.'

Her face hardened as quickly as it had become soft. Criticise someone's nasty habits and they'll always turn on you. She said, 'He told you to fuck off. So stay fucked.'

She made to close the door on me but I held out a hand with my card in my fingers. She glanced at the slip of cardboard but didn't take it. I flicked it into the hallway.

'In case you want to talk to me.'

She said, 'Start holding your breath,' and closed the door.

CHAPTER SEVENTEEN

THE NEXT DAY was Saturday and the traffic back into Liverpool was heavy. It was after eleven in the morning before I stood in front of Mrs Chau's door, staring at a half-moon of stained glass. When I arrived and parked I'd glanced without apparent interest at the house we'd raided a couple of nights previously but there was no change. Before Belinda and I had left we'd switched off the lamps in the attic and I had a vision of those tall spiky leaves wilting and drying out, gradually becoming lifeless. I wondered how long it would be before anyone found them.

When she opened the door there was a moment of recognition followed by the briefest flicker of shock in her eyes. Then she folded her arms and planted her feet.

I said, 'I was told it was your day off. Hope you don't mind me coming like this.'

'The politicians on the television tell me this is a free country, so you can do what you wish.'

'Can I come inside?'

'Not unless I want you to.'

I considered for a moment, then decided if she wanted to play it like that, then I would too.

I said, 'I know you've been taking food to the boy in number 38.' I turned and pointed to the house. 'So why don't we talk inside and you can explain what's going on.'

She coloured infinitesimally. 'I have nothing to say.'

'Are you denying it?'

'I have nothing to say.'

She moved to close the door but I stuck out an arm and stopped her. She didn't persist.

I said, 'Do you know what happens there? Do you know what that young boy does in the attic?'

She looked away. I had the feeling she didn't want to resist me but was under some obligation to feign ignorance.

But still she didn't move and I didn't really want to push her aside to enter the house. I was trying to keep my bullying tendencies in check.

I had one card left to play. I said, 'You know I'll have to tell the Wares about this. The only thing you can do now is be completely honest. I understand you might have got yourself into a situation you couldn't get out of. But things can't go back to the way they were. Now's the opportunity to help yourself.'

Her eyes when she finally turned towards me were black with anger, but she stepped back and I went in.

She led me to a room at the rear of the house that smelled of incense and was dark and filled with cushions. A photograph of a young boy smiled at us from a table. He had his mother's tired eyes but also her intelligence. Perhaps he already knew he was going to die.

She saw me looking at the photo and turned it face down. I didn't know whether it was because she didn't like me looking at him or because she didn't want his spirit to gaze on the scene about to play out.

I said, 'Tell me about it.'

She was still staring at me with intense dislike, but a strange thing happened: a single tear crept out of her left eye and ran down her cheek. She quickly dabbed it with her hand.

She said, 'A man in the Embassy made a promise to me when he took my honour, but he didn't keep it. He was recalled to Britain and I was left to have my child in dishonour. I lost my job because I was pregnant. I had nowhere to turn. A friend of my uncle said that he could get me into Britain and I didn't have to pay. All I would have to do would be to look after some properties for them. They would help me with somewhere to stay, but I would have to find a paying job myself because they wouldn't give me any money. At first I lived in London and looked after two properties in Camden, but then it got too difficult for them and they moved north instead, to Liverpool and Manchester.'

'What did you have to do?'

'Be a housekeeper. Take care of the people they moved in to the houses and buy food and clean and do the laundry.'

'Who were these people?'

'Usually young men. Once there was an older man but he didn't stay long.'

'Did you know what was going on in the houses?'

'I didn't ask. I thought it was something to do with smuggling people into the country—perhaps young women to act as prostitutes. I tried not to think about it or get involved.'

'So this friend of your uncle—does he ever come to the UK?'

'I've never seen him. There's a telephone call when there's going to be a change but I never see the change—it happens in the middle of the night, when there's no one around.'

'And you get paid for this?'

'No, I'm still working off my debt, the payment for the journey here. A small amount of money goes into my account every month to pay for food and cleaning materials. But there's something else …'

'What?'

'My uncle's friend no longer owns the house.'

'Then who does?'

For the first time she glanced away and looked uneasy. I had the sudden urge to shake her until she spoke but I held myself back.

Finally she said, 'A year ago I had a visit from a man who told me he was the new owner. I think he was lying—he doesn't own the house, but he rents it. I saw on the television that a gang of men from my country had been sent back there for trial. But the man who came to see me had taken over my debt.'

'What did he say?'

'He told me the situation would stay the same. There would still be boys coming to the house and I was to look after them, as before. As far as I was concerned, nothing was changed, he said. My responsibilities were still the same.'

'What did he look like, this man?'

'He is about your height and weight. He is European, English I think, but has a cruel face with a curved nose and eyes that don't blink.'

'Does he come here to see you?'

'After that first time, only once more, to check up on me. I've had two phone calls telling me about the change of person in the house.'

I took out my notebook. 'Do you know his name?'

'He calls himself Summer, like the season.'

Wynter and Summer, I thought. This man is playing cagey.

I said, 'Do you know where he lives.'

'I have never found out.' She added, 'I have a great fear.'

'What fear?'

'The second time he came to visit he asked about me and my job. I told him about my work for the Wares and the property in which they live. He became interested and asked many questions.'

'What kind of questions?'

'About the job that Mr Ware does. About the house. About the child.'

She ducked her head and I thought she was probably crying now, as much as her rigid code allowed her to.

Then she looked up quickly and asked, 'What will you do with me?'

'I honestly don't know. You must understand the position you're in.'

'I do. I've made a great mistake.'

'Don't do anything different in your routine. When are you due to go to the house again?'

'The end of the week.'

'Well everything will be settled by then, one way or another.'

She took a deep breath. 'I am ashamed of what I've done. I'll do anything you ask of me. You must do what you must as far as I'm concerned. If Lucas is harmed because of me the shame will be too great to bear.'

There was nothing much to say afterwards so she led me to the door and closed it slowly behind me.

It was the last time I saw her.

I WAS GETTING into my car when my phone rang. It was Bobbie Ware, sounding quietly breathless, as though she'd run somewhere to make the call in seclusion. I couldn't imagine where she'd find an empty space in that vast mansion …

'I need to see you, soon.'

'Hello, Mrs Ware. Nice to hear from you.'

'Don't pull all that good manners bullshit on me. I know what you're capable of.'

'All right, I'm in Liverpool. I can be at your place in about an hour.'

'No! Not here. Haven't you got an office? Somewhere I can see you alone?'

I didn't like this development. So far the Wares seemed to have been working together. If she wanted to see me alone and away from her house, something peculiar was happening. I wondered whether it was connected to Mark Ware's bizarre attitude towards me and the kidnapping of his child. Or whether Bobbie Ware had become infatuated with my subtle detective charms and couldn't bear to be apart from me any longer.

'Can you tell me what it's about? Has there been contact?'

'No, dammit, nothing.'

'All right, we'd be better meeting at my place.'

'If you say so.'

I gave her the address and instructions. 'The front garden's been re-planted so don't wear the Blahniks.'

'Fabulous. I'll see you at two.'

She hung up and I disconnected at my end. I sat in the car staring through the windscreen and thinking about Bobbie Ware. It was always a pleasure to think about her, but I didn't like clandestine meetings and I didn't like it when clients became over-excited.

Especially when I wasn't the one causing the excitement.

CHAPTER EIGHTEEN

SHE ARRIVED FIVE minutes late in a sporty Mercedes with a soft-top. She glanced around at the work that was still continuing to remodel the area where my house had been rebuilt a few months before. The ground was now turfed but I'd decided to have some low walls built, together with a garage, and the foundations for these constructions were in the process of being dug by the builder I'd hired for the job.

I saw her arrive and opened the door before she reached it. She wore a short blue jacket and expensive, tight-fitting jeans. None of the fancy accoutrements could hide the fact she looked grim.

I took her through to my living room and offered a drink but she was all business and shook her head. She placed her expensive-looking bag on the floor and sat on the sofa as if trying to take as little space as possible, trying not to be there.

I said, 'You sounded stressed on the phone.'

'No kidding.'

'It's a tough time. Are you still sure you don't want the police involved? They have counsellors and all kinds of specialists.'

'Are you backing out?'

'Not yet.'

She took this the way it was intended—as a veiled threat. I saw in her eyes that she'd understood what I meant, but then she ignored it. I suppose she thought if it wasn't spoken about it wasn't real.

She said, 'Mark always wants to do things himself, his own way. He sees the police as interfering, not helping.'

'You think differently.'

'I'm not afraid to ask for help, if that's what you mean.'

'Is that why you're here?'

'I don't know why I'm here.'

'Do you think there's something I should be doing that I'm not? Someone else I should be talking to?'

'At the moment we have no idea what you're doing. You talked to Harris and Mrs Chau and Debra, then pissed off her fiancé. We haven't heard from you in two days, so how can I criticise your behaviour?'

I was confused. She was acting like a fireman who's burst into your house to douse the flames, but instead takes a seat to talk about the weather.

And then I began to ask myself whether whatever she had to say was so difficult she couldn't broach it.

I said, 'If you did know why you were here, what would it be?'

At this she bowed her head and took the brightness of her gaze away from me. I looked at the parting in the top of her blonde hair, wondering whether I could see through it to the muddle and indecision that were crowding her thoughts.

I said quietly, 'Do you want Lucas to die?'

Her head shot up but instead of anger on her face there was despair.

'Don't say that!'

'What are you not telling me? You came here with an urgent message that you're not delivering.'

'I know, I know ...'

'Do you? You're right, I haven't told you what I've been doing—partly because I've been too busy to stop and think, partly because I'm finding out stuff that I have to check before telling you or anyone else. But if you're holding anything back I can't do my job.'

Her expression turned scornful. 'I was right, you are backing out.'

'I think you should leave.'

She stood up, but not to go. She walked to the back window and looked over my fish pond and the garden.

She said, 'I think Mark's lying to me.'

I considered that for a moment, giving it the weight she obviously thought it deserved.

'Why do you think that?'

'There are phone calls … oh, this is going to sound stupid. I feel like the betrayed woman.'

'Tell me.'

She continued staring out of the window as though she couldn't bear to look at me as she spoke.

'You know he's still going in to work because the note said he must … so he's getting calls that he hurries out of the room to answer. He says they're from work, but when he comes back he's sweating and avoids my questions. That's not Mark. Work doesn't get to him. Nothing much does, actually. But it's why he's successful. He can make decisions quickly and not worry about them afterwards.'

'You think this is different.'

'I don't know! But he's … what's the word: shifty. I know he's lying to me. I know it.'

'Have you asked him directly?'

She uttered a short laugh. 'No. Believe it or not I'm too scared of the answer. Besides, he would deal with that. I've seen him when he's had to lie—to a customer, or a supplier.

He can do it without missing a heart-beat. And before you ask, no, I don't think it's another woman.'

'It's always a possibility.'

She turned away from the window for the first time and looked at me. 'We don't do that. Do you think we haven't had the opportunity if we were that way inclined?'

She was right. Both of them would have suitors lined up around the block if they gave any hint they were available for fun and games away from the marital home.

I said, 'What do you want me to do with this information?'

She started to say something but then was caught by a wracking sob. Unlike Mrs Chau's subdued tear, Bobbie Ware's crying was open and wild and involved heaving and convulsions. She raised her hands to her face and put a palm over her mouth but still the tragic sobbing emerged. I'd long since learned not to attempt to comfort people other than offering a tissue or a drink of water. I left the room and returned from the kitchen with a glass.

She saw it and took it from my hand, drinking greedily. Even in her grief she was beautiful.

She said hoarsely, 'I had to tell you but now I feel like I've let him down in some way. Is that stupid?'

'You had to tell me because it was the right thing to do. If the calls have something to do with Lucas he should be telling me.'

She nodded. 'He wants to solve the problem himself. He thinks it's his fault, because of his job, his money. He feels guilty.'

'I'll talk to him.'

Her eyes, reddened with tears, flew open. 'No! You can't say anything. I shouldn't have told you.'

'You had no choice.'

'But you do. You mustn't say anything to him because he'd never speak to me again. He'll think I betrayed him.'

'Haven't you?'

Without any hesitation, she slapped me across the face.

The sound erupted into the room and for a moment we stared at each other. Then she put down the glass, gathered her bag and left. My face was still ringing when I heard the Mercedes turn and swish out of the drive.

TEN MINUTES LATER I called Dan. I needed to stop thinking about Bobbie Ware and what she'd told me. I was beginning to feel as though I were playing off one client against another, and as they were married it was going to become complicated. I didn't want to wind up confused about where my loyalties lay.

It was early afternoon and I expected Dan to be asleep: his online time needed him to be awake into the early hours of the morning so he often slept late.

But he answered rather testily on the fourth ring.

'Dad — what do you need?'

I hesitated. 'Just got out of bed?'

'No, actually.'

'Sorry, you're probably doing something …'

'Just tell me what you want and I'll get on it.'

'Don't bother, I'll talk to you on Monday.'

I heard him sigh. 'Come on, what do you want me to find out?'

'Do we have a problem?'

'Only the usual one. The curse of the IT specialist. You treat me like Wikipedia on steroids.'

'Come on, that's not fair. I can't do what you can do. Besides, I thought you wanted to be involved.'

'Being involved means more than answering questions any time of the day or night. Questions you could find the answers to quicker if you just went on Google.'

I wondered if he and Belinda had been talking behind my back again, piling up their complaints about my working methods. He was right, of course: he was so good at what he did I'd started taking it for granted. There'd been a time when he'd seemed eager to work with me, to help me find out what I wanted to know, but perhaps he was growing out of that stage as he saw my work was largely repetitive and low-key. He was starting to grow into his own life.

'Look, I'm sorry. You know I get caught up in what I'm doing and I usually need information straight away. You're right, I don't give you enough credit for what you do.'

'It's not credit, Dad … it's …'

'What?'

'You treat Belinda and me like resources. Like staff. But I'm your son and she's your friend. You should think about that sometime.'

I could still feel the sting of Bobbie Ware's slap on my face, though the actual sensation had faded some while ago. I wondered when I'd become everyone's punch-bag. Or was I just feeling sorry for myself?

I said, 'I'm sorry I'm a bad dad and a bad friend.'

'Stop saying you're sorry. You're not a bad dad. I've had worse.'

He'd been brought up in a series of foster homes before he found out who his real father was. I hadn't known he existed until he turned up in my office. I knew very little about his childhood—he was reluctant to talk about it, though I didn't think he'd been abused or mistreated. Just abandoned.

He said, 'So what is it this time?'

'I need to know more about Mark Ware. How did he get where he is? What's his history? Dig around and see if you can find out something more than the bullshit CVs I read online.'

'When do you need it by?'

'Come on, you know the answer to that.'

'Right—the day before yesterday.'

'And I'll come and see you soon. We can go for a drink or something.'

'Don't force yourself.'

'I'll try not to.'

CHAPTER NINETEEN

I COULD HAVE gone to see Dan that same night. But I didn't. It was Saturday so I stayed in and started watching the last series of *The Wire* on DVD. I'd worked my way through all the previous series in about three weeks. I needed to get out more.

The next morning I was up before seven and went for a run in the growing light, picking my way across the fields behind my house before hitting the road that headed west towards Nantwich. After half an hour I cut left and ran the loop that brought me back to the front of the house, down a narrow track sheltered by trees now in full leaf.

A large black SUV was waiting for me, and as I approached three doors opened and three men climbed out. Two of them were obviously muscle, with thick necks and slick hair and tee-shirts that screamed Look at me, I'm ripped! The third man was the last to stand and the last to look directly at me, first taking in the house, the trees, even the blue sky overhead. I wondered whether he was a poet … but then discarded that notion when his hawk-like features settled their gaze on me. His eyes were dull and the look in them came from a long way distant, passing through layers of speculation and calculation and even contemplation before arriving at acknowledgement. Then the tiniest glint of knowledge lit something inside them and his thin lips twisted sourly.

I recognised him at once from Mrs Chau's description: this was Wynter/Summer, the man who rented the cannabis farm property from Ted Mason. He was a long way south from his patch and it was barely eight o'clock. It must be important.

I said, 'Office hours are Monday to Friday, nine till five, four o'clock on Friday.'

The man spread his hands. 'This isn't an official, office-based conversation.'

His voice was deep and the accent was heavily northern, but not Liverpudlian. Perhaps one of the outlying towns of Manchester—Bury or Bolton, where the vowels come from a different linguistic pool.

I spread my hands in the same way he had. 'I'm tired of having conversations in my garden with people who come to threaten me.'

'Who said anything about threats? Have I issued a threat?' He turned to his men, who were standing next to each other and leaning with their backsides against the bonnet of their car. One was blond and pale-eyed, the other had black hair but the same small features. 'Did you hear any threats, Gordon? Geoff?'

They shook their heads mutely. Well that was a surprise. He turned back to me.

'However, if you want a threat, I've got a good one for you.'

'It better be good—I've had some world-class ones in the last couple of years. You don't want to come up short.'

He ignored the taunt. 'If you don't stop digging into my business, you might find yourself underneath these foundations looking up, instead of the other way around.' He grinned. 'How's that?'

'Three on the Richter scale. What business are we talking about?'

'Yeah, I knew you were going to do that. Professional obligation, isn't it? Deny all knowledge despite the fact we both know what we're talking about.'

'This is where I say, "And who are you?"'

'Exactly. And this is where I say, "Okay, boys, teach him a lesson".'

The boys stood up from the car and came towards me. I suspected I was faster than them if I ran, but I couldn't be certain. They both had a few years on me and despite the breadth of their shoulders they might have been quick on their feet, more like surfers than weight-lifters.

I don't know what their plan was, other than to gang up on me, so I watched to see who made the first move. The one with the fair hair grinned and put himself forward while his darker colleague veered left to outflank me. I tried to keep them both in sight but it was proving hard, especially as I wasn't sure what part Wynter himself was going to play.

They'd distracted me with the blond's movement and I sensed then felt the dark-haired man come close and punch me in the side. The air went from me, but as I doubled over I flew out a straight left arm which caught him in the groin. He whoofed out a breath and bent over himself.

By which time the blond had stepped in and with his left fist caught me a glancing blow on the top of my right cheekbone. It spun me over and I went to the ground, intent on springing up.

But Wynter was on me now. He fell to a crouch and raised his right elbow, bringing it down heavily on the back of my head. I felt a familiar vibration start up and knew later I'd have one of the migraines to which I'm occasionally prone.

I was on my hands and knees and they were dropping blows on my back—deliberate, thought-through and considered shots rather than a generalised free-for-all. It was a controlled melée, which somehow made it more distressing.

After only about thirty seconds or so he called them off.

'Right, lads. Point made.'

The two men hauled themselves up and I heard them brushing down their clothing.

Although I'd spent most of the time on the floor, I felt winded. I rolled on to my back. Wynter was crouching, staring down at me, his dull eyes unmoved and unmoving.

He said, 'My property portfolio is of no interest to you. Get it? I know where you live and I know how to deal with amateurs like you. Stick to taking porno photos of women caught in adultery, or fraudsters claiming benefits. Me, I'm an honest businessman and I advise you to keep your nose out of others' business.'

I had to say something, if only to prove to myself I was still alive.

I wheezed, 'Your arguments are very persuasive, if blunt.'

'Good, you got the general idea. Don't make me have to persuade you again.'

He stood to his full height and the three men climbed into the SUV, reversed once and drove away, leaving me literally in its dust.

AFTER A FEW minutes I felt able to get up, though when I finally stood I wondered whether I'd been optimistic in my thinking. My migraine had started and I knew I was going to have bruises on my sides and back and on the top of my legs where they'd got in a couple of kicks.

I went inside and took some of the tablets my doctor gives me for the headaches, then made a cup of tea and sat on my sofa, still thinking.

There were two possibilities: either Mrs Chau had changed her mind and phoned Wynter, or Ted Mason was more involved than he'd led me to believe. I didn't think Mrs Chau had defied my instructions to do nothing except carry on as normal. But it struck me I knew very little about Ted Mason and his motivations. And I had left my card on their hallway floor, so he had my name and numbers. It would have been easy to track me down from there.

I dug out his phone number from the information Dan had provided and rang it. It was answered after two rings by Joan Mason.

'Ted? Is that you?'

'No, Joan, it's Sam Dyke. Is Ted not there?'

'You! You bastard, what's happened to Ted? Where have they taken him?'

'Calm down … who's taken him? What happened?'

'After you were here Ted phoned someone and an hour later this fuck-off big car turned up with three blokes in it. Ted went to the front door and talked to one of them, evil-looking bastard, then came and got his coat and went off with them.'

'He didn't say where he was going?'

'Just told me to stay put. He wouldn't be long. That was Friday night and not a peep since. What the fuck's going on?'

I didn't know, but it didn't sound good.

CHAPTER TWENTY

DAN TOLD ME the licence plate on the SUV—which I'd had the presence of mind to memorise—came back as a Mitsubishi Warrior belonging to someone called Carter Spring. I'd never known anyone called Carter, which made me wonder about his parents and their aspirations for their son.

Evidently names were an issue for him, too, as he moved between Wynter, Summer and Spring, presumably depending on who he was dealing with. I wondered whether we'd unearth an Autumn at some point, but I doubted it.

Dan hadn't yet finished looking into Mark Ware's professional history but he said he'd have something for me later in the day. I wondered what there was to find and what relation it might have to the kidnapping of his son, if any.

I had time to think about these things because I'd been sitting outside Wynter's house in Wallasey, a two-minute walk from the Cherry Tree shopping centre, waiting to see whether he came out or not. It was Tuesday, two days after he and his men had laid into me, so I'd recovered somewhat from the beating though I was still stiff. I'd asked Belinda to watch him the day before and she'd reported that on Monday morning he'd gone to a local community college, where he stayed a couple of hours before returning home and remaining inside all day. I wondered what he was studying at the college. Perhaps he was a tutor in Advanced Threats.

His street was relatively run-down, though the houses themselves were large semi-detached properties probably dating from the twenties or thirties. The black Mitsubishi stood on his short drive looking conspicuously luxurious against the cracked concrete and worn paintwork of the house and garage.

At nine-thirty he came out of the house just as a Fiat Punto arrived at his kerb. The two big men who'd worked me over climbed out, locked the doors and nodded to Wynter before getting into the SUV. Then he got into the vehicle himself, reversed from the drive and set off, heading south, towards Birkenhead. I let him get a couple of hundred yards down the street before following.

We'd been travelling about ten minutes when I was certain he was going to the same place he'd visited the day before—the Charles White Community College. According to their website they were an integral part of their community and offered courses in a whole range of subjects from construction and electrical engineering through to English, Art & Design and the Performing Arts. Students of all ages welcome. The well-chosen photos showed an essentially redbrick building from the sixties that had been made over with a new, glass-built entrance and the addition of a studio theatre courtesy of the Charles White Trust, set up eighty years ago to help run the college.

We skirted the great industrial wharfs and kept going south, turning finally into a semi-industrialised area on the edge of Bebington. I'd seen the college on Google Street View the night before so recognised it as we drew close. The Mitsubishi turned through a wide entrance and then was out of my view. I parked quickly outside the college property and then crossed the road, moving in to the college carefully. There was no security presence as far as I could tell, though I might have been observed by CCTV. I arrived just in time to see all three men climb out of their vehicle and walk directly into a small office block that I supposed contained a variety of classrooms and workshops. On the campus I counted three other working buildings that were larger and seemed busier, judging from the number of students entering and leaving.

Once they were inside I moved closer and noted the name of the building—Hodson. Then I made a quick tour of the grounds in search of something resembling an administration office.

I found it near the front of the campus, an open-plan office in which two women were industriously entering information into desktop computers. One of them spotted me and came to the counter. She wore spectacles and looked as though she might run the local chapter of the Women's Institute. The bruises on my face seemed to bother her—she looked down at the register on the counter as she approached.

I said, 'Hi, sorry to be a bother, I was asked by Mr Wynter to meet him here.'

'Mr Who?'

'Wynter.'

'I'm sorry ...'

'He said to meet him by Hodson, but I can't seem to find it.'

Now she understood what I wanted but she didn't look happy about it. 'You'll be wanting Dr Church's meeting. It's due to start at ten.' She glanced almost instinctively at the clock on the wall.

'Hmm, I'm not sure. What is it Dr Church teaches?'

'He's not one of the staff, he doesn't teach as such. But he holds regular meetings for people interested in comparative religion. People drawn from the area. It's a kind of outreach programme. For cultural understanding.'

'I see. That's why Mr Wynter thought I'd be interested. I'm actually quite a religious kind of person.'

She said nothing but I could see the doubt swim across her face like the shadow of a cloud across the prairie.

I said, 'So what room is it?'

She became business-like. 'It's in Hodson. Room 3. Go through the front door and along the corridor and it's second on the left.'

'Thank you. You've been very kind. God be with you.'

She gave me another dubious look then returned to her seat.

Outside, I crossed the campus and went through a heavy swing door into Hodson, following the woman's directions. The corridors were empty now and the tiles beneath my feet rang out as I approached the room.

The door was closed but there was a windowed square about nine inches by nine through which I could see into the room. At the front there was a large white-board and facing it were ranks of standard lecture-room benches, sloping down towards a table and a single chair. There were perhaps fifteen people in the room, and they were all watching a strikingly tall, thin individual with no-rim spectacles and straight grey hair and a still, commanding presence. Even through the door I could feel his charisma. He was probably in his forties and was dressed in a cream linen suit that wouldn't have been out of place in Cairo or Casablanca. At first I thought his height and the length of his limbs were due to some flaw in the glass window through which I was watching him. But I soon saw that his arms were very elongated, tapering to thin, bony fingers, and when he walked beyond the edge of the table I could see that his legs were also preternaturally long. His face was oval and his eyes were prominent, the eyeballs protruding and curious behind the barely visible spectacles.

Near the front of the room, his arms crossed on the bench before him, sat Wynter, alone, his two goons absent, probably off somewhere polishing their abs.

I opened the door and went in.

CHAPTER TWENTY-ONE

THE MAN I assumed to be Dr Church was speaking as I entered. He glanced at me but carried on as though unwilling to be distracted. His voice was sonorous and compelling and he spoke in complete sentences though he operated without notes. He walked backwards and forwards in front of the table, looking down at the floor and then lifting his gaze to the individuals in the room when he wanted to emphasise a point.

No one else in the room acknowledged my presence.

He said, 'Of course the universe has no creator or designer. As the particles of which the world is constituted move randomly, they cannot possibly produce anything resembling a pattern and therefore there is no such thing as order or a preordained fate into which we slide like knives into a sheath, or hands into a glove. No celestial theatre director has organised the disposition of the particles of matter, which have coalesced briefly in one place before melting apart in order to form further objects in the world.

'You can recognise this yourself. If you watch raindrops sliding down a window-pane they don't fall in vertical lines. They move, they dodge sideways, they avoid obstacles which are invisible to us. Thus each rain-filled window creates its own design, its own pattern. If the raindrops simply ran in straight lines you could predict their position at the bottom of the glass—but of course you cannot do that.

So it is with our lives, and with the lives of all sentient beings. There is a randomness that pushes them to one side, that makes us unpredictable and so capable of avoiding a fate that has been created for us. And as we jump and joggle about we engage in random collisions with other bodies, thus setting off chain reactions that colour and shape our world.

'And this, my friends, is the source of free will. If everything were predetermined from birth to death, if there were no randomness, if one action produced a precise reaction and so on until the end of time, then there would be no possibility that we could change the course of our lives. We would be living in chains from which there would be no escape.'

He paused his ceaseless walking and turned to face the room straight on.

'You realise that what I've been saying does not necessarily represent my own views. What I've just been describing to you is the thinking that drove the Renaissance humanists to change our view of the world, or so they hoped. The rediscovery of the works of Lucretius and, through him, Epicurus, began the process of liberating humankind from its belief that it had no choice in determining its future. In this new world-view, because there was no pattern or order, because the soul died when the body died, because there was no afterlife of which to be fearful, then it was acceptable not just to avoid pain—which religion had always used as its chief bartering chip—but now to actively seek pleasure. Accordingly we could choose to perform those acts which gratified us individually and were not necessarily performed for the greater glory of God.'

He fell silent and I realised I'd been almost hypnotised by his voice and the rhythm of his words. The other people in the room—all men, I noticed—seemed equally enthralled. Church went on.

'Thus anarchy was born. Since that time, somewhere after the middle of the fifteenth century, we have been in free-fall. Some people say that the power to organise and order your own life according to your own desires brings contentment and a greater feeling of self-worth. But is it not also true to say that acting only in your own self-interest—whether it be financially or sexually—leads only to selfishness? And who is to say that our own desires are always noble and actually enable us to become the best people we can become—the best husband, the best friend, the best colleague? Certainly I would be reluctant to suggest that. And then the argument can also be made that if the beliefs of these Renaissance thinkers—including Galileo, Copernicus and Descartes— were so compelling, why did the very notion of religion survive? Why do people still believe that they will live beyond the grave if that grave is merely a home to worms and earth and is no true container of the soul?'

He raised his arms and stretched them out wide and their true length became evident. They were inordinately long, even for someone of his height and general build.

'Look at me. I have a rare condition that leads to this freakish appearance. It's called Marfan Syndrome and affects one in every five thousand people. Typically it's an inherited condition but I have what is called a spontaneous mutation, and therefore cannot blame my parents. So I have every reason to condemn an unjust God who causes me to be the object of ridicule and scorn. And yet my soul still cries out for an accommodation with a deity who knows me and who will accept me to his bosom when I die.' He lowered his arms. 'That, my friends, is commitment. The great religions ask for your commitment to their faith, sometimes commitment beyond what you think is possible to give. Some of us are able to give that commitment freely—that is where we use our free will, not to indulge in promiscuity of every kind, but to show devotion to a cause greater than ourselves. Now, I will take questions.'

After a brief pause a young man wearing a white scarf raised his hand and in a rather stunned voice asked a question about historical attitudes towards religion. From the back of the room I couldn't hear exactly what it was, but Church took it seriously and replied with another long diatribe about the great religions' requirement for sacrifice and commitment as a sign of one's belief.

After another ten minutes or so the questions lapsed and most of the men gathered their things and filed past me on their way out.

Wynter had turned to watch and saw me sitting on the end of one of the benches.

I smiled at him.

He took the bait and came up the stairs towards me two at a time.

He said, 'You don't take no for a fuck-off, do you? Didn't you get the message?'

'I must have misunderstood. I thought you wanted to make friends, introduce me to your colleagues.'

At this he glanced back nervously towards Church, who was engaged in one more quiet conversation with the ardent-looking youth with the white neckerchief who'd asked the first question.

I said, 'So what's this, then? I didn't take you for a religious man, Carter.'

He was surprised I knew his name and he took a step forward, trying to grab my collar. But this time I was quicker. I grabbed his wrist and with sudden speed twisted his arm and turned him off balance so that his feet gave way beneath him and he clattered to the wooden floor.

The sound rang around the classroom and everyone turned towards us. I noticed Wynter's two men had come in again through a door at the back and two members of the audience had seemingly morphed into acolytes through the simple action of standing behind Church and looking up at me. They were pale-faced and had shaven heads and looked as though they'd found a purpose in life for the first time.

I let go of Wynter's wrist and he slipped a couple of times as he tried to find his feet.

From the front, Church sent the young student away and called up to us.

'Everything all right, Carter? Who's that with you?'

Before Wynter could start to control the conversation I stood up and walked down the broad wooden steps to the front. Gordon and Geoff, the two muscle men, glanced at each other but did nothing.

As I drew nearer Church's size became more obvious — he must have been six feet six or seven and he stood to his full height to look down at me. His eyes protruded slightly and his features were unusually pointed.

He said, 'I saw you come in. I have to say you didn't seem particularly impressed by my little speech. Where did I go wrong?'

I heard Wynter come down the steps behind me and I suddenly sensed I was in the midst of a cabal or cult. The leader was an intellectual with a grounding in abstract religiosity and the followers were probably devout in a particularly hard-headed way.

I said, 'I gave up Sunday School a long time ago.'

'Then why are you here? Were you looking for the woodworking class? Perhaps you found it difficult to tell the classrooms apart. This is Room 3.'

'No, I'm in the right room.'

Behind me, Wynter said, 'You should go. Remember our conversation.'

Church raised a hand and made a shushing gesture.

'Carter, don't be so quick to judgement.' He turned to me. 'So, Mr …'

'Dyke.'

'Mr Dyke. If you gave up your religious studies after Sunday School, what guides your actions these days? What is your system of beliefs?'

'I don't have a system. Call me an ad hoc type of person.'

Church smiled wanly, as if he'd heard this reply before on a thousand door-steps.

'Then let me put it this way, what would you be reluctant to give up in your life? Do you have family? Would it be your wife or your children? Or would it be your house, your car, your profession, your books or music collection? Everyone has something they wouldn't give up if you offered them a million pounds. What would you refuse to give up, Mr Dyke?'

'I didn't come here to discuss my beliefs, Dr Church.'

'Then why did you come here? What have you found so fascinating that even now you can't tear yourself away?'

'You can call it curiosity that led me here. And now I'm here I'd like to know what your intentions are.'

'Intentions? You make me sound like a suitor for the hand of your daughter!' He turned with a smile to the group of men and they all grinned at him.

I said, 'You have a strange little group of followers here. I'm wondering what you're trying to persuade them into thinking.'

The smile left his face. 'You make the mistake of believing that I'm answerable to you. If you're unwilling to accept them, my teachings are none of your concern.'

'Teachings? All I heard was a parade of patronising clichés dressed up in a philosophical wrapping.'

'You think you were patronised? I've barely got up to walking pace in my efforts to patronise you. I think you'd better leave before I break into a run.'

'Don't you want to convert me to your beliefs?'

'In order to do what? Punish the wicked? I can tell you're insistent on remaining a heathen.'

'Is Church your real name or did you adopt it for spiritual reasons?'

A subtle signal must have been given because the other men in the room suddenly appeared to intervene between Church and my scepticism. He stepped backwards and the two shaven-headed men escorted him from the classroom, like a touring rock star being led to the green room where delights lay in store.

Wynter said into my ear, 'Leave, Dyke, while you've still got the use of your legs.'

I turned quickly and brushed past him, knocking him off-balance, though he didn't fall. I wanted to see where Church was going. At the top of the steps I passed the young student Church had dismissed. He hugged his books to his chest and watched with wide eyes as I ran past him. I hoped he wasn't getting sucked into Church's circle.

Outside I ran across the campus and found my car. Moments later Wynter, Gordon and Geoff and the bald men who'd hustled Church from the classroom came out of the

Hodson building. They stood talking on the steps for a couple of minutes, then broke up and went their separate ways. Wynter, Gordon and Geoff left in the Mitsubishi, apparently heading back to Wallasey, and the other men walked off the campus and went in different directions.

There was no sign of Church.

CHAPTER TWENTY-TWO

BEFORE I DROVE back to Crewe I called Dan and asked him to add Dr Church of the Charles White Community College to his to-do list. He didn't sound happy about yet more research but I knew he'd do it more quickly and in more depth than I could ever hope to manage.

When I arrived I knocked even though I had a key—I didn't want him to think I'd just walk in when I wanted. It was bad enough monopolising his time without appearing as though I had some kind of *droit de seigneur* over his property.

He opened up, glanced quickly at the marks on my face, then went back to whatever he was doing. He had an office upstairs, the second bedroom, but he often preferred to sit with the laptop on his knee and listen to music through the good speakers downstairs. A plaintive girl singer without Gillian Welch's profundity was wailing about losing her man. Dan saw the look on my face and used the remote to turn her off.

I went through to the kitchen, looking for something to eat. It was lunch-time and I needed my calories. There was nothing in the fridge except half a pint of milk and two tomatoes that were going off. I looked around and could find no bread or even any fruit.

Back in the living room I said, 'What do you do for food around here?'

His head lifted from the screen. 'You don't like it, go buy something. I'm not McDonalds.'

I raised my hands. 'Sorry. I haven't eaten. Been watching the bad guys.'

'Don't try to guilt me.' He looked more closely at my face. 'Does that hurt?'

'Not much.'

'I've offered to help more if you needed it.'

'You can help me by telling me what you've learned.'

His expression didn't change but his anger came through. 'About who? Ted Mason or Mark Ware or Carter Spring or Dr Sebastian Fucking Church?'

I said nothing and we stared at each other. Then I said, 'I've rather loaded you up, haven't I?'

His head was in the screen again. 'Not a problem. There are some biscuits in the cupboard.'

I busied myself making tea for the pair of us and went back in with a plate of ginger biscuits and the tea cups on a tray.

After a couple of minutes he sighed and put the laptop to one side. He picked up his tea and sipped it.

'Sorry I swore.'

'You're allowed.'

He nodded. 'Okay, first, Carter Spring. Or Wynter or Summer or whatever. And Ted Mason. It seems Mason bought the house from the council a while ago. Prior to that it'd been owned by a Vietnamese guy who was part of a gang who were rounded up for human trafficking and sent back to Vietnam. There's no way the council wouldn't have known there'd been drugs grown in the attic, so someone must have cleaned it up before it was taken into possession by the council to resell. Then whoever took over from the

Vietnamese made sure it was bought by someone on their payroll and just kitted it out again.'

'Perhaps they got Mrs Chau to strip out the paraphernalia. She lived just a few doors away so perhaps she could do it overnight and keep the stuff in her property until they were able to reinstall it.' I thought for a moment. 'Scratch that. It was more likely Carter Spring and his men took everything down. The Vietnamese were done for human trafficking so maybe there was a gap between them being caught and the property being discovered by the police. Then they'd give it over to the council to resell, the product of criminal activity and all that. In the gap, Carter Spring gets involved somehow, sneaks in and strips out the drug equipment before it's found and impounded. Then he waits for the house to come on the market again. Worth the wait because it's a council sale and the price will be cheap. Probably got other places on the go anyway, so it's just a waiting game for this one.'

'So then Ted Mason enters the picture. He served six months for some screw-up with his VAT payments on a printing business he ran. Either he made contact in prison with the Vietnamese party or Carter Spring taps him up when he gets out, giving him most of the money to buy the house disguised as two years' up-front rent.'

I said, 'Why would the council sell the house to an ex-con?'

'White-collar criminal, he had the money, the council didn't want to hang around waiting for someone to make an offer. And once it was off their books they wouldn't care what the new owner did with it.'

'Then Carter Spring sets up shop again, using Mrs Chau as before.' I thought for a moment. 'This means that Carter must have known someone from the Vietnamese crew. She told me that when there was a change, the person who took over said everything would stay the same. And we found a Vietnamese boy looking after the harvest, so presumably that chain is still in place. Same club, different owner.'

Dan took a biscuit. He said, 'You told me Ted Mason's gone missing. What do you think's happened?'

'I think he told Carter that I'd been to visit. They fetched him and then they found me.'

'He's not gone home yet?'

I shook my head. 'His wife can't make up her mind whether to be upset or relieved he's not come back.'

'So assuming they've done something to him, why didn't they do the same to you when they had the chance?'

I smiled lopsidedly at him. 'You trying to get your old man dead?'

'Sometimes I don't understand the criminal mentality. They seem to get their priorities all wrong. They're just not very smart, are they?'

'I've got a bit of a profile at the moment—perhaps that was it. If they did any googling to find me they'd have found newspaper reports and so on. Perhaps they didn't want the hassle. Whereas Ted Mason, poor man, is relatively unknown. No one will miss him, at least for a while.'

'Except his wife.'

'And they're counting on her to stay quiet.'

We drank our tea, almost like a normal father and son. Then he said, 'Doesn't all this bother you?'

'All what?'

'Living on the edge of some kind of mania.'

'I don't understand.'

'Yes you do. Nothing is ever settled and calm around you. There's no such thing as an ordinary day at work. You're always going somewhere, watching someone, getting beaten up or beating someone up. Don't you miss the nine-to-five?'

To show I was taking him seriously I took my time in answering, even though I'd known immediately what I was going to say.

I said, 'I used to do painting and decorating when I was younger, about your age. Not exactly nine-to-five but not far off. I hated it. Knowing there was another wall to paint, another door to strip. When I joined Customs & Excise there was a fair amount of office time but I got out, too, met lots of different kinds of people. The variety became a drug. I needed more. When I left C & E I could have got an office job—in insurance, maybe, a claims investigator or loss adjuster. But it never really crossed my mind.'

He smiled. 'You wanted to be a private eye, taking down the bad guys.'

'To be honest I couldn't think of much else to do if I wanted to work for myself, which I did. I'd met some investigators through work, and while some of them were tattooed dicks, a couple of them were serious, smart and experienced. I could see myself doing what they did.'

'So which are you?'

'What?'

'Dick or serious?'

'Not my call.'

He toasted me with his tea cup. 'I'll let you know.'

I looked around the room at the life he'd made for himself already. He'd parlayed his skills into a mortgaged house, paid-for furniture, a stable existence. Perhaps it was his background growing up in several foster homes that had created in him the urge for stability and a sense of normality. I could understand that the work I did would set him on edge, but maybe that was why he kept saying he wanted to be part of it—to keep an eye on me, to make sure I was safe.

The thought unnerved me. I was supposed to be the one who looked after him, not the other way around. Glancing at him I saw how much he was beginning to resemble me—nearly as tall, dark hair that was almost black, a jawline similar to the one I shaved every morning. The difference was in the eyes: he had his mother's cynical, pale-irised gaze that peered at you from behind long dark lashes.

It did me no good to think about Tara. It only made me feel guilty, though I wasn't actually responsible for what happened to her. I said, 'So anyway, what else have you got for me?'

He sighed and picked up his laptop.

'Okay, Doctor Sebastian Church. An academic doctor, not a medical one. Topic of his doctorate was The Fundamentalist Impact on the Growth of Religious Intolerance. He worked at the college for the first time ten years ago. Then he left to go down to London, where it all got a bit murky. Some teaching here and there, some private tuition, some writing articles for obscure magazines before the Internet made all that redundant. He's been back at the college for three years but doesn't actually teach there now. He gave up his teaching post and for the last year he's been holding meetings on campus for people interested in making contact with other faiths. That's what his website says, anyway, such as it is. At the same time he tried to get involved in local politics, standing as a councillor and failing to win. Lowest votes for a candidate in fifty years, apparently. There's an interview with him in the Liverpool Post when he started his campaign—he comes across as arrogant, full of himself, someone who knows better than anyone else.'

'A politician, then.'

'You should have seen the comments from the locals under the interview online. He didn't come across well. He was eventually thrown out of the local Labour Party, though the exact reasons are hard to determine. Everyone kept their mouths shut.'

'So where's he from, what's his base?'

'I haven't found out. The only address I've got for him is the Administration office at the college. I haven't been able to find him in any local directories, not with that name, anyway. No house address, no telephone number.'

'You think it's not his real name?'

'Bit of a coincidence—Dr Church teaches comparative religion. It's like going to an optician called Seymour.'

'Or a gentleman's outfitter called Taylor.'

'I'm too young to know what a gentleman's outfitter is.'

'Cheeky pup. Does anywhere mention this illness he's got? This Marfan's Syndrome?'

'No, but I looked it up after you mentioned it. It's a genetic disorder that affects the body's connective tissue. You can get problems with the heart, bones, joints. And because it affects the connective tissue linking the body's cells and organs together you also develop these extra long limbs, as if they're being stretched. In the pictures I saw people look very willowy, almost like ballet dancers.'

'Trust me, Church is no ballet dancer.'

'What was he like?'

I'd given that question some thought since I met him in the classroom. I said, 'Highly intelligent. But possibly a bullshitter. Likes the power he has over people because he's brighter than most. Sees himself as a leader but I don't think he can really relate to ordinary men and women, maybe because of his illness. Thinks he's separate from everyone. I think he's dangerous.'

'You think Carter Spring—or Wynter, or whatever the hell he calls himself—works for him?'

'I wouldn't be surprised. Wynter isn't that bright. He might just be able to run an operation like the cannabis farm but even that's a stretch for him.'

'But you told me he asked Mrs Chau lots of questions about the Wares when he found out she worked for them. Wouldn't that imply he was digging for information so that he could kidnap Lucas? That seems to be the link, doesn't it?'

'It might be a link, but it's not the full story. I need to pay some attention to Church. He had himself a little cult developing there.'

'What kind of cult?'

'They were protective of him and they hung on every word he said. I think it went way over their heads but they treated it like holy writ. I think he's one of those very persuasive, charismatic types that can persuade you black is white. If there's an operation, he's the brains. Carter Spring is the enforcer.'

'Okay, if you say so. What will you do, watch him and see where he goes, what he does?'

'First we've got to find him.' I described how everyone else had come out of the Hodson building except for Church. There must have been another route out of the building and maybe out of the college. 'So we don't currently have an address for him, correct?'

'I'll keep looking.'

'Okay, so next … What about Mark Ware?'

Dan switched to a different document on his laptop and glanced through it.

'Interesting character.'

'I've met him. Tell me something I don't know.'

'Well, the big question in the articles I've read is how did he get to be so successful so quickly? First in pharmaceuticals, now in weapons manufacture.'

'It's not hardware, allegedly; it's software. He never sees a bomb or a bullet according to his driver.'

'As if that matters. It's all death-dealing, isn't it?'

'So anyway, he climbed the ladder quickly. He's a clever guy.'

'But it seems to be more than that.'

'Such as?'

'If you dig deeper you find people talking about the deals he made when he was in pharmaceuticals—for example, he spent a lot of time abroad, on the ground, talking to local health officials, hospitals, medical organisations and so on. Very hands-on. And after these personal negotiations, lo and behold, his company's drugs were suddenly welcomed in to the country—which was usually in a struggling economy in the Third World.'

'Sounds dodgy. Any proof of money changing hands?'

'Not that I saw. But that's not all. His last pharma company, Arqevit, was well-known for the junkets they arranged for doctors—conferences in Barbados to discuss the latest test outcomes from new drug products, and so on. All expenses paid for dozens of influential medical journalists and celebrity doctors to go and listen to some speccy scientist read out figures. Then let's hit the beach and party. And it works—the company gets an easy ride in the media and six months later your average GP is persuaded by a salesman's visit that such-and-such a drug is one they should be advising patients to take. Look at this glossy brochure praising its benefits. And it must be true because famous Doctor So-and-So who's written this glowing report is on the television …'

'You're not impressed.'

'I didn't know this kind of stuff went on. It's sleazy and despicable.'

'Got to keep the investors happy by increasing the dividend every year, even if it means cannibalising profits to pay it.'

'One more thing: you know how these pharma companies take years to get their drugs to market—a delay of fifteen years is typical because of all the legislative hoops they have to jump through …'

'I know that: it's for proper testing of side-effects and so on, isn't it? All the science has to be peer-reviewed, various trials, papers published. Takes ages.'

'Exactly. Well Arqevit reduced its pipeline from sixteen years to seven. That's practically unheard of.'

'And they still get their approvals?'

'One or two questions, but yes, all their recent drugs have been passed for use by the American and British review bodies, so they're on sale now at a pharmacy near you.' He shook his head. 'The worst thing is, the media love him and his pretty wife. For which I can't blame them, she's hot. The Tory press like him particularly. His can-do attitude goes down well with the anti-regulation crowd. Cut that red tape and let's get those people swallowing these drugs!'

He looked up from his screen. I could tell he was pleased with what he'd found even while he disapproved with youthful righteousness of what Mark Ware had done.

I said, 'So what are you suggesting?'

'Maybe he's too good, too slick. Perhaps he's given away too much of himself to get where he is.'

'That's not a crime. Entrepreneurs are the new rock stars. Flavour of the month. You might be letting your own prejudices get in the way.'

'Crap, Dad. If all this is accurate, he looks to me like someone who can't tell right from wrong.'

'Perhaps that doesn't matter.'

'Makes you wonder about his son's situation, though.'

'What do you mean?'

'Is this payback for something Mark has done? Was he picked for the kidnapping not just because he's rich, but because he still owed something to somebody, a little favour, a little cash-in-hand?'

I leaned over and patted him on the knee.

'You're really good at this, aren't you? You're beginning to think like a suspicious old fart.'

'That's why I want to do something different. Who wants to end up like you, with a face like a boxer's sponge?'

I couldn't tell whether he was joking or not.

CHAPTER TWENTY-THREE

I HADN'T BEEN to my office for a few days, so Wednesday morning I opened up to gather the collection of junk mail and bills that had accumulated on my door mat.

I'd sat down to read the monthly laugh-fest that is my bank statement when the office door opened and two men came in. They were both smartly dressed in dark suits, white shirts and colourful ties. One of the men had short salt-and-pepper hair covering a blunt, rather large skull, and he brought with him an air of bureaucracy and official authority; the other was marginally younger and his hair was brown and equally short. His eyes were restless and impatient, roaming around the walls apparently on the lookout for threats.

They stood in front of my desk as though waiting to be asked to sit. Instead I stood up so I could look them in the eye.

The older one said, 'I'm Mercer. This is Waite. With an e.'

He stuck out a hand, which I shook. Waite nodded at me and continued to take inventory of my office.

I said, 'Local cop-shop?'

Waite snorted but didn't look at me. Mercer gestured towards the two seats on their side of the table and I nodded and sat down. They pulled out the chairs, undid their suit buttons and sat. Mercer crossed one leg over the other, as if this were going to be a long conversation.

He said, 'Looks like your job cuts up rough from time to time.'

I'd forgotten the marks Carter Spring and his men had put on my face. My ribs had almost stopped aching.

I said, 'You should see the other guy. He can barely walk.'

'Bent over laughing, is he? What do you know about Sebastian Church?'

'Why do you want to know?'

'Don't play games with us, Mr Dyke. You were seen talking to him yesterday morning. Can you tell us the substance of the conversation?'

'There was no substance. It was all froth and blather.'

'That's not what we've been led to believe. What did you discuss with him?'

'I claim client confidentiality.'

'You're not a lawyer and Church isn't your client. You're on shaky ground.'

'Why are you interested?'

Mercer glanced at Waite-with-an-e and adjusted his position. I noticed the crease in his trousers could have sliced bread.

He said, 'I know who you are, Dyke, and what you've done recently. So I'm not treating you as hostile. However, I'm operating under certain constraints so let's just imagine I'm saying the words Counter-Terrorism Unit. That should be sufficient.'

I considered this for a moment. I put that information next to what I knew about Church: his arrogance, his creation of a close group of followers, his use of abstract ideas to fascinate and, possibly, indoctrinate men with unformed minds of their own.

I said, 'You think he's a terrorist?'

'You heard him talk—what do you think?'

'You had a mole in that classroom.'

They were both silent, admitting nothing. I thought back to the men in the room … which one could it have been?

And then I remembered the young man with the white scarf who'd asked the first question, who'd stayed behind after the meeting had finished in order to ask a further question, and had still been there when I raced past him through the back door to catch Church being driven away. He'd remained in the classroom throughout the conversation I'd had with Church and must have reported back to Mercer.

I said, 'I think Church uses his intelligence and even his illness to gain power over people. He's tried to do it politically and failed so now he's trying another route.'

'So you think he's a charlatan.'

'If he believes what he professes, is he a charlatan? Or is he just dangerously misguided?'

'Sophistry, Mr Dyke. We believe he's creating a group of white Muslims.'

'And that's a bad thing?'

'Ten thousand people a year in the UK are converting to Islam. You tell me whether that's a bad thing or not. Bearing in mind the obvious implications.'

'You're sounding dangerously misguided yourself now. Converting to Islam isn't the same as planting bombs on 747s.'

Waite said, 'You know they're called Reverts, not Converts, because Islam is seen as the original faith from which all the others are deviations? So when you switch religion to Islam, you're reverting to your original faith. Shows you how much they think of themselves.'

I turned to him. 'We're all doomed, then, especially the atheists.'

He shrugged. 'It's our job to identify potential terrorist activity. Are you going to help or not?'

'As I said, client confidentiality. I'll keep you informed.'

Mercer said, 'We could just watch you. See where you go, what you do, who you talk to.'

'You're probably doing that anyway. If you can intercept any of these bills on their way to my mailbox, be my guest.'

There was another silence while they switched to plan B in their heads. Finally Mercer said, 'There's something else you should know.'

'What's that?'

'Church has disappeared.'

I felt myself frowning. 'What do you mean? I thought you were watching him.'

'Nobody's perfect.'

'You sound very casual about it.'

'He's on the radar but he's not a centre of attention. Believe it or not we've got plenty of other high-profile trouble-makers to watch.'

'So why do you think he's gone?'

'Anything you could tell us would help.'

I stared at them, not knowing what to make of the conversation. Perhaps they were right and Church was merely a blip on their radar. But if that were the case, why was I getting a visit from men who, to judge by their clothing and demeanour, were high ranking officers?

Waite said, 'Anything to add to our sum of knowledge?'

'As I don't know what you know, it's impossible to say, isn't it?'

'Pretend we know nothing.'

'At least try to make it hard for me.'

'Ha ha. You know what I mean.'

'It's sometimes difficult to know what you mean because you talk in riddles.'

Mercer stood up abruptly, as if he'd had enough of this badinage. A business card had appeared between his fingers and he laid it on my desk, leaving his index planted firmly in its centre.

He said, 'You should walk away from this. I don't care who your client is. Advise them you can't help. We don't want to pull you in. Local rozzers tell us you're in credit. Don't make them out to be liars.'

'Or what?'

'You're out of business.'

CHAPTER TWENTY-FOUR

AFTER THE MEN left I stared into space for a while, wondering where this case was going. Lucas Ware had been missing for over a week now, and still there'd been no contact from the kidnappers—assuming that's what they were. In the meantime I'd followed a trail that led to a dope farm, possible human trafficking and now, it seemed, some kind of terrorist activity. What next—a plot to blow up the Queen?

I called Belinda to ask if she could watch the community college for the day, looking out for Church, but I was taken straight to answer-phone. I left a message but she didn't reply. I presumed one of her other clients was taking her attention.

So I spent some time researching the Counter-Terrorist Unit instead. There were now four such regional units in the country and the men who visited me were probably associated with Greater Manchester Police as part of their CTU. They were particularly involved in gathering information and questioning informants or witnesses. Their role was intended to be preventive, so of course they had fingers in lots of pies, trying to squirrel out useful data. I didn't get the sense they were a bunch of battle-scarred street-fighters who sat in a room armed to the teeth and wearing Kevlar underpants.

That took me till lunch and I debated driving to Liverpool myself to sit outside the Charles White Community College and wait for Church to appear so I could … what? After the conversation with Mercer and Waite, what was I supposed to do? Take Church to one side and ask him some probing questions? He'd made it clear there was no mileage in that.

And then I considered tracking down Carter Spring to see what he was up to. Now I knew he was the real entrepreneur behind the cannabis farm I could talk to someone in the drug squad and have him taken off the streets. While that might give me some personal satisfaction I wasn't sure it would advance the case. And besides, if he were questioned or even locked up he or his men might begin to look further than Ted Mason as the weak link and fall upon Mrs Chau. I didn't really want that to happen.

I phoned Jean Mason again but there was no reply and no answer-phone. I wondered whether she'd gone to the police to report her husband missing. Or perhaps he'd returned and they were out together, shopping.

There were too many unknowns. In the end I went out and bought a sandwich then drove home to eat it. I didn't drive to Liverpool to look for Sebastian Church or Carter Spring, nor did I drive to Ted Mason's house to see if he'd arrived there with a bunch of flowers for Jean.

Instead I ate my sandwich and considered handing the whole thing over to the police and resigning from the case. But I couldn't anticipate where that would leave Lucas Ware. I felt I owed Bobbie Ware more than just giving up, though I didn't know what was driving that obligation. Maybe it was a sense of fellow-feeling because I was also a parent.

Or maybe it was because I was a sucker for female beauty.

IT WAS NINE o'clock when the call from Bobbie Ware came in. I'd been reading and listening to music and berating myself for doing nothing useful all day when my phone rang.

'Mr Dyke? It's Bobbie Ware. You have to come and talk to Mark.'

She was swallowing her words and sounded close to tears.

I said, 'What's happened? Has there been contact?'

'No, nothing, damnit, just come. He won't listen to me.'

'What's the problem? It's a bit late for me to come over now …'

'He's like a zombie, like he's on drugs. And I know he's lying to me. I can tell. He's never like this. I thought about what you said to me the other day—that I was betraying him. You're right, I am, but I don't care now. Lucas is more important than my stupid feelings. You've got to come. He respects you. He'll listen to you.'

I doubted most of that and it sounded to me more like a domestic dispute than anything I should get involved in. As gently as possible, I told her I didn't think I could do anything she couldn't.

Which only seemed to make her more desperate, even close to anger.

She said, 'I can't talk to him. He won't let me in. He's up to something, I'm sure, and I know it's about Lucas. Please come, please …'

'All right, I'll come. It'll take me half an hour. Is he drinking?'

'He doesn't drink. Not at home, anyway.'

'Is he dangerous? Is he likely to hurt you—or himself?'

'Of course not.'

'Is there anyone else with you?'

'Just Harris, in his cottage. We haven't seen Mrs Chau for a day or two but she wouldn't be here at this time of night anyway.'

I made a mental note to investigate that, then said, 'Talk to him if you can. It sounds like he might be entering a depressive state. If he's used to being in charge and getting his own way then being in this kind of situation with Lucas will be killing him.'

'All right. I'll do what I can.'

'How are you?'

'Just come, will you?'

She hung up. I guessed she was probably all right, if a little strung out.

CHAPTER TWENTY-FIVE

WHEN I ARRIVED at the front door none of the downstairs lights was on. But a few seconds after I rang the bell, a light was switched on and illumination began to seep around the edges of the door, the massive chandelier hanging over the checkered tiles throwing out several mega-watts of candle-power.

Bobbie Ware flung open the door and leaned out to grab my arm. She virtually hauled me inside. She was wearing loose trousers, belted at the waist with a large silver buckle, and a short-sleeved pink pullover. Her blonde hair was piled on her head and caught with a couple of long pins. Most women would have looked ragged but she still looked like a model in a Vogue advert.

If she saw my bruises she ignored them. She said, 'Before you talk to him I should tell you I've just had a serious conversation with him. I couldn't take the lies any more.'

'I thought he wasn't talking. That's why I'm here, isn't it?'

'I couldn't sit there and do nothing, expecting you to arrive and solve all my problems. Perhaps I shouldn't have called you.'

'Perhaps not. How did he take it?'

She paused, then said, 'It's like I told you. He won't actually talk about it. It was a one-sided conversation. He didn't deny anything, but then I couldn't accuse him of anything. I just know he's not being straight with me. With us.'

By now we'd crossed the hall heading right, towards the door behind which the staircase led up to their offices. I imagined Mark at his desk, looking at his books and his various sculptures, vases and knick-knacks and wondering what any of it was worth if the life of his son was sacrificed.

As we started up the stairs I said, 'Do you really think he'll talk to me? He barely registered my existence last time I was here.'

The look in her eyes was intense, all of her intelligence and knowledge and history focused on my question. 'He wants to talk about it to someone. I know it.'

'But that someone's not you.'

Now she looked away and paused on the stairs. She said, 'I think he's ashamed. Whatever it is, whatever he's done, he's ashamed. He can't bear to look at me, never mind talk to me.'

She led me along the corridor and stopped outside his office. The door was closed. She tried the handle but it was locked. She tapped lightly and said, 'Mark, I've got Mr Dyke here. Perhaps you'll talk to him if you can't talk to me.'

Then, shrugging with despair, she strode past me and left me alone with a blank door for company.

After a moment I said, 'Mark, Bobbie's worried about you. You know that. She tells me she's worried about your health.' I was silent for a moment, thinking he wouldn't swallow that line. 'And she thinks you've been lying to us. I said at the beginning this would only work if you told me everything. I can't work with my hands tied or if I don't have all the information. So is she right?'

I heard a movement in the room, as though he was shifting the position of his chair. But the door didn't open.

'If you've got anything at all that might help Lucas, don't you think you should tell me? Or somebody? You'll hate yourself if anything happens to him and you had information that might have helped.'

I left that hanging in the air but there still no response. The door was still locked when I tried it.

I said, 'I'll be with Bobbie.'

I exited the corridor and worked my way around to the large sitting-room but she wasn't there and the lights were off. The television was playing mutely on the wall, its huge screen throwing flickering light into the dark space.

Downstairs again I remembered the route to the kitchen and found her there, seated at the large breakfast island, her fair arms showing pale against its black polished surface. A melancholy surrounded her like mist. First her child was taken, now her husband had vanished mentally, if not physically. I couldn't begin to understand what was going through her head. I wanted to touch her but it would have been the worst thing I could possibly do, for both of us, if for different reasons.

She had turned towards me when she heard me come in.

'What did he say?'

'Nothing. You should call the police. Tell them what's been going on.'

'Have you …?'

'Found anything? No. We've tracked down a couple of people but I haven't found a direct link to Lucas yet.' I remembered something she'd said on the phone. 'You said that Mrs Chau hasn't been in for a couple of days.'

'What? Oh, yes. She didn't come back after the weekend. To tell the truth I was glad. I didn't want her long face hanging around like a death-mask.' A thought occurred to her and she frowned. 'You don't think she had anything to do with it, do you? She loved Lucas like her own child.'

'You knew about that?'

'Yes, she told us. I'd hate to think she was connected to all this.'

I hesitated but realised if I expected honesty from the Wares, I had to be truthful myself and tell her about Mrs Chau's dual life.

Bobbie's eyes widened as I explained what Belinda and I had found, and Mrs Chau's link to the cannabis farm. I didn't go further and describe my meetings with Carter Spring and Sebastian Church.

She became animated, her eyes almost glowing with belief. 'But that's it, don't you see? If she knows these people, whoever it is that's growing this dope, then they must be the ones who've taken Lucas. They've done it for the money. We must tell Mark straight away and get the police on to it. They'll be able to find them, won't they?'

'It's not that simple.'

'Why? And why didn't you tell me before? Why is everyone so keen to keep secrets from me? Am I so terrible?'

I had been looking at her as she talked to me. Her eyes were now bright with anger … and then they shifted to one side to look over my shoulder and their intensity softened.

'Mark!'

She stood and went to him and he collapsed into her arms. He hadn't shaved for a couple of days and his usually sleek hair was unkempt. He wore crumpled jeans and a striped business shirt that he'd failed to tuck into his trousers. He was a mess.

As Bobbie took him in her arms, he let out a deep sob and raised his hands to clutch her back. He lowered his head into the cradle of her neck and continued to cry while she patted him and made soothing noises.

Eventually he stood up and wiped his nose and she shuffled him around till he could sit on one of the tall kitchen stools.

She said, 'Darling, tell me what's going on. Please.'

He sniffed again, then took out a handkerchief and blew his nose. Reaching across the counter he poured himself a glass of water from the tap. He glanced at me but looked away immediately, having eyes only for his wife. When he spoke his voice was hoarse at first, then he coughed and it gained some strength.

'They phoned me the night Lucas was taken. On my mobile. They told me they were the ones who'd taken my son and they had a special mission for me. It wasn't money. They told me if I wanted to see my son again I had to arrange for the delivery of two of our systems to a port of their choosing.'

'What kind of systems?'

He turned to me. 'A detection system and a decoy system. The VR5 and the BS12.'

'Which are what?'

'The decoy system is an advanced version of what they used to call chaff, a way of fooling an incoming weapon into exploding harmlessly. The detection system lets you know that something's coming in in the first place.'

Bobbie was growing impatient. 'So you've been in contact with these people for all this time and you didn't mention it?'

'I couldn't, could I? You'd want to bring the police in. I couldn't stop you hiring Dyke but I didn't think he'd be much use against these people. They're organised and know what they want. I didn't think hiring a private investigator would get in their way.'

I said, 'You may be right. But you've not improved my chances. What else do they want?'

'Nothing else. Just for three each of these systems to be delivered to Syria.'

'Syria? Jesus.'

'Why do you think I've dragged my feet? When this gets out it's the end of my career. The end of everything.'

Bobbie said, 'What do you mean?'

'These systems are at the cutting edge—no one else can supply them. And when it comes out I've made it happen I'll be a pariah.'

'Can you even do it? Without raising red flags in your own company?'

'It's what I've been working on for the last week. There was a shipment due to be delivered to Iskenderun on the Turkish coast. I'm trying to get it diverted further south. It's only half of what they wanted but it's the best I can do at short notice.'

I stared at him. He'd been keeping a terrible secret but his own arrogance had undone him. This was a problem he couldn't solve by himself and he didn't know how to ask for help.

I recognised his dilemma.

I said, 'Have you heard the name Sebastian Church?'

'No—should I?'

'I don't know. Who's been talking to you on the phone? Can you describe the voice?'

'Not really. It's disguised, muffled in some way. His vocabulary is extensive, though, and he's quite formal in the way he speaks. He sounds English, which is a surprise.'

Bobbie said, 'Why?'

Before he could answer, I said, 'Listen to me, the pair of you. I'm quitting this case right now. I can't help you any more. You have to call in the police and tell them everything. You've not been honest with me and while I might have been able to help before, now I don't think I can.'

Bobbie was enraged. She said, 'Why? What's changed? Surely it's better now you know what's really going on.'

I said, 'Tell her, Mark. Tell her who you're dealing with.'

He glared at me, then reached out and took Bobbie's hand. He was quiet for a long while as he found the words. Then he said, 'These people … the equipment they want me to deliver, it's matériel to counteract drone strikes. They want to be able to sense them coming and then decoy them so they miss their targets.'

Bobbie was crying now, tears coursing down her cheeks. 'Who? What people?'

Mark Ware lowered his eyes before he spoke. 'It's ISIS, ISIL, call them what you want … it's Islamic State. And they've got Lucas.'

CHAPTER TWENTY-SIX

IT WAS MIDNIGHT when I arrived home, tired and angry. I'd told the Wares again that I was resigning from the case but I didn't think they'd taken it in. Bobbie had asked a hundred questions of Mark but he was in a dark place and couldn't answer most of them.

In the end I left them in their kitchen, arm in arm, stunned in their helplessness. I knew it was unfair to leave them like that but I couldn't see how I could work with them if Mark was so secretive. I had no guarantee the next time a call came in from the kidnappers that he'd tell me; he was so persuaded of his own competence he couldn't be convinced other people might help.

The light on my answer-phone was flashing so I pressed the button to hear the messages. The first was from Belinda, apologising for not getting back to me earlier. As I'd thought, she'd had to do something for one of her regular clients, a large security outfit in Manchester. She'd just started doing legwork for them and wanted to show she was available when they called. And, she added, they paid a better daily rate than I did …

The phone beeped and the time and date of the next message was announced—about an hour ago. It was a man's voice, but muffled, as if speaking through a scarf or handkerchief. I stopped in my tracks and listened.

'Mr Sam Dyke, you will know who this is. We have your son, Daniel. No harm will come to him or to Lucas Ware if you don't look for them. If you persist, I cannot be responsible for what might happen. Do not contact the police. Do not contact the newspapers. Go lie down with the sheep and leave the lions to do their work.'

The message ended.

I felt my heart pounding in my chest as the adrenaline hit me. I snatched up my mobile phone and dialled Dan's number at once. If he was home he'd be online, trading bitcoins for his and my profit.

His mobile rang a few times then went to voicemail. He had no fixed-line phone. I picked up my own land-line phone and dialled 1471 to retrieve the number the call had been made from—but the woman's automated voice told me they didn't have the number.

I texted him a short message but couldn't wait for a reply, so ran outside and climbed into my car. I reversed so quickly I ran over a lavender bush I'd just planted—I heard the scratchy impact—then squealed down the driveway towards town.

It was about seven minutes to Dan's house.

I made it in five.

His car was on the driveway but there were no lights on in the house. I banged on the door then took out the key he'd given me and let myself in. My hands were shaking so hard I nearly dropped the key.

There were no signs of disorder or anything amiss … but he wasn't home. If his car was on the driveway but he wasn't in the house, it was possible he'd walked somewhere or caught a bus.

But it wasn't likely.

It was more likely that the voice on the telephone message was telling me the truth and Dan had been taken.

The Wares had gone through living hell in the last few days and I was about to join them there. I didn't know whether I could hold it together while still doing my job. I'd barely got to know my son and now he'd been snatched from me.

There was an inevitability about the shape of events leading to this moment. Since the first time I saw him I'd guessed we'd arrive at this engagement. Part of me welcomed it, part of me was terrified. This wasn't someone else's case any more—it was mine. And I knew I wouldn't eat properly, sleep well or think straight until I'd got Dan back. I needed all my resources to be working at full power and when I looked inside myself I wasn't sure I could do it. The stakes were too high and the man I was battling was no fool.

Despite his attempt to disguise it, I'd recognised the voice on the answer-phone at once and it had frozen the blood in my veins: Sebastian Church was not someone you took lightly.

CHAPTER TWENTY-SEVEN

AFTER A NIGHT in which I had less than two hours' sleep,
I phoned Howard, a police inspector I'd worked with a
couple of times in the last few years. As he'd grown older
he'd become more suspicious than ever, and when I told him
I wanted some information about Mercer, the man from the
Counter-Terrorist Unit who'd visited my office, I practically
saw him sharpening a pencil in order to take notes.

'Why do you want to know about him?'

'Can I just say it's related to something I'm working on?'

'You can say it, but it won't get you anywhere.'

'All I want to know is whether he's discreet or whether
he's a company man. Can I trust him not to blab private
information to his bosses just so he can get a gold star?'

'How do you know him?'

'He came here with someone called Waite. With an e.'

'Yes, I thought you were clueless.'

'Why?'

'Because, you dickhead, he *is* the boss. Took over last year.
Don't say I envy him, what with all the activity.'

'Why would he come to see me?'

He snickered. 'Because you're famous? Did he ask for
your autograph?'

'Piss off.'

'So come on, tell me what's going on. He wouldn't leave
his office without good reason. What did he want?'

'You know I can't tell you. You'll have to trust me.'

'Last time I trusted you you nearly got a girl killed.'

'This is different.'

'How do I know?'

'Because I'm telling you.'

I heard him sigh and I knew he was looking away, out of his office window, perhaps, shaking his head and cursing himself for having anything to do with me. Luckily I'd helped him on a couple of big cases and, as Mercer had said, I was in credit.

Eventually he said, 'Okay, he's one of the good guys. Straight arrow. Every type of success known to cop-kind. That's why he got that job—imagine the profile of Counter-Terrorism these days. They need hotshots.'

'So if I talked to him he'd be discreet.'

'Well, it still depends, doesn't it?'

'On what I told him.'

'Got it in one. Why don't you tell me, first? Run my seasoned eye over it?'

'I can't. Really, I can't. But there is something you might want to look at.'

'Here we go. Something to my advantage that's also to yours?'

'See if you can track down a Mrs Irene Chau.' I gave him her address in Liverpool. 'She hasn't been seen in a couple of days. I'm worried about her.'

'Scousers are beyond my remit.'

'She's from Vietnam.'

'And why should I worry about her?'

'I think some bad guys might have caught up with her.'

'Which bad guys in particular?'

'Sorry, there's a terrible noise on this line. I didn't catch that.'

He sighed loudly again—it was one of the ways he dealt with my impertinence. 'I'll talk to someone, send a couple of men round.'

'Make them big men.'

'Really?'

I said nothing and after a moment he took the hint and rang off. My phone beeped to tell me I'd missed a call: it was Belinda. I felt myself tighten up as I ignored the message, but I couldn't talk to her yet.

During the conversation with Howard I'd desperately wanted to tell him Dan was missing and I knew who'd taken him.

But like Mark Ware, I couldn't do it—I couldn't bring myself to make Church's threat real by talking about it.

Perhaps foolishly, I trusted myself more than anyone else to find him.

I DUG OUT the card that Mercer had placed on my desk and rang his number. I expected voicemail but he answered quickly.

'Who's this?'

'Sam Dyke.'

'Really? The great non-communicator? In what way can I fail to help you this morning?'

'Okay, I deserve that.'

'Indeed. So do you have anything to tell me about Sebastian Church? Have you come across him during one of your precious investigations? Sorry, that should be private investigations, shouldn't it?'

I'd expected some kind of roasting so I didn't take it personally. I said, 'Why is Church so important to you?'

'More games, Dyke?'

I said nothing.

After a moment he said, 'I'll tell you this: Doctor Church wasn't at the top of our watch-list. We believe he's acting on impressionable minds but he's not, as far as we can tell, rousing them to wage jihad on the streets of Toxteth. He talks about faith and commitment, then he looks for those he can bend to his will and recruits them into his band of merry men. He likes the power, like many of these petty tyrants. Given the physical problems he has, perhaps it has a positive psychological effect on his sense of well-being. Last time we met you asked whether we thought he was a terrorist. The answer to that is no—but given a fair wind he might become one, or influence one or more of his followers to tack in that direction. He's played it very carefully so far, which is why we've only watched him and not taken any action. However, if you have any information to make us change our minds, you'd be rendering your country a service.'

Again I was tempted to tell him what I knew about Church's current activities … but I pictured Dan, and Lucas, tied up and gagged, thrown into the corner of a warehouse or shed … and I kept my own counsel.

I said, 'As a matter of fact, it's not Church I'm interested in. It's one of his men, a man called Carter Spring.'

'Ah yes, Spring, Summer and Wynter. Unpleasant type. Petty crook. He served a few months for smuggling recreational drugs from the Far East. What's he doing now, other than sucking up to Church?'

'I'm on the way to finding out. You can have Church, he's obviously out of my league. But maybe I can help.'

Mercer laughed, enjoying himself at my expense. He might have been one of the good guys, but he had the usual bad opinion of people in my profession.

I said, 'Could we at least meet?'

'I haven't got time. Things happening. I won't say any more, but here's a tip: if you're planning on flying abroad, change your travel plans. Try the train.'

'What the hell does that mean?'

'And they told me you were bright.'

'Manchester Airport or Liverpool?'

'I have no idea what you're talking about. You'll be spreading panic in suburbia. Now, do you have anything concrete to tell me?'

I hesitated but finally said, 'No, not right now.'

'My powers are extensive. I could have you arrested.'

'What good will that do?'

'Get you off the streets and out of my hair. Can I remind you this is my job, not yours? Now excuse me. I have important and highly-classified work to do. Call me again when you have something equally important to tell me.'

He hung up.

I closed the connection on my phone. I was in my office and I could hear the street life outside. It seemed to me as though for the last twelve hours I'd been living in a soundless bubble, my focus so internal I could almost hear my organs functioning.

He'd asked for my help and I could have asked for his. But I couldn't do it.

Mercer had as good as told me that Church was connected to Islamic State in some form—perhaps as a recruiter, or someone who softened up possible recruits. I knew, or thought I knew, that he was going further than that. He wanted Mark Ware to send defensive matériel into the heart of the war zone, presumably to help IS in its push north into Turkey. If they could protect their fighters from allied strikes—from drones or warplanes—then they would have a greater chance of seizing Iskenderun and the rest of Turkey's vast territory.

But what I was concerned about was the safety of my son, and by extension the son of my client. At this point it seemed impossible for me to see further than my own bloodline.

BUT I HAD to tell someone, so I phoned Belinda. She was in her client's offices in Manchester and when she heard my voice she stepped outside.

I told her about the message on my answer-phone.

She knew better than to give me an emotional reaction: she knew what I was feeling. She said, 'You've checked it out, been round there?'

'His car was there but no lights on. Nothing disturbed. They must have taken him at the door, before he could even fight back.'

We both knew he'd have used some of his Tae-Kwon-Do skills if he'd been given any chance to react.

'Okay, you know I'm going to ask—have you reported it?'

I felt my insides churning over. I was in exactly the same position as the Wares—desperate to get my son back but fearful of doing the wrong thing. Belinda would understand the horrible irony of the situation: I was no more likely to call in the police than the Wares had been, despite my advice to them.

I said, 'You know that's not possible. I can't tell anyone.'

'So what are you going to do?'

'What else can I do? I've got to do something myself.'

'I'll come over. You can't find both Dan and Lucas single-handed.'

'I'll manage. You've got your own clients.'

'Oh don't throw that back at me. This is different. They can go fuck themselves if it comes to that.'

'Really, there's no point two of us getting involved. Church is dangerous.'

'Jesus, Sam, this is you all over. You want Dan and me to help when it suits you, but you won't ask for help when it's important.'

'What do you mean?'

'It's like we said the other night. You want us to do the manual labour but you won't let us inside the gates. You don't exactly confide.'

'You're the only person I've told about Dan. Besides, they're my problems.'

'Sometimes other people have better solutions.'

I closed my eyes. What she said was difficult to hear but I knew she might be right.

I said, 'I can't talk about this.'

'Sam, I'll come over. Don't do anything rash.'

'Stay there. I'll call you, I promise.'

'Are you going to tell the cops about Dan?'

'I'll call you.'

CHAPTER TWENTY-EIGHT

WHEN HE BEGAN to wake up he knew the situation immediately. He imagined he should be disorientated and confused because of the drugs they'd used and the change in his circumstances.

But he knew he was a prisoner.

Before he opened his eyes he listened, trying to learn more about his environment. He had flashbacks to opening his front door and seeing two large men wearing black clothing on the doorstep. Before he could slam the door shut they'd stepped in, crowding him in the space at the bottom of his staircase so he couldn't find room to kick or even draw back an arm to strike. And they were immensely strong—one of them had wrapped him in his arms while the other held a soaked cloth to his mouth and nose. The smell had been overpowering and he still remembered the sense of falling, of going limp, and then the blackness.

Now he had a headache and a strong sense-memory of the cloth's smell.

He moved slightly to test his restraints. His shoulders ached where his arms had been pulled behind his back so his wrists could be tied together. It felt as though they'd used thick adhesive tape, wound several times around his lower arms. He was lying on his right side and his left leg also ached. As he moved it tingled and he realised it had gone to sleep because of the awkward position in which he was held.

Blood began to return to the leg and he grimaced in pain as it woke up.

Finally he opened his eyes, trying not to move his head. He was lying on the floor in a small room. The carpet beneath him was musty, unvacuumed, and thin. The curtains were drawn because it was dark inside the room, though enough light was filtering in to show the vague outlines of furniture and other objects. He knew he was on the ground floor—there was something about the solidity of the floor that told him it was concrete, not floorboards.

Facing him was a small bundle of sheets that looked as though they'd been dumped ready for washing.

As he stared at it, the bundle moved and he drew away, expecting to see a small animal peering out, perhaps scuttling across the floor.

Instead he saw the face of a young boy with straight blond hair.

He said quietly, 'Hi, Lucas. I'm Dan. How're you doing?'

HALF AN HOUR later they were both sitting up with their backs to the wall and Lucas was completing his explanation of how to kill the Ender Dragon in Minecraft by destroying the Ender Crystals.

Dan thought it tragic that Lucas had wanted to talk about the Dragon almost as soon as they'd begun the conversation. It was as though slaying a monster had been on his mind for the whole time he'd been held captive.

He said, 'So how many men have you seen here, Lucas?'

The boy made a show of frowning to demonstrate he was taking the question seriously.

'Three. There's the big tall one they all listen to, a big muscley one who brings me stuff to eat, and one with a bent nose who comes and looks at me but doesn't say anything. I don't like him. The muscley one's okay but I don't like the tall thin one either. He comes and talks to me and pats me on the head and tells me not to worry.'

Three men, Dan thought. Carter Spring, Church and one of the big men who'd captured him. He wondered whether more men were gathered outside but weren't allowed in to the house, or wherever they were.

He said, 'What does the thin man talk to you about?'

Lucas looked up at him. Dan felt a pang of empathy, recognising the yearning in the young boy's face, knowing from his own experience what it was like to search for trust in the adults around you.

'I don't know. He uses words I don't understand. He talks a lot about God. He's like the Creeper—I think he's going to creep up on me one night and explode.'

'Don't worry about him. My dad will sort him out.'

Lucas' gaze moved to one side and Dan turned to see a man he knew was Sebastian Church standing over them. He'd arrived almost silently. Dan knew the man was the victim of an illness he could do nothing about, but he was very odd-looking: his face was as elongated as his arms and legs, his eyes protruding and curious behind thin spectacles. He couldn't imagine what Lucas had thought during these last days. It was like being kidnapped by aliens.

Church said, 'Hello, Dan. I'm glad you've rejoined us. You're just in time to witness the suffering that young Lucas is going to endure.'

Dan felt a fear grip his heart. He'd never known a dread so visceral. But he knew Lucas would be feeling worse. He tried to change the subject, to at least prevent Church talking about Lucas.

He said, 'What do you want with me?'

Church grinned, his wide mouth almost splitting his face in two. 'I want nothing with you. You're an insurance policy. Don't think so much of yourself.'

'I don't. But is this the way to get what you want?'

'How do you know what I want? Aren't you the young philosopher!'

'Like all inadequate people you want power and respect.'

Church squatted down so he was facing them. He wore a loose gown that fell from his shoulders, but Dan could see there were jeans underneath. He suspected that like everything else about Church, there was something worn for show concealing an ordinary reality beneath.

Church said, 'That's a nice try, but those attributes aren't the only things people wish for. I don't want power for its own sake. And I seem to have garnered respect without trying for it.'

'So what is it?'

'Think! What is it that all humans want, more than anything else? What drives us to walk amongst people whose heads we would like to tear off? What persuades us to work at jobs we hate, in order to earn money we don't want, simply to visit places we don't want to see and eat food we don't like? What, dear Dan, do I want from you and the delectable Lucas here?'

'I have no idea.'

'It's love! More than anything else I want love. Your love. The love of Lucas. The love of your father. The love of all my enemies.'

'And this is the way you're going to get it? Kidnapping people? Frightening kids to death?'

'Eventually, yes. More important to me is the love of the people I lead. The love of those who give up their souls to Allah.'

Dan shook his head. 'You can't convince me it's about religion. No religion approves of what you've done.'

'There is no religion, only love. We're all born with it but some of us don't know and we give it away or fail to use it.'

Dan felt as though he was losing an argument whose rules he didn't understand. The world he'd created for himself in the last few years was on the point of slipping away, becoming unreal, untethered. He tried to hold on to the here and now and remembered Lucas sitting next to him. He realised that the young boy had moved closer to him and was trying almost to merge himself into his physical being, perhaps thinking that Church would fail to see him.

Church had said nothing more but was still crouched, watching.

Dan said, 'What are you going to do with us?'

'With you? Nothing. With Lucas? Watch ...'

He stood up, reached under his robe to his jeans pocket and took out a penknife, which he opened. Then he crouched down again, this time shifting his position so that he was facing Lucas more directly.

Dan felt Lucas push his back into the wall even while he tried to squeeze into Dan's side. Church opened the knife's blade and waved it back and forth in front of Lucas' eyes, the wide grin illuminating his face once more.

In the guise of positioning himself to hide Lucas, Dan had been shifting his weight to one side. Abruptly he spun and lashed out a leg towards Church's head.

He was astonished when Church threw out an arm and caught his leg, then used its momentum to continue Dan's turn, spinning him so that he wound up face down, his leg bent back and held by Church's weight.

Church said, 'You're not the only one with training.'

Dan felt his breath hard against the mustiness of the carpet. He felt helpless, defeated.

He said, 'Leave the boy alone.'

'You'd rather we took a memento from you?'

'Just leave him alone.'

The pressure went from his bent leg and he sensed Church standing up. By the time he'd turned, one of the muscle-men had arrived. He bent down and picked up Lucas, who shrieked and struggled helplessly.

Dan tried to move but Church had him pinned with an arm.

When the man had left with Lucas, Church stood up, smiled mirthlessly at Dan, his teeth seemingly too large for his mouth, then turned and left the room. Dan could still hear Lucas shrieking in another room.

Then he heard a key turn and the room was dark again.

CHAPTER TWENTY-NINE

CHURCH HAD BEEN told the address of the workingman's club and given the exact time at which he was to arrive: 8:13. Not before, not after. The club had closed down five years before and as they approached in the growing darkness it looked abandoned and pitiful. But the man, known only as Abu, would be inside.

When the car had stopped Church told the brothers, Gordon and Geoff, to get out and have a look through the club's windows. Although they were big and as well-muscled as wrestlers, they weren't the bravest of warriors, and they glanced at each other before crossing the cracked tarmac to peer inside. They had been amongst the first men Church had recruited and they were loyal but rather literal in their interpretation of the world. Church had given them a sense of its mystery even while he clarified their roles for them: they would help him found a school that would continue his mission even when he wasn't there to oversee its progress. They liked that idea—being educators. They thought it cool that other men would look up to them the same way they looked up to Church.

The club had been built in the early sixties and was a long redbrick building with three steps leading up to the entrance foyer and a wheelchair ramp added as an afterthought. Most of its windows were boarded up after local kids had smashed the glass.

Watching them approach the club, Church leaned against the old Ford Fiesta they were using for transport and wished they'd been able to hold on to Spring's big Mitsubishi Warrior—it made more of a statement, but was too recognisable. Spring had left it in the long-term car park at John Lennon Airport, paid up for a month. Everything would be settled by then.

He thought briefly about Dyke. He hadn't known where the idea had come from, but he'd known immediately he was correct: Dyke had walked into his classroom a stranger and left it an enemy. Something had passed between them— a recognition of each other's power, perhaps, and an understanding that they were on opposite sides of a moral divide. From that point onwards he'd made new plans. He'd left the building alone through the downstairs boiler room, whose blank door gave on to an alley way leading to the main road, then climbed into the Fiesta they'd parked there for just such an emergency and driven away.

The door opened and one of Abu's men stepped out, into the shadows at the top of the steps, glanced around, and waved Church over.

Church drew himself to his full height and affected a loose, long-limbed stroll across the car-park, nodding to Gordon and Geoff as they fell in behind him. He felt himself in control, powerful. He wasn't going to allow himself to be cowed by these people.

When he reached the top of the steps the man stood back to let him in, then put out an arm to stop the brothers from passing through the door.

'Only you.'

Church said, 'My men come in or I don't.'

As usual, he was looking down on the person he was talking to, and while the other man kept his gaze firm,

Church could tell he was wavering. After a few seconds he lowered his arm and all three men walked inside.

They had set up a table and chairs in one corner of the room with a battery-powered lamp on it. Abu sat behind it, his long face lit from beneath. He was somewhere in his thirties, wore a full beard and had eyes that were deep but completely lacking in emotion. Two men stood behind him. None of them were armed as far as he could tell—it was too dangerous to move around Britain carrying weapons, especially as they were likely to be on a list somewhere.

But they would probably have knives and maybe one of them would have access to a handgun if called for. After all, Abu had given him one some months ago as a sign of his trust.

Abu gestured for Church to stand still and one of the men came around the desk and searched him. The man who'd been outside crossed the room and began searching Gordon and Geoff thoroughly, brushing his hands over legs, buttocks, arms and chest.

Geoff said, 'You've got to marry me now,' and Church gave him a sharp look.

When the men had finished, Abu said, 'We've got a problem.' His accent came from somewhere in the Midlands, perhaps Birmingham or Dudley, Church could never be sure.

He said, 'I have no problems. It must be your problem.'

Abu said, 'Semantics. The delivery date must be brought forward.'

'Impossible. It's already under way. I can't make the ship travel any faster.'

'Find a way.'

'Make a suggestion.'

'Talk to your man. Frankly, I don't care. Just make sure the delivery arrives before the fifteenth.'

Church folded his arms. He knew there was no argument. This wasn't a negotiation, it was an ultimatum. He felt the blood pounding across his chest. One of the additional effects of his illness was potential problems with the aorta, the large artery that carries blood away from the heart towards branch vessels. He was always conscious of situations or circumstances that might affect his heart's functioning, almost to the point where he could sense its shifting condition.

And the treatment for his addiction wasn't helpful, either.

He said, 'I'll make sure the delivery is made.'

'I know you will.' Abu didn't show any signs of having won an argument—the conclusion had been foregone.

'You could have told me this over the phone.'

'We can't trust the phones. Besides, I wanted to see you face to face again. I wanted to see into your heart, to see whether I can still trust you.'

'And what do you see there?'

Abu paused, but Church knew he wasn't choosing his words so as not to offend. Finally he said, 'I see someone who doesn't know what battle he is fighting. Who is unsure even who the war is against. In your heart you're not decided. Your head is getting in the way. You must ignore the thoughts that you have and rely on what you feel.'

'I know what I feel.'

'Do you? If we asked you to take the head of one of your men here, would you do it?'

Church sensed Gordon and Geoff stiffen at his side.

He said, 'I would do whatever is required of me.'

'Boss—'

Abu laughed. 'See? Your men are not certain about their own commitment, so how can we be certain of yours?'

Church knew there was nothing he could say that would be sufficient persuasion. His actions had to speak for him, and for that he was reliant on Mark Ware and his love for his son. The chain of accountability was spread thin.

Trying to rescue some face, he said, 'So there's a big push coming into Turkey, is there?'

Abu took a tone that Church recognised was one you used with innocents or naïfs. He said, 'What you're providing to us is chicken-feed. Don't ever think you're being helpful. It's a … what do they call it? … a calling-card. A signal of your intent and capability. If you succeed, there might be more for you to do.'

'I want to work on strategy. I want to go to Syria and help with the plan.'

'There is no plan. It is already written. When the Mahdi arrives the Last Hour will come and the world will be at peace. How can you possibly help?'

'I have intelligence and resources. Watching the news reports it strikes me that intelligence is something your cause could use.'

'You have no experience. You are an armchair warrior. Your men here perhaps we could use—but you, you're a freak, one of Allah's experiments. You would be no use to us except, perhaps, as a stretcher bearer.'

'I can't stay here.'

'Why not?'

'I'm known.'

'Of course—the Intelligence Services know all of us. It's our job to confuse them and keep them busy, and not give them direct reason to arrest us.'

'This isn't the Intelligence Services.'

'Who else can bother you?'

'A man. He's an investigator.'

Abu smiled. 'One man? And you think you can offer strategic advice to our cause?'

'I've taken out insurance. We have his son. But I don't think that will stop him looking for me. And I believe he'll find me.'

'Then you kill his son and teach him a lesson for his troubles.'

'I will, when it comes to it.'

Abu said nothing but a smile hovered on his lips.

'Who is this man, this investigator?'

Almost with relief, Church said, 'His name's Dyke.'

'Where does he live?'

Church gave him the address, and the address of Dyke's office.

Abu said, 'You concentrate on the delivery. We'll talk to Dyke.'

'It won't be enough.'

'It better be, for your sake.'

CHAPTER THIRTY

IT WAS TWENTY-FOUR hours since I'd been to the Wares' house but it felt like a week. The lack of sleep of the previous night was catching up with me but I couldn't relax. I'd driven up to the community college and forced my way into the Hodson building, but of course there were no classes. I'd driven around to Carter Spring's house but he had flown, too—the SUV was missing from his drive and when I knocked on his door there was no reply. I even went back to Ted Mason's house to see if he'd returned, but neither he nor his wife answered the door.

Belinda had phoned twice, asking for news, but there was nothing to tell her and nothing I could think of for her to do.

Instead I thought about Mark and Bobbie Ware. I'd phoned them before lunch and told them I'd decided to stay on the case. I didn't mention Dan. Bobbie was effusive in her thanks but I felt she might be wasting her tears of gratitude: there seemed to be nothing I could do. Later that afternoon I also had a call from Mark, thanking me for staying on the case and apologising again for not being honest from the beginning.

I said, 'No more calls?'

'None. I don't like the wait. The first calls told me what they wanted, where they wanted the goods delivered and when they wanted them by. It was all business. I've twisted

so many arms and kissed so many arses to get this moving
… and now it feels like they've lost interest.'

'Where is the package now?'

'On a boat in the Med. I got the systems flown out to one
of our bases in Cyprus and put on the boat for
transshipment. It has to be in Indereskun for the eighteenth.'

'That's six days. Did they say when they'd let Lucas go?'

'He never said anything, never made any promises. Is that
a good or a bad thing?'

'I don't know.'

I told him I'd ring if I heard more and hung up.

As I looked at my watch, which told me it was seven-
fifteen, the phone rang.

'What do you know about this Irene Chau?'

Howard sounded angry.

'Not much, why?'

'The men that went round were highly-trained and
smelled a rat. They broke through a back door, on your say-
so, I might add, and found her missing.'

'You're certain she's not out down the shops?'

'Pretty sure. The big pool of blood on the sitting-room
carpet was a giveaway.'

'Damn.'

'So who is she and what do you know about her?'

I couldn't see any way out of this.

'There's a house in the same street, number thirty-eight.
If you make your way inside and go up to the attic, you'll
find a number of leafy plants. They really shouldn't be there.'

'And what's Chau's connection to the house?'

'The plants were being looked after by a young
Vietnamese boy. He in turn was being looked after by Mrs
Chau—shopping, cleaning, that kind of thing.'

'Jesus Christ, you sail close to the wind. How long have you known about this?'

'Not that long. Maybe a week.'

'And what happened to the boy, this Vietnamese?'

'He's in the system. Child Protection services.'

'It never occurred to you to drop me a line? How long has the Chau woman been missing?'

'I don't know. Maybe last weekend. I've been working on something else.'

'How convenient. Lucky for you she just dropped off the radar. Not so lucky for her.'

He was right. I felt bad for her and hoped she was okay, perhaps the blood was just from some protective wounds as she tried to prevent herself being taken …

I said, 'How much blood is there?'

'Enough. So where can I find this kid?'

I passed on the name of Belinda's friend, which she'd eventually—and reluctantly—told me.

Howard said, 'There may be charges about this, Dyke. You can't conceal your knowledge of a crime and hope to charm your way out of it.'

'Your people can speak to my people.'

He was saying 'Fuck off—' as I hung up on him.

I COULDN'T STAY in the house any longer. I had to be out, doing something, fooling myself that I was on my way to finding Dan. And maybe Lucas.

I drove to Dan's house again. Nothing had changed. Part of me expected to see his upstairs office light on, perhaps some music blaring out of an open window.

But it was as dead and dark as before.

I let myself in again and this time did a proper search. I'd convinced myself that he'd been taken at the doorway so there'd be nothing to work on inside the house.

But it occurred to me that Dan had been researching for me and might have discovered something that he hadn't yet told me. After all, we hadn't been on the best of terms and he might have wanted to 'punish' me by holding something back. It would have been childish, but he wasn't far out of childhood.

I found his laptop and fired it up. We knew each other's passwords and when the system was running I opened his Dropbox folder to see whether there was anything with a recent date on it.

Nothing more recent than two days ago: more information on Mark Ware's biography, culled from some fiery Occupied-clone page in the States. They didn't like him much. His involvement in both Big Pharma and the arms trade didn't endear him to them.

However, on the desktop there was a folder called 'Research'. I opened it up and there were separate folders inside for Mark and Bobbie Ware, Sebastian Church, Carter Spring and Ted Mason.

I read through each of them in turn and found nothing that he hadn't already told me about each of these people.

Except in the folder for Ted Mason there was a simple Word document titled 'Properties'. I opened it up and found a list of ten properties in the Liverpool area owned by the ex-con. This was interesting because I'd assumed Mason was small-fry, buying into one house in order to provide income without having to work for it. For some reason I'd assumed that Carter Spring was the real villain, running the cannabis farm on behalf of Sebastian Church in order to provide funds for whatever kind of cult he was creating around himself. But perhaps the landlord, Mason, was the real power here.

I looked again at Spring's file, particularly at the history of his dealings with the law, and it became apparent that while he was self-important and flash with his money, he'd mostly been caught in low-level criminal activity: a bit of smuggling, a touch of breaking-and-entering, a smidgeon of credit card fraud. I'd assumed that although he was the tenant of the cannabis farm, he'd been the one ruling the roost.

But maybe that was style over content. Acting big to conceal his tiny endowment.

Perhaps Ted Mason had been the one with the upper hand simply by dint of having working capital behind him.

I phoned Ted Mason's number again. I expected his wife to be out but she answered almost immediately. Again there was the disappointment when she heard it was me and not him.

'I've done it,' she said.

'Done what?'

'Reported him missing. He can't have gone for this long without telling me what was up. He's in trouble, isn't he? Ever since you came.'

'Jean, he was in trouble before I showed up. Tell me, how many houses does he own?'

'Ted? Just the two. The others are in his name but it's my money what bought them. We were thinking of selling up and buggering off to Spain, but what with all this referendum stuff we're not sure now. We don't want to land up there then have to turn round and come back because they won't pay our pensions.'

'Do all the houses have people in them, I mean, like renters?'

'Ted deals with all that. I don't know the ins and outs. Why? What's all this interest in my houses? What's it got to do with Ted going missing?'

'Do me a favour, Jean, pack a bag and go stay in a hotel for a couple of nights. Don't tell anyone where you're going.'

I heard her coughing her smoker's hack at the other end, as though my instruction had caught in her throat.

'Why the fuck should I do that? What's going on? Where's my Ted?'

'I honestly don't know. Really, I don't. But you should start thinking about yourself and leave, soon. And if you see that big car in front of your house, don't answer the door.'

'You're proper scaring me, now. Don't ring me again unless you know where Ted is.'

'Just go, please.'

She hung up.

I broke the connection at my end and looked around Dan's study. Then I called Howard on his private number and read him the list of addresses of properties owned by Ted Mason and his wife.

'You might find something to your advantage at those addresses.'

'I'll let you know.'

'I appreciate it.'

CHAPTER THIRTY-ONE

I WAS LOCKING Dan's front door when my phone rang. It was Bobbie Ware, and she was hysterical.

'You've got to come! Please, come! Something terrible's happened …'

'What's going on?'

But she'd dissolved into tears and sobs again.

It was eleven o'clock at night and a forty minute drive to the Wares' house. I wondered whether I could face it.

Eventually she said, 'You've got to come. I can't be alone. I just can't.'

'Where's Mark?'

'He's here … but he can't handle this. I might as well be alone.'

'What's happened?'

'They've been in touch again. And they've sent something. You have to come, I can't talk about it, it's too awful.'

She broke the connection before I could say anything. As I climbed into my car a wave of fatigue washed over me again. Tiredness was like a poison in my veins I couldn't shake off.

But as I drove away from the front of Dan's house, I was awake enough to notice a pair of headlights flick on behind me.

WHEN I ARRIVED she was standing on her front doorstep with her arms wrapped around herself. In the light from the carriage lamp over the door she seemed calmer. She crossed the gravel as I got out of my car.

Before I knew it she'd snaked those same arms around me and was sobbing into my neck. I smelled the shampoo in her hair and felt the slenderness of her arms and raised my own hands to hold her while she wept. Her back was long and slender and contained a tremendous erotic charge: it was like touching a live cable. After a couple of seconds I closed my eyes and then leaned away so I could look at her.

She kept her face down and I knew she was deliberately avoiding me, avoiding the embarrassment. She sniffed a few times then found a tissue in her sleeve and disengaged herself, stepping back to wipe her nose.

We stood in silence for a moment, listening to an owl in the woods behind the house. I thought I could hear the sounds of voices and music, and realised it must be Harris, the driver, watching one of his DVDs, the sound carrying further than normal in the warm night air.

I told myself it was a good job the moon was covered by a sheet of thin cloud otherwise I might not have been able to control my romantic inclinations towards this ravishing woman.

She looked past me, over the immense grounds. 'We know they've taken your son.'

I stared at her but her features were unreadable.

'How do you know? What have they said?'

'Let's go inside. We've got to talk.'

She turned back to the house.

Inside, she closed the door behind me then led the way upstairs. Mark Ware was sitting on one of the cream sofas staring into space. On the coffee table before him was a cardboard box, opened. Bobbie Ware sat next to him and took his hand. I sat opposite them. The air in the room here was as chill as a December morning. I felt my own temperature falling.

I said, 'What have they sent?'

Bobbie lowered her head and put a hand over her eyes. Mark seemed not to have heard. Then he woke and looked down at the box again. He glanced up at me, then reached forward and slid the box across the table.

I had a sick feeling in my stomach before I opened the flaps of the box. It was about six inches on each side, made of cardboard, and had no label.

Mark Ware said, 'It was found on the doorstep tonight. They didn't call. It might have stayed there until tomorrow morning.'

I knew they hadn't hired any security because they didn't want to draw attention to their situation. But in this instance it might have been useful.

My mouth dry, I opened the box fully.

A small ear, bloodied on the cut edge, lay on a small bed of straw.

I looked up to find them both watching for my response. I said, 'We can't be sure whose this is.'

Bobbie Ware exploded in anger. 'What are you talking about! It's Lucas' ear! They've cut off the ear of my boy and sent it as a … as a warning, or something. Are you stupid?'

Mark put his hand on hers and squeezed. She glanced at him as though she didn't understand what language was being spoken, as though she'd just woken to find herself in a foreign country.

I said, 'They've taken my boy too. I'm sorry to be blunt, but the fact is we don't know whose ear this is.'

Mark remained impassive; Bobbie looked away, colour flooding her face. Mark said, 'When I spoke to you earlier you said you're still going to help us. Is that true? Or are you backing out after all?'

'How can I give up now?'

'All right. When we found the ear Bobbie and I had a discussion about whether to call in the police anyway. But because you said you'd carry on we thought we'd leave it with you. I couldn't bear all the mess.'

Bobbie seemed to have taken control of herself. For almost the first time she raised her eyes to mine. 'We're placing a lot of trust in you. You can't let us down.'

I wondered if the little show by the front door, the crying and the leaning in to me, had been an incentive, a little extra motivation. There was no doubt she knew the power of her sexuality.

Then I realised that was an ignoble thought. She probably had no idea what she was doing most of the time. My own thinking had become slightly deranged since I knew Dan was missing.

I said to Mark, 'Bobbie said downstairs you already knew about Dan. How?'

'There were two messages with the ear, in the box, folded up.' He reached into his pocket and pulled out a sheet of paper. He handed it over and I read it quickly. It was a computer print-out on plain A4. It was addressed to Mark Ware and said the timing had changed: they wanted the delivery three days earlier. And he had until six o'clock on Saturday night to confirm it would be done.

I looked up at him. 'That's two days' time. Can you do it?'

'Impossible. I've been dealing with some very dodgy people to get this arranged, calling in some favours. If I rush them now they'll walk away, leave the ship floating off the coast of Cyprus.'

At his side, Bobbie had shifted again and she started crying gently, without any fuss. It was as though she'd begun a slow lamentation, a mourning plaint that was offered up to whoever might be listening. There was no reason to it and there was no way she could be placated.

As if to prove this fact, she suddenly reared up and hit Mark on the arm with the flat of her hand.

'Bastards, bastards, you're all fuckers. My poor boy! What are they doing? Make it stop!'

'Bobbie...'

'Oh shut up, he's not even yours, you fucker, just shut the fuck up ...'

She laid her head in her hands again, sobbing ferociously.

Mark Ware knew I was looking at him. I couldn't read the expression on his face, but Bobbie knew exactly what she'd said. She stopped crying abruptly and stared at me, her expression bitter.

'It might have been different if Lucas was his, but he wasn't. I was already pregnant, wasn't I, dear?'

'We don't have to go through this again now —'

'Why not? Everyone should know. The contents of my womb are an open secret, aren't they?' She turned to me. 'Oh, the scandal! His mother and father wouldn't bear it, would they? Dear Marky boy taking someone damaged for his wife and heir ...'

'Bobbie, stop.'

She ignored him and spoke to me.

'I was at university, away from home. Look at me. I'm gorgeous. I had men crawling all over me. So of course I got pregnant. I'd already started seeing Mark before I knew it. They thought it was a plot to trap their wonderful son.

Which of course it wasn't. I had better prospects than him lined up.'

Mark said to me, as though explaining a complicated narrative, 'They knew she was pregnant by someone else. Or at least they thought they knew. We agreed to marry so quickly it must have looked peculiar. They happened to have guessed right. I suppose my own parents felt I wasn't man enough for her, this golden goddess.'

'Oh, Mark.' Her voice had softened. 'You did a good thing. You married me even though Lucas wasn't yours.'

'I've never been enough for my own parents.'

By saying this he hurt himself more than anyone else ever could. I saw it in his eyes.

She looked at him but said nothing, and after a while the tension became too much for him and he stood up and left the room, striding quickly away without looking back. I wondered whether his apparent apathy at the end of my first visit was because Lucas wasn't his child, though that seemed an excessively cruel thought. There was no reason for him not to love Lucas as his own. My relationship with Dan had shown me how feelings change when you become a parent — however belated that had been in Dan's case.

After a moment's consideration, Bobbie stood up and followed Mark out of the room.

I stared at the black sky through the french windows. The contents of the room were probably worth several thousand pounds, if you included the paintings, the furniture, the pottery and the glassware.

It meant nothing to me. I was wondering what the second note had said, and trying to stop myself from coming to conclusions.

TEN MINUTES LATER Bobbie reappeared with two cups of coffee. She placed mine on the table then leaned back on the sofa and cradled hers in both hands.

We avoided looking at each other. She had the brittle air of someone waiting for an opportunity to snap. I couldn't blame her, but I didn't want to be the one to give her cause.

A couple of minutes later the door opened again and Mark came in. Bobbie moved over as he sat down, as though she didn't want their clothes to touch. Where before he'd given the impression of being purposeful despite being powerless, now he seemed drained of all direction.

I said, 'You should know Mrs Chau is missing. I knew she hadn't been turning up for work so I had someone look into it. There's blood on her carpet and she can't be found. It looks bad.'

Bobbie said, 'It goes on and on, doesn't it?'

'I think she might have been the link to the kidnappers.'

Mark roused himself and said, 'She's toast. If she's still alive I'll have her fucking deported.'

'She didn't know. I think she was involved in something else.'

'What?'

I gave them a brief rundown on the cannabis farm and Mrs Chau's part in taking care of the housework.

'So who are the crooks? Surely you should be talking to them.'

'It's better you don't know. Besides, they've gone into hiding.'

There was a pause. Then Bobbie said, 'Why hadn't you told us any of this? Why are we only finding out now?'

'Because it's better for me to be out there working on it rather than sitting here reporting on it.'

There had been a brown leather portfolio case on the table since I'd arrived. Mark opened it and pulled out a sheet of paper. 'You should see this.'

It was the second note, printed like the first on a sheet of plain A4. It was addressed to 'Mr Dyke' and said,

By now you know we've been telling the truth. Your son is with us. If you're reading this, you have already defied us once. You have brought the consequence upon yourself.

I re-folded the note and put it in my pocket. Church had been smart all the way. He'd known from the beginning I suspected him and that I'd made the link through Carter Spring to him and the kidnapping. He must have known there was no other connection from him in the other direction except through Spring to Mrs Chau, which led directly back to the Wares.

He might have suspected I was on to him because of the cannabis farm. But if I were connected to the Counter-Terrorist Unit the house in Liverpool would have been raided earlier and he and his group would be behind bars by now. The fact that nothing had happened told him I was acting independently and had given him just enough time to organise his flight into hiding. With the Wares under threat of losing Lucas, he must have felt he still had enough leverage to continue with the bargaining … so long as he could keep me out of his way.

But if he even suspected the CTU were involved he'd know he was playing a high-stakes game. He was either an IS fanatic—which somehow I doubted—or he had an exit strategy in place.

Mark Ware said, 'What do they mean when they say you've defied them once?'

'Because of the message they left on my answer-phone. It told me to stop helping you. If I'm reading this note then it means I'm here, obviously, and I've ignored their advice.'

'So what will the "consequence" be?'

'I have no idea. I don't want to think about it.'

'I want to help. I want to do something.'

'Absolutely not. You don't know these people.'

'I can't just sit by the telephone while they're … doing things to Lucas.'

Bobbie said, 'Mark …'

'No! You can't stop me. Have you any idea how useless I feel? Maybe my parents were right—I'm not a real man. All I can do is order people around, as though I know what I'm talking about. But most of the time I don't.'

'Getting hurt won't make you more of a man.'

'Perhaps it will make me feel different about myself. Perhaps it will make me feel something, full stop.'

Bobbie put her hand on his arm and he glanced at her.

She said to me, 'You're going to carry on helping us, aren't you?'

The chill I'd felt when entering the room had now seeped into my bones. I realised it was more mental than physical.

'Of course.'

'You must feel as bad as we do.'

'I must do, mustn't I?'

'So what are you going to do?'

'I'm going to punish the wicked.'

CHAPTER THIRTY-TWO

IT WAS PAST two a.m. when I turned into my drive and pulled up in front of my house. I sat for a moment in the car, listening to the turbo tick down and wondering what I should do next.

The obvious thing was to talk to Howard, try to keep it quiet. See if he could use his resources to hunt down Church and Spring and the rest of the men. They would have left tracks somewhere. Half a dozen full-grown men don't just vanish without leaving family, friends, houses, vehicles … although having said that, my impression of Church was that he was clever enough to have planned ahead.

It also occurred to me that I had no idea what his ultimate goal was. From what I'd seen of his lecture at the community college, he was simply recruiting, using religion as a cosh to beat waverers into line. Mercer—or was it Waite?—had said he was gathering together a group of White Muslims. What did that mean? Was the implication that Church was acting in the same way as a host of fiery imams at mosques around the country, promoting the IS version of Islam to enlist young men into a cause they didn't really understand?

At least until they were bivouacked in a dilapidated house in Raqqa, forced on pain of death to grow a full beard and listen to Coalition jets whistling overhead.

Was Church that much of an ideologue? Or was there something else in the mix … some financial gain? He surely didn't think he would ever leave the country. He was too unusual a figure to pass through Border Control without them spotting him. Though of course he might leave through unofficial channels, making his way by boat to Spain then crossing through to North Africa.

If he stayed in the UK, what was in store for him? Probable capture and then maybe an attempt to make a martyr of himself, another rallying point for people who saw in him a persecuted standard-bearer for religious transcendence ...

I was out of the car by now, fishing for my keys on the doorstep.

There's a moment just before a physical confrontation when you hear an intake of breath, or a shift in the air flow. If you're alert and practised, you know you have to move at once.

I darted to the right and watched from the corner of my left eye as a huge blade came swinging down, striking the stone step of my doorway.

I spun and put distance between myself and whoever was holding the machete.

There were two men of average height, both in loose trousers and the kind of flowing shirts you might wear at a martial arts class. Only this wasn't a class. It was deadly serious. I knew this because one was carrying a long, curved machete while the other held a short but wide knife in his hand.

I carried my house keys.

The two men wore black scarves around the lower halves of their faces but their features were dark, bearded. They didn't look like anyone I'd seen with Sebastian Church.

The man carrying the machete said, 'It's a shame you're not a religious man, Dyke. You might find it useful about now.'

'You've come a long way to deliver that message. West Midlands—Dudley, perhaps?'

They began to separate so they could come at me from different angles. I backed away so that my car was behind me, acting as a kind of protective shield and preventing them from covering both my front and my back.

The one carrying the machete adjusted his grip and said, 'You're going to hell, Dyke. Where people like you belong.'

He lunged with the machete in front of him, trying to impale me against the car. I twisted to the left, putting him between me and his partner, and knocked his hands down with my right hand, then hit him a downward blow with my left. His momentum and the weight of the sword took him forward but he caught himself and swirled towards me again, the blade passing just in front of my stomach. I stepped in quickly and punched him hard on the nose, keeping an eye on the other man, who was still behind and hadn't had the good sense to circle around to my blind side.

But now he did, holding the knife in his right hand and beginning a slicing motion that, I saw, was coming for my left shoulder.

There seemed to be no way to avoid it because the man with the machete had already fought off the pain from my punch and was raising his weapon again. Any moment it was going to be level with my stomach.

I couldn't avoid both knives and so chose to go for the larger, kicking with my right leg towards the man's midriff and finding a satisfying connection, pushing him backwards.

I waited for the searing pain of the broad knife in my shoulder …

But it didn't come.

Instead I heard a muffled cry and heard something metallic hit my front door and skitter away. The knife.

In the half-second it took me to regain my balance and turn to see the other man, I understood that someone else had joined the fight.

I turned and saw Harris, the Wares' driver, grappling with the second attacker, pulling his scarf from his face while exerting a huge bear-hug with his other hand. He was stronger than I'd imagined from seeing him amongst his soft furnishings. The attacker's arms were pinned to his side, making it difficult for him to break free.

Harris said, 'Let's see who you are, you bugger.'

But the man twisted and turned and eventually managed to break free of Harris' grip, darting away and running behind my house into the dark fields beyond. All this took about two seconds. When I turned back to check my own opponent he'd got to his feet and disappeared too. The odds were suddenly too great.

Harris and I stood staring at each other, sucking in great breaths and listening out for the sound of the men returning. I didn't think they would.

Eventually Harris said, 'This is where I say I'm getting too old for this shit. But that would make you Mel Gibson.'

'You watch too many films.'

'I like films.'

We paused again as we gathered our breath.

I said, 'It was you following me.'

His hands were on his knees while he inhaled deeply. Then he stood up and nodded. 'Guilt's a terrible thing. I thought you might lead me somewhere. You seemed to know what you were up to. I thought I might be able to do something. Help out.'

'You could have mentioned it. Instead of scaring the shit out of me.'

'You'd have told me to get lost.'

'Probably.' I took another look into the darkness that surrounded us. 'Did you know those two were here?'

'I was parked on the road opposite the entrance to your drive. I saw them turn up and hang around before you went out to the Wares. They were dropped off and they skulked around in the woods for a while as if wondering what to do. Amateurs. They didn't follow you when you left so I thought they might still be here when you got back. So when you came out from the Wares I trailed you, just in case.'

'That was a brave thing to do, considering the stuff they were carrying.'

'I went on a course. Unarmed Combat for Dummies. Got me out of the office for a day.'

We grinned at each other. We'd both been on courses more useful for getting you out of the office than actually teaching you anything.

After the adrenaline rush I was beginning to feel cold. I said, 'Come in and have something.'

He nodded, then crossed to the knife and picked it up using his handkerchief. He peered at it. 'I can talk to some people. See if there are any prints we know.'

We went inside and I switched on the kettle and turned on all the downstairs lights, checking out each room as I did so. Harris followed me after a moment and looked in a couple of the rooms. I heard him rifling through my thin collection of DVDs and Blu-Rays. Then he found me in the kitchen.

He said, 'This is a weird place. It's got the shape and size of an old house but everything looks new. All the walls are straight. The woodwork's still shiny.'

'It burned down some months ago. Some characters I was investigating tried to teach me a lesson. There was a cop involved, so the police reimbursed the insurers to have it rebuilt. I didn't really want to move.'

'I think I read something about that. A lot of stink about what happened to the cop. Bad apple and all that.'

I didn't disagree with him. The man had nearly got me killed.

We sat with coffees in the sitting-room. I said, 'I heard your TV playing out at the Wares. Did you leave it on for their benefit?'

'I do it from time to time while I bugger off for the night. Got a woman I see in Manchester. Keeps them happy to think I'm around. DVD changer. Plays three films one after the other. Had it for years and just found a use for it.' He sipped his drink. 'So, who were those men?'

He'd suddenly gained some heft in his voice and attitude. I saw the ex-policeman come to the surface like a sea-creature coming up for air.

I said, 'Believe it or not, I have no idea.'

'A random act of violence?'

'Not exactly.'

I told him about Church and his men, about Mrs Chau and her link to Carter Spring and thence to the community college and Church's meetings. Then I told him about Ted Mason and his property empire and my belief he might be the one behind the expansion of the cannabis farms.

He said, 'So because this man Church is doing a bit of light preaching you think Islamic State is involved? Bit of a stretch.'

'Not my idea, though I was getting there. The Counter-Terrorism Unit gave me a heads-up.'

'I suppose these jokers did have a machete. Like a calling card.'

'I didn't see them when I visited Church. One of them said I was going to hell, so I guess he was a true believer. I think they were outside muscle, brought in to teach me a lesson.'

'By putting a crease in your head? Drastic.'

We both took some time to drink our coffee and think about what had just happened. My fatigue had returned and was giving me a headache.

He said, 'You see now why the Wares should have told the local rozzers? They'd have tied all this up in a bow. If *you* found out Irene Chau was connected, they would have done, too. It could all have been sorted out quick sharp.'

'You don't have kids, do you?'

'What's that got to do with anything?'

'It changes the way you look at things. I can't blame them wanting to keep it quiet. It's a miracle they called me.'

He raised his coffee cup as though in salute. 'They wouldn't have done, if it wasn't made easy for them.'

'What do you mean?'

'Who do you think told Bobbie Ware about you in the first place?'

CHAPTER THIRTY-THREE

I WOKE UP the next morning feeling as though Harris and I had lost the fight. I'd barely managed two or three hours' sleep, my arms and legs ached and I felt bruised all over. The lack of sleep and the spending of nervous energy was taking its toll. It was as though I'd been drugged and couldn't come out from under.

I finally dragged myself out of bed and forced myself to eat breakfast while watching the news on TV. It was particularly interesting because there'd been a major alert at Manchester Airport. It had been sealed off and sniffer hounds had been brought in. Two men had been hauled out of the queue for a plane on its way to Munich, but whether they were the men Mercer was looking for or just some random possibilities, I couldn't tell. It was on all the channels so everyone was taking it seriously. I remembered the hints that Mercer had dropped and realised he must have known what was going to happen some days before. Counter Terrorism was all about gathering information: the action scenes you saw on the ten o'clock news were the end of the process, not the beginning. I'd caught Mercer's attention by talking to Sebastian Church, but something more pressing had come up in the interim.

It was Friday morning. Mark Ware had been told he had until six p.m. on Saturday to guarantee the delivery of the equipment would go through. Presumably there'd be another call and Mark would have to swear on his son's life—literally—that the delivery would take place.

And then what? Church would let Lucas and Dan go free? Somehow I doubted it. There were high stakes being played for here, and kidnapping was almost as bad as premeditated murder when the courts passed judgement—Church would think he may as well be hung for a sheep as a lamb. If he got rid of the two boys there'd be no evidence connecting him to their deaths … so where was the problem? He was probably using a throw-away phone for the calls to Mark Ware and the printer that had printed the notes was no doubt already in a landfill somewhere, so it too would be useless as evidence.

As for my own so-called investigation, where was I going? The previous night Harris had agreed with me that calling in the police was the best way to move forward … but he also saw that it was impossible, both for the Wares and for me. It was too risky. If Church had eyes on the Wares' house and they saw a sudden burst of visitors, however innocuous, then the boys' throats would be slit and all would be lost. Church and his men would probably slip out of the country and turn up again in Syria, rousing the rabble against Western capitalism in favour of a version of a religion that was now thought to be fourteen centuries out of date.

While I shaved, my mind wandered to Dan, and what he was going through. I supposed he was being kept with Lucas. He was clever and feisty so I hoped he was containing himself and not aggravating his captors too much. It might be okay to do that if you had full control of your limbs and your actions. Not so much if your hands were tied behind your back.

I hoped they saw him as a bargaining chip with me and not someone they could punish for his own sake. In effect they'd be doing it to punish me, not him, and that thought made me sick with worry for him.

I had a day and a half in which to find Church and neutralise him. I had no clues, no one to talk to and no one to investigate. All I could do was go over old and stony ground to see if anything new had grown there.

Because I was looking for a lecturer at the Charles White Community College, I thought it might be useful to find out exactly what they knew about him. It might be nothing, it might be everything.

As long as it was *some*thing.

THE SAME TWO women were seated at their computers in the Admin office of the college. The one with the Women's Institute demeanour listened carefully while I explained that it was extremely urgent I find Dr Church.

When I finished, she said, 'I'm sorry, I can't give out the personal information of staff members.'

'You told me he wasn't a staff member.'

'In this respect he has that status. The rule applies.'

'You may not believe this, but it's a police matter.'

'You're right, I don't believe you. Fetch a policeman with the requisite authority and I'll see what I can do.'

'Do you enjoy your job?'

'Not much.'

'I can see why. Is there someone with more seniority here? An admin officer or a manager?'

'He'll tell you the same thing as me.'

'I'd like to hear it in person.'

The woman's face twisted as she scowled: I'd challenged her authority, never a good move towards a bureaucrat. But she reached out a hand to the phone on the desk and pressed an extension number.

'Mr Wilson? There's someone wants to speak with you in Admin.' A pause. 'A Mr Dyke. It's about Dr Church.'

She put the phone down. 'Two minutes. Please take a chair.'

She turned before I could even thank her.

Three minutes later, a man with a grey suit and a relaxed air pushed through the double doors and caught sight of me. I stood up and shook his hand.

He said, 'Dave Wilson. Vice Principal.' He glanced towards the two women, their backs still pointedly turned away from me, and said, 'Let's go somewhere friendly.'

He led me back out of the Admin block, across a short path into a building I could tell immediately contained a canteen or restaurant—there was a smell of vegetables over-cooking and the metallic clatter of large kitchen equipment being moved about. We walked through a door into a hall full of thin plastic chairs and Formica-topped tables, the walls covered with college notices and, here and there, colourful paintings. Half a dozen students were scattered about, mostly staring at their phones and texting.

We went to a counter and bought coffees, then Wilson took me behind a partition into an area where the chairs and tables were of slightly better quality than in the main concourse.

He said, 'Executive dining suite. Chefs come from miles around to try our steam puddings. Please, sit.'

I did so and explained I was looking for Sebastian Church as a matter of urgency. I couldn't tell him why but it was extremely important that I found him.

Wilson hadn't touched his coffee. He probably had insider knowledge.

He said, 'Sebastian Church is a mystery, isn't he? He
worked here for a few years, you know, back when I was just
starting. Something of a rock star on campus, what with his
exotic looks and high-wattage brain-power. Taught some
humanities courses, English, Sociology. He covered the
waterfront, so to speak. Bright man. Everyone knew he had
this ailment, Marfan Syndrome, but he never let it get in the
way. He managed the symptoms and led an ordinary life, or
so it seemed to me.'

'Then he quit?'

'He got a better offer. Went off down south somewhere
for a couple of years, learned those London ways. I'm not
sure what he did, but he came back a bit of a zealot. Shifted
his sympathies towards religion. Especially comparative
religion—you know, the differences or similarities between
them, their histories and so forth. Well we couldn't really
find a place in the syllabus for him and he didn't want to go
back to doing what he was doing before. To be honest I
thought he'd go somewhere else, try the bright lights of
Manchester, the university there. But he stuck around here,
in the area. Then asked if he could run some open classes for
locals, try to get more integration into the different cultures
that were beginning to spring up.'

'Did you have any idea what he was doing in his
classroom?'

Wilson shrugged. 'Not really. I leave that to the
academics. I'm management. Can't you tell?' He gestured
towards his expensive suit. 'To be honest, I'm still not sure
why we're talking about him.'

I weighed him up and decided to take a chance. I had little
time left for niceties such as client confidentiality now.

'We think he's kidnapped a child. In fact, two people. One
of them is my son.'

He frowned. 'Church? Why on earth would he do that?'

'His motives aren't clear. But when I saw him in action I thought I was watching someone in the grip of a strong belief system. Add to that the fact that some of the men he's been mixing with have been growing drugs, and I've been physically attacked twice in a week, and a child's ear has been delivered to his parents ...'

He grimaced. 'All right, all right. I think it's all a bit far-fetched but I suppose you've done your homework. If it's that serious, why aren't the police here, searching the place for evidence?'

'Because the kidnappers said both youngsters' lives were forfeit if we brought in the police. I'm taking a risk telling you this much.'

'I don't come across private detectives every day. You understand this is hard to believe.'

'I don't care whether you believe me or not. I need his address.'

'You know it's against our regulations to give out the private addresses of people affiliated to the college. I'm sure Doris told you that in no uncertain terms.'

'I understand that. I'd feel the same in your position. But this is different.'

'The situation's moot, anyway.'

'Why?'

'Because we don't have an address for him.'

IF I'D THOUGHT about it clearly, I'd have realised that Church would arrange his affairs so that he vanished as completely on paper as he had in person. If he really was the man behind all this mayhem, then he was ahead of me every step. Of course he wouldn't have known it would be me on his trail when he started planning—he probably thought there'd be a quiet police investigation, that the Wares would ignore his message, contact the police, then stand by and watch the boys in blue start searching for him.

But whether it was someone private like me, or official agencies, he'd anticipated that someone would come for him, either before his deadline or after it.

So he'd hidden himself.

He started having his post delivered to the college. He told them he was moving house but hadn't acquired the new address yet. I presumed that should anyone check with the utilities he'd have cancelled his accounts and whatever address they referred to would now be empty. He probably used online banking and whatever post they sent him would be lying inside his abandoned property.

I felt myself growing angry. If there was no paper trail there'd be little chance of anyone finding him—neither me nor the Counter-Terrorist Unit. He could be in London by now, or Cardiff, or Tenerife. He knew his physical appearance was a weakness so he'd gone underground and arranged it so he could survive, like a mole, with little light or outside stimulus.

I said, 'Damnit. He could be anywhere.'

Wilson said, 'I doubt that.'

'Why?'

'He needs his treatment—he gets it from a local unit, so he can't travel far.'

I sat up in my chair. 'Why kind of treatment? Is it for his condition?'

'Not as far as I know.'

'Then what, for Christ's sake!'

Wilson hesitated. 'I can't say. His health is his own affair.'

'Not when the life of my son is on the line. Tell me now or you'll regret it.'

He must have seen something in my face. He went pale and lost the smooth administrator's serenity that had rested benignly on his features.

'Okay, okay … I happen to know that when he came back from London he was addicted to heroin. I don't know how that happened — perhaps it was connected to his condition. But when he came to see us about starting again here he was open about it and said he was on a programme. Methadone. It meant he had to go to a unit, talk to a counsellor, then he'd be given his dose, which he had to take there and then.'

'And you still let him near kids?'

'Not really. We allowed him to use the premises as part of his rehabilitation. He doesn't come into contact with anyone under eighteen. That's part of the deal. We thought we were doing a good thing, though in hindsight we might have been too optimistic.'

I stood up. I had to get out of there. 'Do you know where he gets his treatment?'

'An out-patients unit a few streets away.' He gave me the address, which I wrote down.

'How often does he go?'

'Once a week. Methadone stays active longer than heroin. I happen to know his appointments are Friday afternoons. Today, in fact.'

'Don't say anything to anybody about this. It'll be over in a couple of days and either I'm wrong and he'll turn up again next week, happy as larry, or I'm right and you'll see it on the news.'

SOMETHING WILSON HAD said resonated with me. He'd mentioned his assumption that I'd done my homework, and I wasn't convinced I had. I thought for a while until I managed to bring the missing piece of information to the front of my brain, and when I was back in my car I phoned Belinda. I caught her at a free moment and asked if she could help me.

She recognised the change in my approach. I was actually asking for her help. I just knew she was impressed.

So she said she could and I told her what I needed and gave her some directions, and when she was confident she understood, I asked her for a phone number.

CHAPTER THIRTY-FOUR

THE NUMBER BELINDA gave me finally connected. I asked if I could speak to Jo Deddicoat and after a long wait was finally put through.

She sounded exactly as I expected a social worker to sound—tired, harassed and short of time. 'Who is this?'

I explained who I was. It didn't go down well.

'So you're the one who dumped this kid on me at seven o'clock in the morning? Belinda's got a lot of payback for that.'

'Don't blame her, it was my idea. We couldn't think what else to do and there was no way we could take care of the boy.'

'I get that. But seven o'clock in the morning? After I'd been up till two o'clock in a house in Birkenhead trying to convince two kids not to run away from their foster parents for the fourth time … bad timing, guy.'

'Can we meet?'

'Only if it's here. I can't go anywhere this afternoon, I've got more paperwork than God.'

She told me where the office was and I said I'd be there in twenty minutes. I would rather have been with Belinda but time was running short and I couldn't be in two places at one time. Besides, it was my own fault for not thinking things through in the first place and considering all the sources of information I had at my disposal.

FOR A CHILDCARE officer Jo Deddicoat looked more like a punk—two studs in her nose, a ring in her lower lip, coal-black hair swept up on one side of her head, a black tee-shirt advertising The Replacements.

She was standing outside her office—one of the large Victorian piles in Liverpool town centre converted to council work—smoking a cigarette and peering around furtively in case she was spotted by her manager. She looked about twenty from a distance but grew more mature as I got closer, winding up at about thirty-five.

'Jo?'

'Walk around the corner with me.'

We walked twenty yards, the loud traffic preventing much in the way of conversation. There was a narrow street between two buildings and she went down it then leaned with her back to the wall and took another drag.

She said, 'Filthy habit. Have to keep it from the kids, setting a bad example blah blah. Most of them are already smoking by ten. My clothes probably reek anyway.'

'Thanks for seeing me, but why the cloak-and-dagger?'

She eyed me up and down. 'Belinda's a mate but I don't know you, do I? Can't have you walking into the office demanding to see kids when we're trying to protect them from being exploited. Besides, my boss tells me the police have been in touch. They want a word with the youngster too. Did you give him up?'

'I had no choice, and the man in charge is doing me a favour.'

'Better be a bloody big favour. My boss doesn't like interference from that quarter.'

'He's helped me out before and I might need him again.' She shrugged as though it was no skin off her nose. I went on, 'I need to see the boy, ask him a couple of questions.'

'Why?'

'He's connected to some bad stuff—more than the cannabis farming. If it's of any interest to you, there are two boys whose lives are in danger.'

Her eyes narrowed and she picked a sliver of tobacco from her lower lip.

'What boys?'

'One of them's my son. The other's only ten, my clients' boy. That's all I can tell you.'

'What do you think Lanh knows?'

'So you got a name from him?'

'Promise them a go on Playstation and they'll tell you anything. At least at first. Then he clammed up again. Perhaps you don't understand these kids, but they don't know who to trust. They're like animals who've been beaten—they want to believe you're safe but they're on their guard anyway.'

'Where is he now? Can I see him?'

'I doubt it.'

'Why?'

'I had to give him up to Immigration in the end. No papers. No relatives. No one to vouch for him.'

'Will they send him back?'

'To be decided. Got to keep the numbers down, dontcha know. Send 'em back to where they came from, let them sort themselves out ...'

'Who do I talk to if I want to see him?'

She stubbed out her cigarette on the wall then threw it on the street. Not such a good citizen.

'I'll text you a number. I don't have it with me. What do you want to talk to him about?'

'I wish I knew. But it has to be soon. I'm running out of options.'

Surprisingly, she put a hand on my arm.

'Belinda said you're one of the good guys. Don't give up. I'll do what I can to help.'

I smiled at her knowing that my smile was pained and not genuine. She gave a little wave then turned the corner and went back towards her office. Ten minutes later my phone notified me of a text. There was a name and a number.

I CALLED THE number from a quiet coffee shop and got through to the name Jo Deddicoat gave me — Lionel Stevens. You don't come across many Lionels these days, maybe because the name has a ring of lower-middle class officiousness which this representative exemplified. He said No in a variety of ways and then told me to go through 'proper channels' if I wanted to talk to someone being held as an illegal alien by the Immigration Service. I had no idea what 'proper channels' might be, so I phoned Howard. If he couldn't get through himself, he'd know someone who could.

He said, 'I can't go there, Dyke. Separate world. Different universe, Immigration. Numbers, targets, ship 'em out. Or keep 'em till they stop squealing, then send 'em back.'

'I just want to talk to one boy.'

'This anything to do with those properties you pointed me to?'

I felt he was giving me an opening. It was probably done on purpose but he made it sound casual.

'Might be, why?'

'All but two of them had little miniature forests in the attic. Funny, that. Caught a few young lads, too, and one young lady. Of oriental extraction. No English spoken.'

'The boy I want to talk to speaks English, though he doesn't let on. He might know something to your advantage.'

'Doesn't everyone?'

'So if you were to have a word with someone, who in turn might have a word with Mr Stevens, would you like to listen while I ask some questions?'

He gave his little bark of a laugh.

'I think you've got this the wrong way round. I'll be the one inviting you to the conversation, if the mood so takes me.'

'As long as I can speak to him I don't care whose name is on the invitation.'

'What's the boy's name and where is he?'

I told him the name that Jo Deddicoat had given me and passed on Lionel Stevens' number.

I said, 'I know you've heard this before, but I'm on a very short deadline here. If you could organise it for this afternoon it would be helpful.'

'Government agency, my boy. Than which only icebergs move more slowly. You'll be lucky if it's the middle of next week.'

'That's too late. There might be two dead boys on his conscience if he doesn't pull his finger out.'

'I'd recommend I do the negotiating on this, if that's going to be your opening gambit.'

'Just get the fucking appointment, Howard. My son is one of those boys.'

He was silent a moment.

Then he said, 'I'll sort it. Stay near your phone.'

CHAPTER THIRTY-FIVE

HE TOOK SENSIBLE precautions but had no reason to believe anyone would be following him. As far as he was aware, no one remembered his weekly appointments except the pharmacist and his counsellor—after all, his medical records were confidential and these days they took that seriously.

Carter Spring had wanted him to at least take a couple of men with him to the Unit, but Church had said that would only draw attention to him. It was better if he snuck in without fanfare, spoke to his counsellor, Alf, drank his fix, then drove home. He had no fears he would be seen by Dyke or anyone else, despite his height and unusual appearance. Besides, he'd keep an eye out and be careful.

As was often the case, he drove through the suburbs of Liverpool wondering what was going on in the heads of the average people he saw on the streets. Where did they think they were going? What was their ultimate goal in life? Ever since he'd been conscious of his condition he'd thought about his future and what meaning his life would have. It could be cut short at any moment, so it was imperative it meant something, otherwise why was he here?

He asked himself, as he'd done so often, whether he was a bad man. What did that mean? He'd done bad things from time to time, but did those behaviours categorise him absolutely? Did it mean his whole character and personality were evil? What about the times he'd given money to beggars at Euston Station? Or the time when he was seven years old when he'd stopped a group of kids torturing a cat? Didn't those things count on the credit side?

But casting his mind back to when he was a child was unfortunate … it brought back a number of actions he'd committed that by any stretch of the imagination were bad — even evil. He'd subsequently placed the cat he'd rescued in the washing machine , for example, to see how it would cope.

It didn't.

Luckily he'd had time to take out the sodden corpse and walk it three streets away to dump it in an alley where no one would see it and associate it with him. It was a good experiment, though, because he was able to measure exactly how long it had taken the cat to die.

He'd then tried the experiment with his three-year-old brother … but his mother had come home in time to see him setting the controls while Andrew's face was pressed against the glass.

They'd put it down to the stress of his condition. Marfan. Who was this mysterious Marfan? He'd often promised himself to research the progenitor of his ailment but each time he came close he backed away, as though he didn't really want to know. As though it would ruin the mystery. He knew Marfan was a French doctor but that was all. Of course he'd read about the full range of symptoms and had been taken to clinics when younger where he met others like himself, but that had been pointless: he didn't see himself reflected in them. He was always smarter, more self-aware, more ready to see the condition as a sign of being extraordinary.

Eventually he'd come to see it as a sign of being Chosen.

It was true he often asked himself whether there was something wrong with him, something not related to the condition, a psychological flaw. But he always convinced himself that in fact he was different because he was superior. He'd always amazed people with his intellect, and when people recognised he had brains they assumed he was good, even noble. The idea that he could harbour evil thoughts never occurred to them.

So he used his brains. He sought camouflage in his studies, his growing reputation, his ability to talk in complete sentences, unlike the people who listened with their mouths dragging on the floor as he told them about the worlds to come.

He arrived at the Unit and parked as close to the entrance as he could manage so he wasn't in the open too long. He closed his eyes and prepared himself for the discussion he would have with Alf. His counsellor was always casual but intent, trying hard not to pressurise him while at the same time needing to convince himself that Church wasn't backsliding, that he was attempting to stay on the straight and narrow.

In fact Church hated himself for succumbing to the addiction, a situation that developed during his brief stay in London. There was a time when he'd suffered the typical joint pain associated with the condition and had sought release. It was unfortunate that heroin turned out to be the drug of choice, the one that worked best, and his life had got out of hand for a while.

Until he found his purpose. He might even describe it as his Calling.

And eventually he'd fought the addiction and left London and enrolled himself on a programme to get clean. He was lucky that many of the other symptoms only manifested weakly in him—he didn't have so much of the curved spine or the eye problems that were symptomatic of the syndrome, though he'd noticed an occasional blurriness from time to time …

He stared out of the window and thought about the next few days. Assuming Ware delivered tomorrow night, he'd be able to contact Abu and tell him the deal was going through. From that point he'd begin his own extraction. Carter Spring would get him as far as the coast, then he'd lie low in the hold of a yacht owned by a wealthy convert and cross the channel, eventually heading south to reach northern Spain. After that he had a series of contacts who would get him into North Africa.

He'd met Abu at a gathering in London sponsored by Jamaat-e-Islami, Bangladesh's major Islamist party, and after a number of cautious and secret conversations had offered to source the kind of electronic equipment that IS sorely needed. At that point he had no idea how he'd do it: he just recognised it was something he could take responsibility for.

JEI claimed officially to be solely a religious organisation, but it supported the writings of Syed Maududi, the founder of Jamaat Islamism, the largest Islamic organisation in Asia. In a series of books and writings, and with the example of his life, Maududi had created the ideological and theoretical basis for the complete Islamisation of the world. Church liked the fact he'd exhorted his followers to 'strive to change the wrong basis of government and seize all powers to rule.' There was no quarter given in that statement, no negotiation or compromise.

Church had been gripped by a kind of belief he'd never experienced before. Maududi had been absolute in his assertion that Islam was the only path, and that those who were not Moslem could not benefit in any way from the established state. Sharia law would regulate all community life and there would be no argument with Allah's word.

For no reason that he could explain, Church found this absolutism liberating. He had immediately devoted himself to supporting the cause however he could, using whatever gifts he found within himself.

At their last meeting in the working men's club, Abu had been dismissive of his chances of becoming involved in Islamic State's strategic thinking, but he knew he'd be able to convince them. He had a track record of recruiting young jihadis and he'd proved his worth with the acquiring of matériel that would help the senior leaders counteract or avoid drones or other, more lethal, weaponry.

He mused briefly on the brotherhood that awaited him when his destiny was fulfilled. He'd had a real brother but after the incident with the washing machine his family had said they couldn't cope and he'd been taken into care. He'd lost contact with his family who, despite their sympathy with his condition, couldn't see past one single incident …

He shook his head. Allah knew what was in his heart and knew he would fight and fight until the Caliphate was established globally. His intelligence was worldly and analytical, but he'd known for years he must commit himself to a higher cause if he was to live forever, in some form.

He climbed out of the car and went inside. Alf was waiting for him and shook his hand. They moved into a consulting room and Church talked to him for half an hour, lying fluently, then was given the bottle his system craved. He took off the top and drank down the thick green liquid that would ease the tremble in his limbs.

God, the stuff tasted awful.

But now he was ready for whatever came next, however bloody it might be.

CHAPTER THIRTY-SIX

SAM HAD TOLD her he couldn't risk Church spotting his car near the Unit, but Belinda thought her bright pink Volvo had an equal chance of catching his eye. The difference being, they hoped, that neither Church nor his men knew who she was.

So she'd parked it tightly between two larger cars and positioned herself inside so she could see the entrance and the front door of the building through the skimpy foliage. It was a low redbrick structure that didn't advertise its presence except with a list of opening hours and, like many official buildings in Liverpool, was surrounded by high security fencing of pointed bars and complete with sliding gate. She had no doubt there was CCTV watching the front, too, a small man in a peaked cap and a pretend uniform seated somewhere behind a bank of three screens. These days even the National Health Service had to defend itself.

It was mid-afternoon and traffic was beginning to pick up as people knocked off for the weekend. She'd been fortunate she'd been able to escape from the office of Hereford, the agency in Manchester for which she'd been working for the last few days. This branch office was mostly engaged in identity checking for large organisations—making sure that employees were who they said they were—rather than anything more surreptitious. She'd been told American companies were very keen on this at the moment.

But Hereford was one of the largest agencies in the world, perhaps second only to Kroll, and their clients had a variety of needs. So from time to time, they explained to her, they needed someone to go knock on a door and ask a few questions: nothing dangerous or underhand, but it had to be a personal contact. Then she was asked to come back to the office and write up the details of the contact on one of their secure computers. It was all very high-tech and bureaucratic and not exactly what she'd signed up for when she'd decided to try her hand at private detection. In her eyes the job was about helping people in difficulty, not acting like a member of the Stasi. However, they paid more than Sam did and the work had the prospect of being regular.

Before she'd parked she'd driven the streets where the Unit was situated to make sure she had the geography right. As far as she could tell, this was the only entrance. The place had its own car-park but she'd seen a couple of people parking on the street before walking through the gates, so she assumed there was a hefty parking fee if you went into the grounds.

She'd been there half an hour and was beginning to wonder whether Church would come, when, as she watched, an old car went straight through the gates and parked in one of the administrative slots near the front doors. It was a tan-coloured Nissan Sunny that seemed too small for the long man who climbed out of it. His hair was thinning and his features were sharp beneath his glasses and he looked around quickly before crossing the short distance to the front entrance. He was probably six and a half feet tall and Belinda had no doubt it was Sebastian Church.

She texted Sam immediately: *He's here.*

She didn't know where Sam was and she knew he hated texting, but the reply came back in less than a minute: *Watch and follow. Nothing else.*

When he'd asked whether she could do this job he'd made it clear he didn't want her to tackle Church—there was too much at stake, including the safety of Dan and the other boy. But it gnawed at her that she couldn't storm through the front door, punch him in the solar plexus and batter an answer from him. Sam had said he was clever enough to have put some kind of fail-safe plan in place in the event he didn't return to his hideout. He'd also said he suspected there were heavier hitters involved, maybe a group of home-grown jihadis like the ones who'd attacked him the other night. There was a bigger picture here and he didn't know how extensive it was.

So he didn't want to extract Church straight away. They needed to know where he was returning to. Then they'd formulate a plan.

Now she knew he was in the building she made herself comfortable and rotated her rear-view mirror so she could see the entrance without having to turn in her seat. From what she understood of the process Church would have a consultation and then be permitted to take his drug. Then he'd leave. She wondered whether there was an imposed time-lag after he'd taken the drug for the initial effects to wear off, or whether he could get directly into the car and drive. Did methadone even give you a high? Or did it just stop the craving? Something to investigate later …

AN HOUR AFTER he went inside, Church reappeared. He seemed no different. He still behaved as though he believed in his innate superiority and the beadiness of his gaze suggested not much in the outside world came up to his high internal standards.

He climbed into the Nissan as though it were a top-spec Mercedes, respecting its seats, reversed it, then exited through the gates and turned east, not even glancing in her direction.

Belinda gave him a few seconds then eased out of her parking slot and followed.

She soon realised he was heading towards the A59, which would take him through the Wallasey Tunnel under the Mersey and into central Liverpool. She made sure there were a couple of cars between them and then eased back, keeping the Sunny well in sight. The day was bright and clear and warm and at last she found she was enjoying investigation work. This was what she'd thought it would be—trailing bad guys while knowing she was doing a Good Thing.

She wondered why that was important to her. A stint in the army, driving enormous machinery, had left her confused about what was right and wrong, and often these days she found herself weighing up jobs depending on whether she approved of them or not. She recognised this was a bizarre practice—she was using a moral code to justify secretive behaviour: for example, gathering information about people who were simply leading their lives. Or, in this case, someone so far only suspected of illegal activity. Was she so much better than them, in the end? Did her perception of Justice trump their belief in what they were doing? In other words, was she nobler than Church just because she felt Right was on her side? Or was that self-justifying cant? If he had a religious conviction that told him his behaviour was vindicated, could she honestly say she was a better person than him?

She couldn't even say that his promised use of violence meant he was a lesser being—hadn't she just felt the desire to go after him and beat him up?

She gave up that train of thought: whenever she tried to compare her own sense of right and wrong with another person's, she became confused. It was never as simple as she wanted it to be.

She wondered where Sam was and what he was doing. She'd found herself worrying about him over the last few weeks and now Dan was missing he must be on a very short fuse. Like everyone else, it seemed, her first thought had been to get the police involved. But if he was right and there were elements of Islamic State involved, she could understand why he would want to keep the investigation operating with a low profile. Nobody wanted to see terrible videos popping up on YouTube showing terrified young boys being executed, or worse …

She slowed down as the toll-booths to the tunnel came into sight. She filtered until she was in the same lane as Church, then threw her money into the collection bucket, waited for the orange bar to rise, then pulled away, still keeping him in sight a hundred yards ahead. He didn't speed up or change lanes swiftly or do anything else that might have suggested he knew he was being tailed. Sam had said he was cocky and certainly he seemed to think he was superior to everyone else: his body language even while driving a car said as much.

She thought that would change when they took him down.

They came out of the tunnel and Church took the slip-road heading north. They entered an area of Liverpool that was still showing signs of recession and despair: they drove past shuttered pubs and soulless high-rise apartments, past building works that looked as though they'd stalled as soon as the first ground was broken. Then they bore right towards Anfield football ground and at the first junction Church turned immediately right again, now heading south, into an estate of tightly-packed houses that looked as though they dated from the boom years of the eighties.

Before she arrived at the first junction she knew she'd lost him.

She looked right and left and then drove slowly onwards. Now she'd entered a warren of white-painted estate houses that looked like the temporary structures used as army barracks. She passed them by and tooled around for a while, turning left and right until she'd criss-crossed the whole estate, but she didn't see his vehicle on any of the house forecourts, and couldn't even be sure that he'd stopped here—he might have simply passed through on his way to somewhere else. The houses were in unforgiving rows, long terraces of two bedroom properties with postage-stamp-sized front lawns and single-car garages built into the bottom storey.

Damnit, she'd let Sam down.

She stopped the car and texted him: *Lost the target in Everton. Still looking.*

She hoped that if she continued to drive around she might come across Church's vehicle, but she didn't hold out much hope. Church might not have known he was being followed, but he'd been cagey nonetheless.

Sam was right—he was smart as well as dangerous.

CHAPTER THIRTY-SEVEN

I SAT AT my office desk and stared into space. I was still waiting for a call from Howard and I'd heard nothing more from Belinda. I was tired and wrung out. I could barely lift the pencil I'd been playing with, never mind drum up the energy to chew its end.

Outside, the streets of Crewe were empty except for revellers looking for somewhere to revel. Crewe itself wasn't much help—a few pubs, a night-club, a cinema complex. Not exactly Leicester Square.

It was past ten o'clock and I didn't know where to be. If I went home I was frightened of missing a call to the office; if I stayed in the office I thought I might miss a call to my home. I really should work out how to use call-forwarding, I thought.

Thankfully my mobile phone was mobile and accompanied me everywhere. It rang out, crashing through the silence of the office and I swiped its screen to answer.

Bobbie Ware's voice sounded in the speaker. The last time she'd done this she'd been frantic and almost hysterical as a result of finding an ear on her doorstep. This time she was calm, as devoid of energy as myself.

She said, 'Mr Dyke?'

'The same. How are you holding up, Bobbie?'

'Not well. No more contact so far as I know.'

'And Mark?'

'That's why I said, "so far as I know". Mark's gone missing. I haven't seen him since he went out this morning. I'm so tired, Sam. I can't seem to get any rest.'

'He hasn't phoned or left any messages?'

'The definition of missing is that I don't know where he is. Is that hard to understand?'

'Is Harris there?'

'I think so. I haven't seen him but his car was parked around the back when I looked out my office window earlier.'

'Okay. Do you think Mark has gone somewhere of his own free will or not?'

She thought for a moment. I could almost hear her contemplating the idea that her husband might have been kidnapped as well as her son.

'Looking back, I think he's up to something. After you left last night he was quieter than usual. Almost monosyllabic. He couldn't stop looking at the ear. Took it to his office. He came to bed late and didn't read, turned his light off straight away. When I woke up he was gone.'

'When did you begin to think he was actually missing?'

'I was nervous after his behaviour last night so I phoned him this morning. He didn't answer his mobile and when I tried his office direct line his secretary picked up and said he hadn't come in. I still thought he might have a meeting or something, you know, hoping against hope. But he didn't come home tonight.'

'It's late. Why didn't you call me earlier?'

'I was still hopeful. I thought he might have been wandering around, getting his head straight.'

I thought for a moment. I didn't know what to tell her. Mark was probably in the same state of mind as the rest of us—on edge, wanting to do something but unable to, thinking about what he could have done differently. Worrying about what was going to happen tomorrow.

I said, 'He knows he has to ensure the delivery of the goods. Or at least appear to. Has he said anything about that?'

'Nothing. But I know him—it's a problem he's been working on, so he goes into a shell and focuses all his energy on it. And knowing him as well as I do, it'll be achieved. But will they keep their word? Will they let our boys go?'

I wanted to be truthful but I couldn't leave her without hope. I said, 'It's hard to know. It'll depend on whether they've kept themselves hidden, especially from Dan, who's pretty sharp. It might also depend on how they see their mission—whether it's simply to get hold of the goods or to teach us a lesson.'

She caught the implication of this.

'What do you mean, "teach us a lesson"? I thought we were dealing with some kind of home-grown terrorists trying to help their pals in the Middle East. What are they trying to teach us?'

'You've seen the news. They might be bloodthirsty and psychotic, but they're doing it because they think *we're* evil and their version of history is right, not everyone else's, including current Islamic thinking. It's a history lesson as much as a morality tale.'

She sighed as though it were all too much for her. 'I'm scared. I want it all to end. I want us to go back to who we were before. I want to get out of this monstrosity of a house and find a nice little four-bedroomed place in Altrincham. And I want my son and my husband back and no more involvement with these people, whoever they are, whatever group of bloodthirsty animals they belong to.'

I said nothing. There was nothing I could say to make her feel better.

She added, 'And what about you? Have you got anything? Anything at all? It's been days and you've said nothing about what you've found out—or even *whether* you've found out anything. Are you just taking our money and sitting in your office waiting for tomorrow night? Can't you *do* something?'

'I'm going to hang up in a minute because you're tired. And when I do I want you to call Harris and let him know that Mark's not there. You don't have to ask him to stay in the house or keep you company, or anything like that. I'm sure you're safe. Just tell him you're alone in the house. He'll know what to do.'

'Are you sure? You're placing a lot of faith in a fat old bobby. I'm not sure I trust him.'

'You can trust him. Just call him then get some rest. Mark will probably call tomorrow, if only to let you know he's all right.'

'You still haven't said what you're going to do to get my son back. I thought I could trust you. Now I'm not sure.'

I said, 'You can trust me. It'll be okay. This time tomorrow night it'll be over.'

I hung up and put the phone down. It rang again immediately.

Howard said, 'We're on. Eleven-thirty tomorrow morning. I had to twist some arms, so make sure you're there.'

'I'll be there.'

He gave me directions to the office and then hung up. I was putting a lot of faith in a small Vietnamese boy, but what else did I have?

CHAPTER THIRTY-EIGHT

I WAS OUT of bed and having breakfast the next morning when Mark Ware called.

'Dyke? They've been in touch again.'

His voice was taut with strain.

'Where are you? Bobbie's worried.'

'I've already spoken to her this morning. I'm in town. I couldn't stay in the house any more, it was driving me mad. Everything was driving me mad. Even Bobbie.'

'What you did wasn't fair. You should have told her.'

'Well, we don't always do the things we should do, do we? I should have taken more care of my family from the beginning instead of chasing ... whatever the hell it was I was chasing.'

'This isn't the time for self-pity.'

'Oh, I'm not pitying myself, trust me. I don't blame anyone else for the mess I've made of things.'

I didn't know what to say to that so I ignored it. He was beyond argument.

I said, 'All right, that's something you're going to have to sort out with Bobbie afterwards. What did the kidnappers say?'

'Not a lot, as usual. The call came at midnight last night. They just repeated that I had until six o'clock tonight to confirm the goods will be delivered.'

'Did they say anything about the boys?'

'I don't think you understand how these calls work. I answer, they check it's me on the phone, then the person with the masked voice talks. They don't ask questions, they don't let me ask questions. The only thing he says at the end is, "Have you understood?", to which I have to reply Yes. That's it. I tried ringing back once but got a message that the number wasn't recognised. I suppose they took the SIM out of the phone straight away to destroy it. I haven't heard the sound of Lucas' voice so I don't even know whether he's alive or not. So in answer to your question, no, he didn't say anything about Lucas or your son. I have to act as though he'll be true to his word, don't I?'

'So you're somewhere in town … do you have any plans to go back to see your wife?'

There was a pause, then he said, 'Not right now. There are some things I have to do before tonight. I've told Bobbie I'll see her afterwards. I know it's bad leaving her alone during today but I can't help it.'

'You're not going to do anything stupid, are you?'

'I've already done that. How can I make it worse?'

'You strike me as unpredictable. Plus the fact I don't know where you are or what you're doing.'

'Never mind me—what are *you* doing? Is there any hope of finding these people before tonight? I have to say you've been very uncommunicative about how you're following this up.'

'At this point the less you know, the better. I know who the kidnappers are—'

'You do? Who is it?'

'—but I don't know *where* they are. I'm working on that today.'

'I'll ask you again—who are they? Should we tell the police now so they can arrest them? Or is it too late?'

'I don't want to risk spooking them before I'm in a better position to control the situation.'

'Don't risk my son's life.'

'I'm not risking his life—nor the life of my own son.'

'Of course.'

We said goodbyes and hung up. I wasn't entirely sure why he'd rung me or what he was up to. The reason he gave for being away from Bobbie and the house sounded spurious, though I supposed it might be true that he had last minute details to confirm about the delivery. At least he'd spoken to her.

But whether that conversation had made her feel better or worse would be difficult to say.

I COULD TELL Howard was burning with frustration because I wouldn't disclose anything. At one level he could treat this as a conversation about the cannabis farms and Lanh's involvement; at another, he knew I was working on something I wouldn't—or couldn't—discuss. And it was giving him stomach ache.

We sat in an immigration lawyer's office off Dale Street in Liverpool, waiting for Lanh to be brought in. He was already an hour late and no one had offered any explanation. I could barely keep my own frustration in check—time was going by and I couldn't hold it back.

This was the solution that Howard had worked out with Immigration to let the meeting take place. The interview would be recorded and there'd be a representative each from Immigration and Child Protection in the room. They wouldn't say anything unless the conversation strayed onto their territory. Both officials knew we were going to be asking the boy questions about his involvement in the running of the cannabis farm near Sefton Park, and there were no quibbles about that—after all, he'd been caught more or less red-handed in the operation. Still, he had some rights and he needed to be protected as far as possible. Who knew what danger he might be in as a result of talking to us?

Howard was wearing a pale suit that looked to be of a higher quality than he usually wore at work. He saw me noticing it.

'Wedding this afternoon. A sign of my dedication, this. I should be at home telling the missus she looks wonderful. Perhaps vacuuming the car, taking it down the car wash. Instead I'm stuck inside a room with the Silent Detective, the one who says fuck-all and wants everything back in return.'

'I've told you everything I can.'

'You mentioned something about two dead boys last time we met. If a person says something like that, it's likely to pique my interest. Funny thing is, it did. I started wondering why your boy would be in danger. Asked around about any unusual activity. Anything online, the kind of thing he gets involved in. It seems he's not been seen for a day or two. Not in the usual forums he goes to. Not doing any trading on that Bitcoin thing.'

'Jesus, you been in touch with the NSA? Does Snowden know about this?'

'That's all smoke and mirrors. We can get the info if we want. But in this case there's no info to be got, is there? So is that what you're doing, trying to find out where he is? I can help in that department, you know.'

I studied him briefly. He sometimes gave me a hard time but he knew by now I often came up smelling of roses. Either by accident or good fortune we'd shared some serious results over the last few months.

And yet …

I still couldn't bring myself to tell him about the Wares and Church and the kidnappings. I was sailing so close to the wind I was through the other side—concealing evidence of a crime was no joke—but when it's your own son being held captive by men with no conscience it alters your perception of right and wrong and the whole notion of justice.

He must have seen the tension in my face because he shrugged and turned away.

He said, 'Don't say I didn't ask. We've been here before, haven't we? You get up to some rum stuff then make a phone call at the last minute and I come to your rescue like the damn Seventh Cavalry.'

I said, 'I've got nothing for you. Maybe later.'

'Prick teaser. I may not take the call this time. Let you stew.'

I was prevented from replying by the door opening and the woman from Child Protection coming in with the boy I now knew was called Lanh.

When Belinda and I had taken him from the house he'd been wearing threadbare jeans and a white tee-shirt under a denim jacket. He'd kept the jacket but had been given new jeans, a different tee-shirt and new sneakers.

He still had the same attitude. He walked in and took a seat at the end of the table as if this was yet one more in a long line of interviews he'd undergone since being taken from the house. He gave no sign of recognising me and gave Howard only a cursory glance. As soon as he sat down he took a stick of gum from his pocket, put it in his mouth and started folding the silver wrapper meticulously. It was a way of keeping his eyes down and away from ours.

The woman from Child Protection had taken a seat in the far corner and another man from Immigration had come in behind her, nodded at us each in turn and stood in an opposite corner, arms folded. Even I was intimidated so god knows what effect it had on Lanh.

When we were all settled Howard nodded briefly at me and I leaned forward in my seat.

'Okay, Lanh, we all know you speak English so don't pretend you don't understand me. I'm here with this man not to get you in trouble, but because I need to find someone and you might be able to help. Okay?'

He didn't raise his head from the paper folding. His long fingers worked quickly and skilfully on the pleats he was creating.

I said, 'I know you remember me because you had my chicken nuggets.'

He didn't look up but a swift grin passed over his features.

I said, 'I understand if you're scared. You were probably forced to work in that house and had no way of escape. Now you've been kept in another place you can't get out of and you've been asked lots of questions and you don't know why. I get that, but this is really important to me and it'll help you find a way out of this mess.'

I stopped talking and let him take this in. I became aware of the other bodies in the room, the shifting of the woman's legs on the chair, the rustle of the Immigration officer's clothing as he unfolded his arms and placed his hands in his pockets, the faint rumble of noise from other offices in the building. It was Saturday morning but amazingly the lawyers were still at work.

Lanh stopped folding the wrapper and looked up at me.

'I'll talk to you if you want.'

'Great, thanks.'

'But he has to go, and the others.'

Both Howard and the Immigration officer started talking at once but I raised a hand and they stopped.

'That's not possible. They're here to protect you.'

Lanh made a snorting noise. 'Too late. I'm dead already. Whatever you do, they'll kill me.'

'That's not true. I know who they are and they're going to be caught. You'll be safe.'

'Where? Here, or back home? I'm not talking with them in the room.'

I turned to Howard.

'Let's do it his way.'

We all knew the conversation was being recorded anyway but he had to put up an objection.

He said, 'No way. You can't talk to him without me here.'

'He won't talk at all unless we're alone.'

Howard looked up at the Immigration officer and after a pause, nodded. The man, who was in his forties and had seen it all before, shrugged and opened the door. The woman from Child Protection came over and said to Lanh, 'Remember what we talked about. Behave yourself.'

Lanh rolled his eyes like any teenager being told off. The woman looked at me without expression and then followed the other two men out of the room.

The door closed. Lanh stopped folding his gum wrapper and put it on the table.

He said, 'They'll listen through a microphone, won't they?'

CHAPTER THIRTY-NINE

I SHUFFLED MY chair closer to his and said, 'You're a smart kid, but we're both in trouble, you and me. It's possible you'll be sent back to Vietnam unless we can find a way to keep you here.'

'What's your trouble?'

'I've got a son, and he's been taken as a hostage to stop me doing something.'

'What?'

I glanced up at the ceiling, towards the recording device that neither of us could see. I watched the understanding light up his face: I couldn't talk freely. Now we were on the same side.

I said, 'I can't tell you that.' I leaned back in my chair. 'How come you speak English so well? Did you learn in Vietnam?'

He made a face indicating I was stupid. 'I don't remember Vietnam. That's a long time ago. Six years.'

'Where are your parents?'

He shrugged. 'Back there. They sent me here with an uncle. He pretended I was his son when he came here on a visit. When he went home he left me behind with a friend. I lived in London in a big house with an older boy. He looked after me and taught me about the plants and stuff. Then they brought me up to Liverpool.'

'Didn't you want to get away?'

'Why? Where to? I didn't know anybody except Mrs Chau, and she's an old woman. Anyway, I had my DS and Playstation and TV and food.'

'You didn't have any friends.'

He shrugged again. I began to see it as a defensive gesture when he wanted to avoid painful questions—he acted as though he didn't care as a way of concealing any hurt.

I leaned forward again. 'Tell me what you did in the house.'

He looked around the room and puffed out his cheeks. 'This is boring. Can I go now?'

'Not yet. Tell me … how did it work with the plants?'

'I didn't do much. Just checked the temperature and the water. Old lady Chau came and brought food and shouted at me for not doing something. Then she'd go round with the machine … what do you call it … the hoover. She'd bring clean clothes. Sometimes she talked to me in English, to practise. But I watched English TV all the time. I like Dave. Funny programmes. And Top Gear.'

'What about the boss? Did you see him?'

'There was a man with a nose like a bird. Mr Carter. He'd come every few weeks and look upstairs. Then he'd walk around the house, look in the fridge, as though he was checking old lady Chau was doing her job. He gave me some money every time but I never went out so I never spent it. Can I have it back? It was under my bed, in a box.'

'I don't know. I'll find out. Anybody else come to the house?'

'He sometimes came with another man.'

'What did he look like?'

The boy made a noise with his lips. 'I don't know.'

'Was he very tall and thin? Did he wear glasses?'

He frowned. 'No, not really.'

I'd expected him to identify Sebastian Church, but I was wrong.

Then Lanh said, 'Mr Carter called him Ted. I remember because it was like Father Ted, on TV.'

'Ted Mason?'

Lanh shrugged. 'I don't remember.'

Mason had told me he knew nothing about what was going on inside the house and that he was trying to go straight. But I'd since found out he owned more than one property, and according to Howard several of those properties also contained cannabis farms. So he wasn't being entirely honest despite my pushing him around like a thug.

I said, 'Can you tell me anything else about the men? Did you see what car they were driving, or did they mention any addresses?'

The boy stared at me. 'It was weeks ago. When they came in I went away, into the other rooms. They didn't like me listening. Can I leave now?'

It was ridiculous to expect him to remember anything useful. He was a kid without any interest in the doings of the men he worked for. Everything he did was to protect himself and keep out of trouble. What a shocking life he'd led.

I said, 'Are they looking after you?'

The shrug again. 'I like the food, but I want my DS back. It's mine.'

'I'll see what I can do.'

I stood to leave and he looked up at me.

'What's going to happen? Will they send me back? I don't want to go back. I like it here.'

'It's out of my control. I'll talk to someone but it's not my decision.'

His dark eyes turned moist and he looked away. I thought of Dan and the good fortune he'd had after his miserable upbringing, and wondered whether Lanh would get the same opportunities. I doubted it.

I said, 'You'll have to behave yourself if you want to be treated properly. It'll be hard but it's your only chance.'

He didn't look at me but he nodded. I hated to see a youngster so alone and miserable. I leaned forward and put my hand on his shoulder briefly but still he didn't turn. I hoped someone would give him a break.

I left the room and closed the door behind me. The woman from Child Protection was in the corridor and she went straight in after me.

I WANTED TO get away before Howard saw me but he was too wily for that. He got to me by the Fire Exit door just as I was pushing down the bar.

'All right, so Mason is the owner of all those houses, isn't he? We'd best have him in for a chat. Call me suspicious, but I think you're trying to have your wicked way with me.'

'Have you been to see Mason yet?'

'Getting our ducks in a row. Evidence. He's on the agenda now, first thing Monday morning. What can you tell me about him?'

'Can we talk about this later?'

He folded his arms and sighed.

'Let me lay out the cards for you. What I know so far is that you called me to ask about the head honcho of the Counter-Terrorist Unit, then let slip that I should look up this Irene Chau woman. Shortly after that you said I should investigate several properties owned by someone called Ted Mason. You also told me that the lives of two boys are in danger, including that of your own son. Right so far?'

'Get on with it.'

'Then we have this little conversation with Chairman Mao in there and it seems Mr Mason is indeed involved with the wacky baccy factories. So putting my enormous analytical brain in gear, it seems to me that you've got yourself involved with some high-end drug smugglers who may well have taken your young Dan as a prisoner, possibly as a hostage to keep you off their back. With your usual grim resolution you've decided to ignore them and keep going anyway, never mind the potential consequences for your own flesh and blood. How am I doing now?'

'Fifty per cent. Are you done yet?'

I saw the surprise register on his face. He thought he'd scored higher than that. His mind started to tick over.

'So as usual there's more to you than meets the eye. Perhaps I should just sling you in the pokey until you tell me what's going on.'

'Would that help?'

'Probably not, but it'd give me enormous satisfaction.'

'Every minute you keep me talking here is one minute further away from you finding out what's happening. I can't tell you anything because I've got nothing useful to say. Nothing that you could do anything with. Time's short. I promise I'll let you know what's happening as soon as I can.'

'How soon is that likely to be?'

'I can't say.'

'No, you never can.'

I was taller and bigger than him and he could never have taken me in a fight. But he knew he was an officer of the law and I would have had to submit to him or face a very difficult few months being dragged through the courts for resisting arrest, assaulting an officer … etc.

Thankfully something ticked over in his mind and he turned away, towards the main offices, waving a dismissive hand behind his back.

He said, 'Go get Dan, and for Christ's sake don't break any more laws.'

I hesitated, then said, 'I owe you one.'

He muttered, 'Several,' under his breath as he turned the corner. I pushed open the Fire Exit door and left.

I'D TAKEN OUT my phone to ring Belinda when it rang in my hand. Unknown caller.

'Sam Dyke. Who's this?'

'You know who it is, Mr Dyke. It's your adversary, the criminal mastermind you've been chasing for a while. How's that going for you?'

'I'll tell you at six o'clock. Where are you now?'

Church laughed quietly, almost gently, enjoying himself. I imagined putting a fist through his pointed nose. Then I got a grip on myself.

He said, 'I really should have carried through my promise, you know. I had an idea that taking young Daniel wouldn't actually deter you. You haven't got sufficient imagination to consider the amount of fear and pain he'll suffer. But the time is getting closer, and then you'll know it. Then your imagination will run amok feeling every ounce of his torment and wondering what you could have done to prevent it. And the answer, of course, is nothing. I would have mistreated him whatever you did, whether you gave up the chase or not. But then you knew that, didn't you? That's why you continued.'

'One hair of his head, Church. Just one hair. You'll wish you hadn't been born.'

He laughed again, this time with more steel.

'Have you seen me? Do you understand my condition? Don't you think I've visited that particular repository of thoughts in my time?'

'Your condition doesn't excuse you or your behaviour. That's all down to you.'

'What—am I evil? Is that what you're saying?'

'I don't believe in evil. I don't think you're a representative of an abstraction. And I don't think an evil spirit has invaded your body. You're just a man whose intellect has been separated from any sense of right and wrong. You say I've got no imagination. Well, look in that mirror. At least I know what bad behaviour looks like. I don't think you have any idea. It's just what you do on a daily basis because you've trained yourself not to know any different.'

'An interesting philosophical point. Did something go wrong with my sense of self at the mirror-stage of my development? Did I fail to separate from the bosom of my mother at the right time, and thus become over-attached and therefore co-dependent? Or did I separate too soon and see myself as isolated, with no connection to the wider sphere of humankind? Discuss.'

'What happens at six o'clock?'

'Nice change of subject. Don't let the evildoer indulge his sense of paranoia. It's a binary situation, isn't it? Either Mr Ware will have fulfilled his side of the bargain, or he won't. Let's both hope he will. The alternative is too painful to contemplate.'

I was starting to call him names when the line went dead. I leaned back in the seat of my car and closed my eyes. He was doing it deliberately, taunting me to make me angry and throw off my thinking.

And it was working.

CHAPTER FORTY

SATURDAY AFTERNOON TRAFFIC was thick through Liverpool and although it was only a few miles to Ted Mason's house it took me the best part of forty-five minutes to get there. I drove past dull housing estates and past the grey brick of West Derby school, out into small country lanes and then back into middle-class suburbia. Eventually I found the turn off into the leafy estate where the Masons lived and I sat and watched the house for a few minutes, seeing no signs of life. I don't know what I expected to see, exactly, because most suburban streets are lifeless until a front door is opened or a car arrives. The idea that children could play outside on the streets is now very passé.

I went to the front door and knocked and Jean Mason, cigarette in hand, opened it quickly. She hadn't looked on top form when I first met her: now she was worse — unkempt, unmade-up, her face a map of worry and despair.

She said, 'Oh, it's you. I thought I told you to piss off.'

'I decided to ignore your kind offer. I take it you haven't heard from Ted?'

'What do you think? There'd be balloons and bouncy castles outside if I had, wouldn't there?'

'Can I come in?'

'What for? I've only got one husband for you to fuck up, and you've done that.'

'I might be able to help find him if I can see his things.'

'The bizzies have already done that. I told you I reported it, didn't I? They come round and asked a lot of nosy questions. Haven't heard a blind word from them since.'

When Howard had spoken to me he hadn't mentioned this—that some of his colleagues had been to the house. It was likely to be a completely different station, though, so he probably wasn't aware they'd visited the house. He was chasing Ted because he thought he was a drug trafficker; the other unit would be looking for him as a missing person and wouldn't take it seriously for another day or two.

I said, 'Did they take anything away?'

'Like what?'

'Ted's papers, records, stuff like that.'

'You're joking, right? He doesn't let anyone near them.'

I took a step forward so that she would have to back up, into the house. Then I was able to get into the hallway and close the door behind me.

I said, 'Look, Jean, despite what you think I want to find Ted for the right reasons. Not to stitch him up but to help him.'

'You're a right Good Samaritan, you, ain't you? What am I supposed to do if he doesn't come back? All them houses, all that business? I can't do that.'

'What is it he does?'

'Rents them out. Gets rent money. But he has to look after them, too, fix plumbing, nail down floorboards, get the roofs sorted. That kind of stuff.'

'Nothing else?'

'Not that I know of. Why? What are you saying?'

I took her hand. 'I'm sorry, Jean, but I think he's mixed up with some bad people.'

'That ugly-looking beggar with the hook nose, walks around with those two steroid mountains?'

'Them and others. I need to look at his books if I'm to have a clue where he is. Can you point me to them?'

She took a long drag of her cigarette. She looked about sixty but could have been twenty years younger, the cigarette grimace etching lines into her cheeks and her top lip.

She said, 'They're in here.'

She turned and led me into the kitchen, then reached up into a cupboard that had been built above the extractor unit over the gas rings. Not an obvious hiding place. She pulled down a blue ring-binder that bulged with plastic envelopes containing sheets of paper and letters, with sections separated by coloured dividers.

I took it to the kitchen table and sat, turning the pages carefully. I'd seen from the clock on the wall that it was four forty-five and I had an hour and a quarter left. I tried not to let it distract me.

The papers were mostly ledgers of rent payments, with occasional letters between Mason and the renters. At the back of the file, in a separate section, were utility bills for all the houses, neatly arranged for water, gas and electric, and community tax. I counted eleven houses in total and I spotted the address of the one where Lanh had lived.

I went through the other addresses and found each of the houses that I'd read out to Howard over the phone and which he'd raided. I'd been hoping there'd be one that hadn't been mentioned on the other list, one we'd missed. But they were all there.

After the payment ledgers and before the utility bills was a section of random letters—a payment to workmen for replacing a door, for painting a shed, for putting in a fold-down trapdoor like the one I'd found in the first house.

Then there was a section dedicated simply to supplies of building materials. There were invoices from B&Q, from Wickes, from Jewsons for deliveries of bricks, of sand, of wooden beams. Each invoice named the delivery address.

Which is where I found a discrepancy.

One of the addresses was new and hadn't been mentioned on the ledger of rental properties. I flicked to the front of the book to check I hadn't mis-remembered: number 18, Dewhurst Close, wasn't there.

Jean Mason had been looking over my shoulder. She said, 'Is that important?'

'Do you know this place?'

She peered more closely at the address.

'Never seen it before. New one on me. Where is it?'

'I don't know. Have you got a computer?'

She left the kitchen and I followed her into a small downstairs room kitted out as a study, with a rolling leather chair, plain wooden desk, a couple of bookcases. She moved a mouse on a mat and the flat screen of a desktop computer came on. The screen wallpaper showed two children, a boy and a girl, aged about ten. The faded colour of the photograph suggested it was probably ten or fifteen years old when it had been scanned in.

She said, 'The kids. Both at college now. Beth's doing French … can't remember what Jason's doing. Something with computers.'

'Nice kids.'

She said nothing but took another drag. I opened up Google Chrome and clicked the app link to take me to Google Maps, then typed in the address of the delivery. Half a ton of sand and several bags of cement had been delivered there six weeks before. Evidently it wasn't a habitable dwelling so maybe Ted was having it done up prior to letting it out, adding to his portfolio without telling Jean.

But the map shifted on the screen as it zoomed in on the address. It was south of Everton, where Belinda had lost Church, and perhaps it was a place where Church and his cronies could hide out, off the grid.

The problem was, if they weren't there I had no time to investigate anywhere else.

I RAN FROM the house and climbed into my car. Dewhurst Close was about four miles from my current location, according to Google Maps. I typed the address into my GPS and while it found the satellites I speed-dialled Belinda. She knew the deadline and answered quickly.

I said, 'Where are you?'

'On my way to Liverpool. I thought you might need help.'

'Find 18, Dewhurst Close, it's a bit south of where you lost Church yesterday.'

'I'll be there in about forty minutes. Don't do anything rash.'

I glanced at my dashboard clock—she'd arrive about twenty to six: cutting it fine, but I'd need her support if I had to force my way into the house.

We hung up. The satellites had found the route and I chose first gear.

CHAPTER FORTY-ONE

IT WASN'T FAR, but it took an age: Saturday afternoon shoppers returning home, people driving to the newsagents to buy lottery tickets, party-goers driving to meet friends before going out for the evening … those four miles were the longest distance I'd ever driven.

By the time I reached the bottom of Dewhurst Close and had parked discreetly, it was almost 5:30. By counting houses I found number 18, but I could have used what I'd learned at Jean Mason's kitchen table to direct me: the sand and concrete that had been ordered and delivered still stood in piles in the house's front yard.

The street was a 'Close' in that it was a dead-end, culminating in a circular sweep around which a number of houses gathered like diners at a round table. Number 18, a semi-detached white-fronted sixties model, sat at the very bottom of the circle and seemed to be a work in progress. The front garden wall had been demolished and it appeared that the sand and cement were being used to rebuild it. More than that, a garage was being added to the side and it seemed to me that some kind of construction was going on at the rear, too. Mason was going to a lot of work to render an unattractive house even less attractive. Rents in this part of the city weren't going to be high, so I didn't see how he expected to get his money back any time soon.

I looked closely at the house next door, the one to which number 18 was attached. It was identical but in reverse, its front door to the left of the façade as opposed to the right. I realised that these two houses and all the others in the Close had once been flat-roofed and had been topped off by a kind of artificial gabled roofing some time after their original construction—a trick often performed by housing associations to make their properties appear a little more appealing as well as protecting the original flat roofs from the weather. It was likely that Mason had picked up the house cheaply if the housing association had been forced to sell by the changing economic climate.

On the pavement outside several of the houses were small, sporty cars and I suspected the inhabitants of the Close were either young couples or single men without much disposable income, what income they earned being spent on their small, sporty cars and large TVs.

My phone rang: Belinda.

'I'm thirty yards behind you. Shall I come?'

'Do it quietly.'

'Always.'

Thirty seconds later my passenger door opened and Belinda slid into the seat, closing the door gently. Her hair was tied behind her, ready for action.

'Which house?'

'The one with the sand and cement in front.'

'How many inside?'

'Church, maybe Carter Spring, two big men he had with him when he beat me up. I don't know if there are others. Probably.'

'You got a plan?'

'Does "kick the living shit out of them" count?'

'Not very detailed. Do you think they're armed?'

'Don't know. A different two men had a go at me Thursday night. Different clan—machetes and knives.'

She turned and looked at me more closely, searching for wounds.

'How d'you do?'

'The ex-copper Harris turned up. He'd seen them watching me, thought he could help. We drove them off but they might be inside, I suppose, whoever they are.'

'Machetes.'

'I know. Do you want to wait till I invite Howard to the party?'

She looked at her watch. 'Only ten minutes now before he calls. Has Ware delivered the stuff?'

'I don't know, but it's irrelevant. I think Church is nuts enough to kill Lucas and Dan anyway.'

She opened her mouth to say something but then closed it. I knew she was about to say, 'If they're not already dead,' but thought better of it in my presence.

Instead, she said, 'What's behind the house? Just garden?'

'I think so. Then the gardens of the houses in the street the other side.'

'So we can't sneak up from the back or get a look at what's inside.'

'If the boys are there they'll probably lock them in a bedroom. The house has got double-glazing by the look of it, so they could just lock the windows and lock the bedroom door. Dan would have got out if he could. Or helped Lucas to get out.'

She must have heard something in my voice because she put her hand on my arm.

'Keep it together, Sam. We'll get them out.'

I nodded as if I agreed but I didn't convince myself.

Time was passing. Eventually I said, 'I can't see anything else for it. Knock and enter, deal with what comes up. Is that mad?'

'Totally. But we've got no choice.'

First I called Howard. He answered quickly.

'Dyke—what now? The pudding's about to be served.'

'I might need back-up. Number 18, Dewhurst Close. Can you get Mercer and his men to turn up?'

'What's going on?'

'Well, terrorism, obviously. Plus kidnapping, possible murder and extortion. And did I mention terrorism? You might not be interested …'

I cut him off before he got to his first swear word.

I glanced at Belinda, ready to open my door. Her eyes were fixed on something straight ahead.

She said, 'Who's that?'

I turned to the house and saw Mark Ware walking through the gate of number 18. From the angle at which he'd arrived, it looked as though he'd come through the garden of one of the neighbouring houses. Before I realised what was happening he'd knocked on the door and it had opened.

I had climbed out of the car and was racing towards the door when I heard the first shot, followed by an agonising scream.

CHAPTER FORTY-TWO

DAN LOOKED OUT of the rear bedroom window. He and Lucas had heard the first shot and the cry of pain that had followed it. Now they listened hard. There was another shot and the sound of men shouting. He realised that Lucas was holding his hand.

They had been put in the bedroom that morning, their hands tied behind them, but they'd been able to untie their knots by standing back to back and straining their fingers. Dan had untied Lucas first, who'd then untied his own ankle bindings and turned around to untie Dan's wrists.

They'd soon discovered they were still trapped. The window was double-glazed but was locked and unbreakable. The door to the bedroom was also locked.

Lucas had asked, 'What are we going to do?'

'I have a plan.'

'Will we be able to get away?'

'I don't know for sure, but I think so. If someone comes in the door, stand well back.'

'Can you fight?'

Dan grinned. 'I have my moments.'

They had little sense of the house itself because whenever they'd been moved they'd been blindfolded. He knew there was an empty room downstairs, where he and Lucas had been kept, and there were at least two more rooms on that floor and probably a kitchen. Upstairs there was this bedroom, which was empty of furniture except one chair, and a toilet, which he'd been allowed to visit twice during his captivity. He didn't know how many other bedrooms there were but there must have been enough to sleep Church and his men.

He'd counted five men altogether, judging from the voices he'd heard, but he didn't know whether they were all in the house or if there were others he had no knowledge of. If this was Sam and Belinda causing the noise downstairs — or even the police — he hoped they knew what they were up against.

His first priority was to protect Lucas. He was the bargaining chip and presumably the last line of defence if Church's men went down.

Unfortunately, he didn't know how he could stop them taking Lucas if they came for him. He might get in a couple of kicks and punches, but the big men who'd manhandled him upstairs were like house-bricks stacked together and forced into clothes: impregnable.

Lucas had stepped back from the window. He said, 'What about that?' and Dan turned.

Lucas was pointing to a small trapdoor in the corner of the ceiling. Dan had seen it that morning when taking inventory of the room, but supposed it was locked or nailed down in some way. Besides, there had seemed little point in aggravating their captors by trying to hide in the loft.

But things were different now. If there was a raid taking place downstairs then it might be an advantage if Church or his men couldn't find Lucas immediately.

He said, 'Let's try something,' and carried the spindly chair underneath the trapdoor and stood on it. He placed his hands on the wood and took the strain slowly, pushing upwards against the thin wooden trapdoor. It gave way with a hollow pop, showering him with dust.

He raised the trapdoor and slid it sideways. He couldn't lift himself into the attic space because he wasn't high enough to get leverage on his arms, but he could tell the space was sufficient for Lucas to hide in.

He stepped off the chair. 'I want you to go up there and stay until I call you down. Is that okay? You're not scared of the dark, are you?'

'Course not.'

'Good. It shouldn't be completely dark anyway. And you'll be safe.'

'All right.'

Dan was impressed by the youngster's stoicism, especially in light of what he'd been through.

He picked up the boy and assessed his balance. It was going to be tricky to stand on the chair while carrying a ten-year-old boy, then lift him high enough for him to climb inside, but he couldn't see another way of doing it.

He raised Lucas so that his right arm was beneath his buttocks, around the boy's knees, then stood before the chair.

He said, 'I'm going to step on to the chair and lift you in one go, and I want you to grab hold of the side of the hole up there. Do you know what I mean?'

'Yes.'

'If I lose my balance, or if the chair tips over, hold on and I'll sort myself out and come up again and grab hold of you. Okay?'

'Yes.'

'Here goes …'

He took a firmer grip of Lucas, took half a step back, then stepped forward again, raising his leg so that it landed on the seat of the chair. He was glad he'd been doing some strength and agility work at his Tae-Kwon-Do class—just getting marginally fit again helped. He straightened his legs and raised his arms so Lucas could grab the edge of the trapdoor … and suddenly the weight of the boy was released as his hands found purchase.

Dan quickly shifted his balance and put his shoulder under Lucas's knees and heaved again, the chair wobbling beneath him.

Lucas tumbled through the hole and a moment later his face appeared against the darkness.

'We did it!'

Dan stepped off the chair and moved it to one side. 'Good work, young man. Now slide the door in the hole again and go and sit in a corner. I'll call you when I can.'

The boy slid the door back and hammered it in place with his small fist. Dan picked up the chair and swung it against a wall. It shattered into half a dozen pieces that would now be useless as a hoist.

He turned and waited for the door to open.

CHAPTER FORTY-THREE

BEFORE I REACHED the front door there was another shot. I ducked instinctively but there was no sign the bullet had come out of the house. As I ran I realised that Mark Ware had been carrying a handgun in his right hand, so he must be the one responsible for the shooting.

And while I was thinking that, I was also wondering how he'd found the place. Judging from his angle of attack he hadn't followed me, and if he'd arrived and stayed hidden and simply watched me sitting in my car with Belinda there was no way he could identify which house we were looking at.

So he must have got hold of the information some other way…

Of course: he was a defence contractor and would have contacts with other purveyors of electronic equipment. Doubtless one of them distributed equipment that included the ability to track cell phone calls. When Church had called Mark last night his call must have been monitored and Ware had spent the day arming himself and staking out the property — maybe waiting to see if I or anyone else turned up before the six o'clock deadline.

I was at the front door now. It was open and I pushed it gently. I could smell the gunshots and almost hear their echo.

The door swung open into a large room in which a series of actions had frozen in place. The room was as wide as the house and had been extended backwards, presumably as a result of the work Mason had been doing. Floor-to-ceiling picture windows at the back showed a garden mounded with lumps of concrete, turned-over earth and empty bags of cement.

In the centre of the tableau was a group of five men. One of the men was dead—it was either Gordon or Geoff, the men who'd beaten me up on Carter Spring's instructions. He was laid out on his back with a red stain in the centre of his chest.

Next to him was Mark Ware, who was alive but cradling his left arm and groaning softly. On the other side of him was the second weight-lifter, Geoff or Gordon, also still alive but holding his thigh and swearing as he tried to stop blood leaking through his fingers. Next to him was a squat figure I didn't know. The fourth man I recognised was Carter Spring. No sign of Sebastian Church.

Now they noticed Belinda and me and the faces of the living turned towards us, including Spring and the squat man, who were apparently unhurt and were standing over Mark Ware as if about to give him a kicking for interrupting their Saturday afternoon. They didn't look particularly tough but they were acting as Church's Praetorian guard so it was possible they had some skills. At least they weren't armed.

Until Spring bent down and picked up a machete from beside the wounded weight-lifter. He must have dropped it when Ware shot him.

And then I saw why Ware was groaning—his left hand was severed at the wrist. Perhaps he'd shot the first weight-lifter and then been attacked by the second. Ware had managed to shoot him too, in the leg, but his other hand had been cut off by the machete, perhaps at the same time as he'd fired. He'd dropped the gun to wrap his wrist in the bottom of his shirt, which was a bloody mess. He would soon pass out from shock.

But that meant there was a gun lying around somewhere.

Belinda said, 'Do you want machete-man or should I take him?'

'I'll do it.'

'You have to get in close.'

'I know.'

And at that moment the tableau was broken and we all went for each other.

From the corner of my eye I saw Belinda step quickly towards her target, the stocky man who was in his twenties and looked fit. He said to her, 'Want some of this, do yer?' and went into a crouch.

He'd be no match for Belinda.

Meanwhile Spring had stepped forward, machete in hand. This was the second time in less than a week I'd faced someone wielding one of these long knives. It was getting to be a habit.

Spring was nearly as tall as me and looked relatively light on his feet. He was unshaven and his eyes were rimmed with red: I suspected he'd been missing some sleep lately. He was chewing gum, giving him the appearance of someone on a training exercise to whom this encounter wasn't important … but he didn't seem entirely comfortable with the machete in his hand, as though he couldn't decide which way to hold it—hanging down, for slashing manoeuvres; or straight ahead, for stabbing. He settled for swinging it backwards and forwards in front of me, an amateur's pose.

He said, 'Didn't learn your lesson, did you, Mr Dyke?'

'Didn't like the teachers.'

He smiled, and as his confidence got the better of him he let his machete-arm droop. I took a rapid step forward and before he could get up the impetus in the arm, I aimed a punch towards his kidneys.

He was quick enough to turn and big enough to take the blow without too much discomfort. He'd started to raise his weapon so I flicked out my left hand and whipped it across his nose. It caused an instant's pain but no permanent damage. He stepped back.

I glanced quickly to my left, to see Belinda launching herself towards her opponent's upper body—she was going for his windpipe or his eyes, two of the key areas of attack in krav maga, which tries to disable an opponent as quickly as possible. The man raised his hands just in time to deflect her but she regained her balance and stepped back, facing him sideways with her weight slightly on her front foot, a classic stance. She was only average in height and build but would use her weight against the man's vulnerable joints.

I hadn't lost track of Spring and felt him coming towards me. He'd raised the machete to try to bring it down on my head, perhaps thinking that because I was big I was too slow to get out of the way.

My own training, though, kept me limber and I side-stepped him, using my trailing hand to grip his arm as it came slashing past and force the machete to point downwards. I tried to bend his arm behind him but he was too strong and stepped back from me, slipping slightly. The floor beneath us was tiled, and I had the sudden realisation that the intention for this house was to turn it into a mosque or madrasa, somewhere Church's disciples could be indoctrinated. That was the reason for all of the building work. I wondered whether he'd bothered to get planning permission.

It also meant his own plans had changed. The building materials had been delivered weeks ago but not much had been done: the kidnapping had suddenly become urgent, so getting hold of Mark Ware's electronic equipment had risen up someone's priority list and construction work had slipped down it. Whoever the equipment was being delivered to in the Middle East must have had needed it desperately.

Spring had changed strategy: now he was moving the machete from hand to hand, as though it might confuse me. But I knew he was right-handed so would almost certainly choose to come at me with that hand raised.

It also meant he would be less adept when it was in his left hand.

I said, 'Where are the boys?'

He grinned. 'What boys? No boys here, only men.'

From my left I heard a crack as Belinda broke her opponent's arm. This acted as a distraction to Spring, and he stood momentarily with the machete in his left hand. I took two quick paces and got inside his reach, knocking his left arm down with my right and punching him with all my weight behind it with my left fist. The cartilage in his prominent nose gave way and blood spurted from his nostrils. He tried to raise both hands to his face but I'd now grabbed his left wrist with both my hands and had moved behind him, taking the arm with me. He let out another yelp and dropped the machete, which I kicked away. He tried to turn towards me but I hooked a leg around both of his and pushed. He fell forward and I landed on top of him with a knee. His head hit the tiles and he was out.

Belinda said breathlessly, 'How you doing, Sam?'

'Got him.'

'Me too.'

I looked across to where she also had her man face down on the tiles. He was sobbing, his broken arm twisted behind him where Belinda held it.

I looked around the room. One man dead, another sitting upright holding his leg but deathly pale, two face down.

And Mark Ware. He was going into shock, his left wrist wrapped tightly in his shirt, his eyes staring ahead while he tried to block out the pain. He was sitting on a threadbare sofa, the only piece of furniture in the room except for a television. Bean bags and cushions were scattered around, some of them having been kicked about during the fight.

Belinda had pulled her man's tee-shirt down from his shoulders and used it to pin his arms behind him. He let out agonised cries as she manoeuvred him into position.

She said, 'I'll look after yours and get Ware fixed up. I presume you're Mark Ware?'

He knew he'd been addressed and he turned towards her dumbly. Then he nodded. 'That's me.'

Belinda said, 'Sam. Go.'

'I'll be upstairs if anyone calls.'

CHAPTER FORTY-FOUR

HE'D THOUGHT IT would be a good idea to meditate before six o'clock, before he made the final phone call. It would help him cope with whatever Ware said. He didn't think Ware would let him down, given his son's life was at risk, but you could never be sure.

So he needed to be in an appropriate state of mind when he made the final contact, and freeing his mind of extraneous clutter would be perfect.

When he heard the first shot, and shortly after the second, a deep despair came over him. He knew at once it was over, and he also knew he would now have to perform a series of actions that were essential but not to be welcomed. To take the life of a young boy didn't sit well with him, though he knew it was the price that the Wares had to pay for failing to follow instructions. The Dyke boy would go too, as a lesson to Dyke Senior. He wasn't yet sure what the lesson was, but he knew it was necessary.

He stood up from his meditation cushion and went to the top of the stairs. He called down for Gordon, then Geoff. There was no reply, but maybe if they were in the other side of the house they couldn't hear him.

He felt himself getting angry. This wasn't how he'd seen it in his mind's eye. He thought there might be an occasional bump on the road but he'd planned it so meticulously he didn't see how there could be a problem now, so late in the day.

However, he wouldn't let the plan be defeated without his putting up a fight. A martyr must always be alert for the moment of glory.

The two houses at the bottom of the Close had been knocked into one—at least on the first floor. Downstairs the living room and kitchen of number 18 had been gutted and retiled for the teaching space, and they'd been on the point of knocking through a door to number 17 so they could begin equipping it with the video training room and the new kitchen. The upstairs work had been finished first: a series of small bedrooms that were almost like cells except for the master one, which they'd stripped of furniture and given over to the hostage boys. At the end of the corridor a single flight of stairs led downstairs, so whoever was coming for him would have to come up those first. He stood waiting there for a moment, listening to the sounds of combat— grunts and yelps and then a loud cry, followed almost immediately by silence.

He would have to hurry.

He walked back to the small bedroom he'd been using as his meditation room and got the weapons he'd set aside for a moment like this—the Heckler and Koch USP Compact 9mm pistol that Abu had given him and a saw-edged hunting knife he'd bought off the internet. There was a heavy finality in their weight and practicality. Once you had them in your hands you were almost committed to using them.

He walked back to the bedroom containing the boys and unlocked the door. He had little doubt they'd been able to undo each other's bindings so he turned the knob and pushed, swinging the door wide, then stepped back.

The door slammed shut, as he thought it might, the young Dyke taking an opportunity to resist.

He pushed the door again and this time stepped into the room with his pistol raised. He spun as he sensed a movement to his right and stepped away in time to avoid a swinging foot — the young man certainly had some skills, but perhaps not enough experience in using them.

He said, 'Stand still or I'll shoot you.'

The young man had come to rest with one foot forward, his arms hanging loose by his side. There was a focus and intent in them that Church appreciated even while he disliked the problems this attitude was causing him.

A quick glance around the room confirmed what he'd sensed: Lucas Ware was missing. The door had been locked, the window was impregnable. Another glance upward told him the story: they'd managed to get him into the loft space above. Clever. And it left him no option.

He said, 'Take off your tee-shirt.'

'What if I don't?'

'I'll shoot you in the leg and you'll bleed to death.'

'You're going to kill me anyway.'

Church shrugged. 'Maybe. Is young Ware in the attic?'

'Vanished into thin air. One minute he's here, the next he's gone.'

'The tee-shirt, please.'

Church heard the tread of a footfall on the stairs — it was a new flight made of bare, uncarpeted pine that hadn't settled yet and groaned with every step it received.

'Turn around. Hands behind your back.'

The young man did so and Church quickly wound the tee-shirt into a strip and ran it around the other man's wrists, pulling it tight and knotting it.

He heard the door to the small bedroom next door — the first in the corridor — being opened. Whoever had come this far would find something they didn't expect and Church smiled grimly.

Then he pushed the pistol into his pocket and took out the hunting knife. He positioned himself so the young man was between him and the door, his left hand gripping the bound wrists, his right snaked over the other's shoulder with the point of the blade directly on his bare chest, just below the ribcage. He was considerably taller and could see over the younger man's head.

He planted his feet and waited for the door to open.

As he did so, he began to push the blade into Dan's chest.

CHAPTER FORTY-FIVE

THE STAIRS WERE new and bare wood and creaked every time I took a step.

I began to have the sense that the house wasn't laid out as I expected. The knocking down of the walls downstairs in number 18 had made one large space but left no room for a kitchen or laundry or anywhere to eat, judging by the furniture we'd seen.

Now, as I slowly headed upstairs on the new staircase, I began to see the corridor I was approaching was longer than the width of the house should have allowed … and then I realised: they'd knocked through the connecting wall and into the house next door. Church or Mason must have bought both numbers 17 and 18 to make them into a larger base of operations. Housing out here was cheap, especially if bought from a struggling housing association, and the cannabis farm profits would have made the purchase of two houses almost an incidental expense on the balance sheet.

When I reached the landing at the top of the stairs I halted and listened. I heard Church's voice from one of the rooms but I couldn't be sure which one. The upstairs had been remodelled. In this house I would have expected three bedroom doors and one for the bathroom. Two bedrooms would have faced the front, perhaps one of them being a small box room or child's bedroom. Facing the rear garden there would be the bathroom and another bedroom.

But having knocked through the intervening wall to next door, they'd created a long corridor with doors coming off it on both sides, with no indication which door led to a bathroom—presuming there was one—and which doors led to bedrooms. I supposed if they were going to use the place as a teaching or training centre they'd need a dormitory-type arrangement to house the trainees.

Facing me directly on the landing was the first closed door. I tentatively pushed it open, waiting for a shot or some kind of assault. I had no idea how many men had been in the house when Belinda and I had entered. For all I knew, each door might conceal a number of waiting opponents, like one of those old computer games with zombies milling about behind the doors.

The door caught on the carpet and I pushed it further. It opened into a cell-like room containing two bunk-beds and a small set of drawers under a window.

On the floor was a large pile of clothes.

I was about to turn away when something made me look again. I saw with shock they weren't just clothes, and a spike of fear ran through me. I realised there were two bodies lying on top of each other. Their legs were intertwined but their heads were covered.

I stepped inside and bent quickly to inspect them. I moved a pullover from the face of one of the bodies—it was Ted Mason, his face white and long dead. He looked more peaceful than he had when I'd met him.

I moved him to one side and revealed the face of the other body: Irene Chau, her features pale but also bloody, as though she'd been knifed or perhaps hit by the machete. By contrast with Mason, her expression was one of terror, her eyes wide and her lips pulled back fractionally from her teeth. I felt something open up in my chest as I thought again of Dan and what he might have experienced in the last few days.

The bodies having been kept in reasonably sanitary conditions meant they hadn't begun to rot, but still there was a stench of death in the room, a dark, fusty odour that anticipated the smell of the earth to which they'd eventually return.

I stood up and peered into the corridor. Still no movement and no sound.

Then I heard a loud groan from the room next door.

CHAPTER FORTY-SIX

I MOVED ALONG the corridor, my chest thumping. Somewhere in the distance I heard the wail of an ambulance and guessed that Belinda had called for help. Mercer and his men would probably be on their way, too, though they might be taking it more quietly because of the instructions I'd given Howard.

It was all over for Church, but did he know it? Had he done anything to Lucas or Dan before the deadline, or was that groan—however disturbing—a sign that at least one of them was alive?

My senses became hyper-alert. Now I could hear Church talking quietly behind the next door on the corridor though I couldn't make out what he was saying. From downstairs I could hear Belinda talking to Ware, trying to keep him awake and out of shock. I could even hear children playing outside, in their gardens. As so often, a private horror story was being played out against a typical suburban background. Was there really any such thing as normality?

I put my hand on the doorknob. I didn't know what I was going to face inside and I had an unspeakable fear of confronting it.

Then I heard another groan, louder this time and more full of pain.

I went inside.

Dan was facing me, bare from the waist upwards, his hands held at his back. His chest was pale and streaked with blood.

Sebastian Church stood behind him, wearing some kind of flowing garment that looked vaguely Eastern. His height meant that he gazed at me over the top of Dan's head. In his right hand he held an evil-looking knife that he had buried some distance into Dan's left side, as though about to rip it sideways in an act of hara-kiri.

Dan's face was twisted in pain and he tried to turn against the blade. But Church had him in a tight grip and Dan couldn't move.

Church seemed to be forcing the blade slowly into Dan's body.

He said, 'Welcome, Mr Dyke. I'm sorry you find me in this situation. Unfortunately the young Ware has disappeared so I had to use a substitute.'

'Let him go, Church. This doesn't get you anywhere. It's over.'

'Oh, I know, I know. But there has to be pay-back of some sort, doesn't there?'

'You've already killed two people. Don't make it three.'

'Why not? Three's a nice round number. Even a holy number. Christ and the two thieves. The Father, Son and Holy Ghost. Etcetera.'

Dan uttered another groan and I knew that Church had increased the pressure on the knife. There were two yards between us in the room and I knew if I made a move he would simply push further into Dan's chest then draw the knife out and go for me.

Dan was slumping now, letting his weight drop a little so that Church had to support him. His long right arm snaked over Dan's shoulder while his left held on to his jeans belt, holding him upright. The blood from Dan's side was running freely down on to Church's hand, past it and down Dan's jeans to the floor.

There was a sudden burst of men's voices downstairs and I knew that Mercer had arrived. I hoped the ambulance was close by.

A change came over Church's expression. His lightweight glasses seemed to turn opaque and his mouth became thin and hard.

He said, 'All right, enough of this,' and I saw him gathering his strength, hoisting Dan with his left hand to get better purchase …

Which is when Dan moved. Although he must have been in enormous pain he'd shifted his weight under Church's grip so that he could pivot on his right leg and bring up his left.

Falling away as he turned, his left shin rose in a blur and smashed into Church's face.

Church uttered a grunt and fell backwards to the floor, pulling the knife from Dan's side. I was on him instantly, falling on him to seize his knife hand with my left and pummel his face with my right.

I'd read that sufferers from his condition were often fragile and suffered a number of related physical problems. Church, however, had done what he could to maintain a level of fitness and he was able to turn on the floor and use the length of his limbs to shift from underneath me, even as I held on to the wrist in which he gripped the knife. He slowly moved his legs and arced around me and eventually straddled my waist. He stared down at me, no more than a foot from my face, his wide mouth in a strange, obsessive grin, his knife hand forcing its way towards me. He seemed to have gained strength from somewhere inside him, as though his self-righteous beliefs were coursing through his muscles like adrenaline.

He said slowly in a voice as low as a growl, 'You don't get it, do you? I love you and we're all going to hell.'

I had been fighting the downward pressure of the knife with my left hand when suddenly he took the strength from it and allowed me to push him away. He fell on to his back once again.

Now it was my turn to squirm on top and straddle him, still holding his wrist, using all my strength to keep it down against the floor. I thought I had the measure of him now.

So it was shocking when he slowly put strength into his right hand again and flexed his elbow, drawing the knife inwards between us. There was nothing I could do to stop its movement. I watched as if from a distance as he placed the point of the knife over his own chest. I realised too late what he was doing.

He said, 'Done!'

Then using a swift and almost graceful motion he wrapped his left arm around my back and pulled me onto him.

With my weight on top of his hand, the knife found a way through his ribcage and pierced his heart. He died instantly.

I ROLLED AWAY and drew in a huge breath, then remembered what I had to do. I scrambled over to Dan's side. He was on his back with his tied arms beneath him. His eyes were closed and he was breathing heavily. The knife wound looked deep.

I ran out, to the head of the stairs, and was on the point of shouting when Howard appeared below, followed by Waite-with-an-e.

He said, 'What do you need?'

'Ambulance. And a lot of luck.'

EPILOGUE

THE AMBULANCE CREW had been efficient and packed Mark Ware's hand in ice as soon as they realised the situation. They'd given him massive doses of pain-killers and then set about dealing with his wrist. When it was clear one of the paramedics could cope with his injury the other one—a woman in her twenties—raced upstairs and started staunching Dan's wound. He was still conscious but not very intelligible. He kept muttering something about the 'upstairs' and I didn't understand what he meant until I looked upwards and saw the trapdoor.

Eventually I'd been able to persuade Lucas to come out by telling him I was Dan's father.

Otherwise I think he might still be up there.

I'D BEEN EVERY day to the hospital but it didn't get any easier. Dan had been lucky the knife hadn't punctured a lung, but it had been very close. In the end it was a serious stab wound but one from which he would recover with only a scar to show.

They kept him sedated for a couple of days but on the third day he was awake and his wary eyes watched me enter his room and take a seat next to him. The hospital had fancy electronic stations that hung by the side of the bed and which patients could use to watch television or make phone calls—

for a small fee. He pushed a button to blank the screen and pushed it away.

He said, 'Is he dead?'

I nodded. 'How much do you remember?'

'I got in a good kick but it nearly killed me. I think I passed out. I remember a nurse or someone hovering over me.'

'The paramedic. She gave you painkillers and stopped the bleeding.'

He closed his eyes for a moment and I thought he was going to sleep. But then he opened them again.

'I keep feeling the point of the knife going in. Deeper and deeper—'

'Don't.'

'—and I remember wondering whether he would ever stop, or whether you'd ever get there, or whether this was it and I was going to die on a building site.'

'I'm sorry we were late. We had to get past some thugs.'

'You and Belinda?'

'She was great. She probably saved Mark Ware's hand.'

He looked puzzled and I realised he knew nothing of what had happened downstairs while he was being tortured by Church. I explained quickly how Ware had tracked the last phone call from Church to the house and gone inside with a gun he'd sourced that afternoon, shooting the two big men and killing one of them.

And losing his left hand in the process.

'Bloody hell. Is he all right?'

'He's been flown somewhere for an operation to try to reattach it. Switzerland, I think. They say there's every chance they can do it. Money's no object, of course.'

'It would be cooler to have a robot hand. Or print a plastic one—they can do that nowadays.'

'You're such a nerd.'

He pulled a face. 'I saved your backside in there. Not many nerds do Tae-Kwon-Do to competition standard.'

I nodded in agreement.

There was a silence then that stretched out for more than a minute. I was happy to say nothing and just be with him and to know he was alive and would be well.

Eventually he said, 'How about Lucas? Is he okay?'

'He's fine. They've all gone off together to Switzerland or wherever it is.'

'He was pretty good. Did what I told him and didn't seem too frightened. They took him out of the room once and he went nuts—I thought they were going to kill him before the deadline. But then they brought him back with a change of clothes.'

'They delivered an ear to the Ware's house. It was meant to be Lucas' but it turned out it belonged to Mrs Chau. They'd already killed her so they just cut off her ear. She was small and female so if you didn't look too closely you might mistake it for a young boy's. Maybe they took him out to compare his ears with hers, to see if they could get away with the substitution.'

'Wouldn't his mother know?'

'She glanced at it but then wouldn't look again. She didn't want to believe they'd done such a thing. His father obsessed over it, though. Took the ear away and kept it in his office. I think he was eaten up because he couldn't be sure—he didn't know his own son well enough to know whether it was his ear or not. Partly explains why he took things into his own hands at the last minute. He didn't trust me to do my job and he was always one to do things personally.'

'Please don't use the phrase "hands-on".'

We glanced at each other and suppressed guilty smiles.

There was another minute's silence.

He said, 'I've been lying here wondering whether there was anything I could have done differently. How about you?'

'I might have gone to Howard and Mercer earlier, got them there with some men so we could get past the guards downstairs quicker. I like to be hands-on, too.'

'Well, that's you all over, isn't it? Keep everything to yourself, trying to solve everyone's problems and just winding up creating more.'

'You're right, but I can't help it. It's in my blood. I don't like asking for help.'

'Look at me. I'm a good reason why you'd better learn to.'

I had a great reply to that … but a nurse came in and told me I had to leave.

So I did.

I DROVE OUT of the hospital car-park thinking I'd go back to the office. Then I decided to go home instead and catch up on some sleep.

But I had second thoughts and turned on to the road leading out of Crewe towards Sandbach and the motorway.

I kept turning over in my mind Church's almost-last words—about loving me and we're all going to hell. I wondered what he meant, and whether he was aware of any kind of contradiction in what he'd said. I thought perhaps it was his summary of his own spiritual or religious creed— and the creed of many who thought they were acting in the best interests of humanity by killing those who didn't subscribe to their own particular belief set, leaving behind them millions of innocent dead.

I didn't understand it and I didn't understand those who thought like that. It was taking on far too much responsibility for the fate of other people, who had the right to direct their own destinies.

Five minutes later I was on the M6 heading north. I put a new album by Gillian Welch in the CD player, forced my way into the outside lane and hit the gas.

I wanted to be alone for a while and have no responsibility for anyone.

Not even myself.

ACKNOWLEDGEMENTS

Sebastian Church's lecture in Chapter 21 owes a lot to Stephen Greenblatt's *The Curve: How the world became modern*, W.W. Norton and Company, 2011.

Thanks to Linda Hoey for suggesting Lucas Ware's name – good choice!

And final thanks to my old pal and fellow author John Haines for vital information about Liverpool, particularly for suggesting the different locations for where the action could take place. Check out his books on Amazon! The final choice of locations was mine so apologies if I upset anyone.